ALSO BY BREE BAKER

The Seaside Café Mysteries

Live and Let Chai

No Good Tea Goes Unpunished

Tide and Punishment

TIDE AND PUNISHMENT

BREE BAKER

Published by Poisoned Pen Press, an imprint of Sourcebooks
P.O. Box 4410, Naperville, Illinois 60567-4410
(630) 961-3900
sourcebooks.com

Printed and bound in Canada.
MBP 10 9 8 7 6 5 4 3 2 1

To Lanita

CHAPTER ONE

Merry Christmas," I called to a pair of newly arriving guests. "Welcome to Sun, Sand, and Tea." I rushed to shut the door against a wave of icy air and fought a head-to-toe shiver. I'd laced the seashell wind chimes above my front door with sleigh bells days ago, and tonight they'd barely stopped ringing.

It wasn't like our island to see more than a quickly vanishing flurry of snow this time of year, but a late-season tropical storm off the coast of Florida had ruined our normally mild weather. Unusually low temps, heavy winds, and precipitation had conspired to dump several inches of snow over our small town last night and most of us weren't sure what to do about it.

Charm was a small coastal town on a string of barrier islands off the East Coast. The islands were known collectively to most as the Outer Banks. For me, they'd always been *home*.

My newest guests, a couple I'd known all my

life, greeted me with hearty hugs and handshakes. A younger, unfamiliar face smiled behind them. Mr. Waters, the general store owner, kicked snow from his boots while his wife dusted tufts of powdery flakes from her hat and shoulders.

I opened my arms again, this time with greedy hands. “Let me take your coats.”

Mr. Waters was quick to comply, and I grabbed a hanger from the overstuffed rolling rack behind me. “Leave it to Everly Swan to plan a Christmas party on a night like this,” he teased. “Charm hasn’t seen this much snow in forty years.”

I hung the coat with a smile, thankful I’d had the forethought to borrow a rack from the local cleaners for my party. While I hadn’t predicted the snow, I knew folks would be more comfortable without dragging their wrappings around all night, and my café hadn’t come with a coat closet fit for one hundred. “In my defense,” I told Mr. Waters, “I started planning this party in September. Besides, I think the snow adds a little ambience. Don’t you? And it didn’t keep you away, so I’ll call that a win.”

He chuckled. “From the looks of the parking situation out front, the weather hasn’t stopped anyone.”

His wife grinned and passed me her coat, one arm suspiciously behind her back. “That’s because no one on this island is fool enough to miss a Swan holiday buffet. We were thrilled to see the flyer. Your grandma used to make your family’s special cookies every year, and I counted the days until I could get my next hit. I swear that woman was magic in the kitchen."

"She was." My grandma had loved to cook and bake. She'd practically raised me in the kitchen, and I was honored to follow in her footsteps. Unfortunately, we'd lost Grandma last year. I hadn't been around to say goodbye.

I hung Mrs. Waters's coat beside her husband's and turned back to find her arms outstretched. What looked like a three-foot, red-and-white-striped baseball bat lay across her palms. "This is for you," she said. "It's a peppermint stick!"

My eyes went wide. "Wow." I accepted the giant gift with a little grunt of effort. "Thank you."

"You're welcome. We thought you could crush it up and add it to all those amazing cookies you've been churning out over here since Thanksgiving. What's a lady have to do to get a few dozen on order?"

I hugged the candy to my chest and smiled. "Just let me know what you'd like and I'll do my best to get them to you by Christmas," I said, unsure it was physically possible to take another order with only nine days to go.

"Excellent!" She clasped her hands and beamed. "Now let me introduce you to our surprise holiday gift." She pulled the young, dark-haired woman who'd arrived with them against her side and smiled proudly. "This is our niece, Lanita. I don't know how, but she and her mother, my normally loose-lipped sister, managed to keep Lanita's visit a secret until my doorbell rang and I found this lovely young lady outside!"

"Hello," I said, offering my hand in greeting. "I'm Everly Swan, and this is my iced tea shop. It's nice to meet you."

"Thank you," she said. "I'm staying with my aunt and uncle over holiday break."

Mr. Waters clapped her on the back. "Lanita is a senior at Duke University this year. She's going to be an anthropologist and study people."

"Cultural development," Lanita corrected with a shrug. "People are interesting on their own, but I'm especially fascinated by their interactions and the ways they develop societal constructs."

I laughed. "Well, you're going to love it here. There are plenty of interesting interactions to observe."

Lanita's wide brown eyes seemed to lighten behind her dark-rimmed glasses. "The snow," she whispered. "Everyone is acting as if they've never seen such a thing before."

"We are a beach town," I said. "Most folks move here to get away from weather like this. We're not equipped to deal with it."

"Materially or emotionally?" she asked with a broad smile.

"Both!" the Waterses and I answered in unison.

Lanita laughed, and her sleek bobbed hair danced around her chin.

I envied the fashionable look—cat-eye glasses, angled bob, adorable fringe. Unfortunately, my wild and wavy locks were barely manageable in the cold, dry winter and downright crazy in the humidity of summer. Even on a good day, my hair gave Albert Einstein a run for his money.

"I don't mind the snow," Lanita said. "I grew up in the mountains and my SUV has four-wheel drive, so this is nothing. I've been passing out my number in case anyone needs a ride. I'm calling it a Pick-Me-Up. It's like getting an Uber or a Lyft except I'm the sole proprietor, only driver, and just opened for business after seeing two golf carts slide off the road this morning. The extra cash is great, plus I'm getting a crash course in entrepreneurship and an earful as I drive folks around. Lots of uncensored truths flowing in the backseat if you know what I mean."

I could only imagine.

My door chimes rang once more, and a gust of frigid wind whipped through the foyer, pressing my skirt against my knees.

Lanita passed me a pink sticky note with ten digits printed across it. "If you ever need a Pick-Me-Up."

Mrs. Waters released her niece and rubbed her palms together. "I'd better have a few cookie samples so I can pick some favorites for my order."

Mr. Waters took his wife's hand, and they hurried through the archway to my seaside café and iced tea shop. Lanita and I followed.

I prayed silently not to drop the peppermint and break my toe.

Warm scents of cinnamon and vanilla pulled me

through the crowded space inside Sun, Sand, and Tea and lifted my spirits further. Dozens of familiar faces laughed and chatted merrily around the smattering of chairs and tables. There were twenty seats in total, five at the counter and fifteen scattered across the wide-planked, whitewashed floor, ranging from padded wicker numbers with low tables to tall bistro sets along the perimeter.

The café stretched through the entire south side of my home's first floor. The previous owner had strategically knocked down several walls, opening the kitchen and formal dining area up to a large space for entertaining. It was a decidedly modern concept for a home that was more than 170 years old, but it made a stunning setup for my shop. I'd recently traded the hodgepodge of yard sale and thrift shop furniture I'd started out with for a top-of-the-line set of reinforced wicker pieces in shades of the seaside. Pale blue for the sky and water, gray and tan for the driftwood and sand. I used throw pillows and accents in bright yellow, orange, or red to reflect the other things I saw frequently through the windows, like sunsets, kites, and Frisbees. Tonight, I'd added a heaping helping of holiday accents in shimmering blue, white, and silver.

My great-aunts, Clara and Fran, beamed at me from behind the counter where they busily loaded the dishwasher with dirty place settings and restocked the little countertop buffet with fresh cookies and dinnerware. Aunt Clara patted my hand as I stowed the giant candy stick in the pantry. "You've outdone yourself. Folks can't seem to stop smiling or saying wonderful things."

I bit back a goofy grin. Just ten days until Christmas, and unexpected weather aside, the party had gone off without a hitch.

"People are especially impressed with your tree," Clara continued. "It's the perfect amount of sunshine and whimsy. Just like you." She kissed my cheek, then turned back to the buffet.

I gave the fat Carolina pine standing before my rear wall of windows a prideful look. I'd raided a dollhouse store in the neighboring town of Duck and bought all their miniature summer decor on clearance. Then, I'd spent an afternoon hot-gluing hooks onto everything from dried seashells and starfish to brightly colored buckets and shovels, tiny beach balls, floppy doll hats, and striped flip-flops. I'd even foregone the traditional tree skirt in favor of a few strategically arranged beach towels and had stacked gifts on a pair of child-sized Adirondack chairs for punch.

"I couldn't have done all this without you guys," I said, "and thank you again for the lovely gnome."

"Of course," Aunt Clara cooed, obviously pleased with my appreciation for her new hobby. "I knew the moment I finished painting him that he was meant to live here with you."

I forced my smile in place as I nodded, though I wasn't in love with references to him "living" here.

My great-aunts had always been a bit eccentric, but Aunt Clara had recently taken a worrisome step toward the deep end with a sudden gnome obsession. She'd started painting the little garden figures shortly after Halloween and hadn't stopped. Now I had a particularly large and festive-looking one guarding my front door. Thankfully, she'd painted him in green pants with a red hat and matching curl-toed boots, so come January first, he could take a year-long vacation to the storage shed. Aunt Clara's kindness was duly noted, but the gnome creeped me out.

"Parking is a nightmare out there," a newly arriving woman said. She shook snow from her crown of red hair and frowned. "We had to park halfway to Timbuktu tonight. There must be forty vehicles outside."

"It's a full house," I said, trying and failing to recall the woman's first name. Unfortunately, I recognized her face. If Mrs. Dunfree, the current mayor's wife, was here, that could only mean one thing: trouble was afoot. "May I take your coat?"

"Please." She unbuttoned the long wool number and passed it my way. She was very thin, her face drawn with distaste as she regarded her white suede ankle boots, darkened by a long walk over the snow-covered ground.

I caught my breath at the sight of her husband moving through the crowd in our direction. Mayor Dunfree was Aunt Fran's current nemesis. He was also the man Aunt Fran planned to run against in the next mayoral election. Worse, she planned to make that decision official with a public announcement tonight.

"You might want to invest in some additional parking," he said smartly, loading his coat and hat into my arms. "It's ridiculous to expect folks to walk so far for a little iced tea."

I highly doubted the good mayor had decided to come out on a night like this for iced tea, but I smiled politely and nodded. "I'd love to add parking. Do you think the town council will approve a private lot so near the beach and boardwalk if I let them know the mayor suggested it?"

He grimaced. The town council rarely approved anything new. In fact, the mayor and his minions worked diligently to keep everything in Charm the same as it always had been.

Mayor Dunfree smoothed several long strands of gray hair across his otherwise bald head, then reached for his wife's hand. "Shall we?" he asked, pulling her into the crowded café.

Aunt Fran motored around the counter in my direction. "I can't believe Mayor Dummy showed up here," she hissed, grabbing my elbow and dragging me out into the foyer.

I bit my tongue and selected hangers for their coats.

Aunt Fran's eyes were narrow and tight. "I'd bet my good britches someone told him I planned to make my announcement about running for office tonight. He's probably here to bust it up."

I hung the coats quickly, then squeezed her hands and willed her not to panic. "What can I do?"

She tracked him through the crowd with her gaze, face growing redder with each passing moment. "I don't know."

"You can always hold off," I suggested. "Make your speech on New Year's Eve."

"No." Aunt Fran huffed out a long breath, then marched back the way she'd come.

"Wait," I stage-whispered after her, but it was too late. She'd caught up with the Dunfrees at my café's service counter.

I dropped my head forward with a groan. It was my first Christmas home after too many away, and I'd wanted to make it memorable with a big party, not host a septuagenarian showdown.

Mayor Dunfree and his wife occupied a pair of bar stools across from Aunt Clara, who was busy keeping the trays stocked.

Aunt Clara smiled brightly. "Welcome. Merry Christmas," she said. Her cream-colored silk blouse had a high collar and long sleeves. She'd pinned a pearl-and-diamond brooch to the neckline that nearly matched her silver and blond hair. She looked a bit like an angel in the glow of twinkle lights draped overhead.

Aunt Fran went to stand by her sister's side, creating a dramatic visual contrast.

I'd often thought of my great-aunts as a human yin and yang. Vast personality differences aside, most of their wardrobes were handmade or handed down and well past the point of vintage. Aunt Clara's closet was overrun with shades of cream from eggshell to tan, while Fran's clothes were mostly black. Clara's fair hair, light complexion, and pale blue eyes seemed to match her sweet spirit, while Aunt Fran's olive skin and dark hair and eyes seemed to support her no-nonsense personality.

I looked more like Fran than Clara, but my natural disposition lacked ninety percent of Fran's verve.

"What brings you out tonight?" Aunt Fran asked the Dunfrees. "I'm surprised a party at Everly's place would garner a visit from the mayor."

Mayor Dunfree nibbled his way through a pile of cookie selections before him. "I have an announcement to make," he said. "And the flyers said everyone was invited."

Aunt Fran's eyes narrowed into slits.

I could practically read her thoughts from where I stood. *He* had an announcement to make? And he planned to make it *here*? *Tonight?*

Aunt Clara smiled kindly. "Of course everyone is welcome here. We're just surprised to see you. That's all."

Mayor Dunfree stopped chewing. He shifted his gaze from Aunt Fran to Aunt Clara. "What's with all the gnomes outside your shop?" he asked. "They're everywhere, and I saw another one on my way up the porch steps out front. Is that one of yours too?"

Aunt Clara beamed. "Why, yes! I'm painting a gnome garden at Blessed Bee. Each day I add a little something new, and soon there will be lights and signs to brighten shoppers' days."

I grabbed two mason jars and filled them with ice and tea for the Dunfrees. "How about a drink to go with your cookies? I sweetened these naturally with apples and honey from my aunts' garden and hives."

Mrs. Dunfree accepted the offering and sampled the tea carefully, then smiled. "Thank you. It's lovely."

The mayor ignored the jar I'd set before him. "The gnomes are nearing eyesore territory, not to mention a potential tripping hazard. Why are you painting garden statues in the winter?"

Aunt Clara leaned over the counter and grinned conspiratorially. "I got the idea from a Christmas legend in Norway. They call the gnomes *Nisse* and the *Nisse* assist with daily farm chores in return for kindness and a bowl of porridge with butter on Christmas morning. Isn't that nice?"

Mrs. Dunfree slid her eyes in the mayor's direction. "It must be nice to have help with chores."

"I'll paint you a gnome," Aunt Clara offered.

I suppressed a shudder. Aunt Clara had a habit of leaving the tale of the *Nisse* unfinished. She never mentioned that when the farmer forgot to add butter to the gnome's porridge, the gnome killed his best cow in retaliation. I didn't have a cow, but I had a fluffy white cat and loyal seagull, and no room in my life for a vengeful gnome.

Mayor Dunfree dusted crumbs from his puckered lips. "Why don't we mingle, darling? I've heard enough about gnomes."

His wife slid off her stool and took his arm. The jingling of seashells and sleigh bells turned me on my toes.

"Merry Christmas," I called, hurrying to welcome my newest guest and hoping the mayor wouldn't provoke Aunt Fran again before I returned.

A group of islanders were hanging coats in the foyer when I arrived. I welcomed and hugged them one by one, then answered a dozen questions about the Swan holiday cookies. When I confirmed the cookies would only be around for the holidays, despite the fact I had opened a year-round café, everyone wanted to place an order.

I finished as quickly and graciously as possible, then went to check on my aunts.

Aunt Clara stood before my boom box at the far side of the room and lowered the volume on my favorite holiday CD.

Aunt Fran waited impatiently beside my tree. She tapped a spoon against her tea jar when the music was low. "Can I have everyone's attention?"

Slowly, the drone and tinkle of voices quieted. The crush of guests looked in Fran's direction.

"As most of you know," she began, "I'm a lifelong resident of this town and a member of the founding family. I'm also the newest member of our town council. I care deeply about this place and everyone in it, which is why I believe there is a need for change."

A few heads nodded. One or two faces looked toward the exit. *Change* wasn't a word Charmers knew what to do with. We were better prepared to deal with snow or an alien invasion.

"I believe that even a place as close to perfect as Charm can use a little revision from time to time…some occasional sprucing," Fran continued. "Specifically, I think it's time someone takes a close look at the policies and procedures that govern our town and seeks ways to improve them. I'd like very much to be that woman."

Most of the guests clapped softly. All kept an eye on Mayor Dunfree, who'd risen while my Aunt Fran had spoken.

She hitched her chin in defiance, blatantly ignoring the only man on his feet. "Next fall, when the ballots go out, you will see my name in the running for mayor of Charm, and I hope you will vote for me. Vote for change."

Aunt Clara led us in a tentative round of applause.

Mayor Dunfree strode forward, clapping aggressively as the crowd's enthusiasm died. "Very nice, Miss Swan," he said, moving into Aunt Fran's personal space, probably (mistakenly) assuming she would step back. Instead, he settled for standing close enough to rub shoulders with her. "I commend your bravery, especially as someone who's only been on the town council a few months and therefore so admittedly new to politics. It's inspiring to see you willing to toss your wildly inexperienced hat in the ring."

Aunt Fran scowled.

"Speaking of change," he continued, turning on his

heels to face the crowd. "I'd like to take this opportunity to let you all know change is already on the way. I've decided to run for reelection next fall, with a partner."

I furrowed my brow. *A what?*

Dunfree extended one arm toward the crowd, and I stopped short at the sight of my childhood nemesis, Bracie Gracie, a.k.a. Mary Grace Chatsworth, emerging from the crush of people. Bracie had moved away when we were in middle school, immediately improving my adolescence, but had unfortunately returned to Charm this September. I was trying to release my old grudge, but Bracie had once told all the kids at school that Grandma raised me because my deceased mother had actually run away to be a circus clown.

"It wasn't long ago that I'd planned to step down from office, but when I couldn't bring myself to do that, I struck up a deal with Ms. Mary Grace Chatsworth, who has recently returned to her beloved hometown. With your votes, there will be a deputy mayor for the first time in Charm history. I believe that with her insights of youth and my decades of experience, we will make this town a place every Charmer will be proud to call home."

Fran took a step away from Dunfree and Bracie. She nodded cordially at the room, her cheeks crimson with humiliation as folks shouted questions to the pair who'd crashed her speech.

"I need a minute," she whispered, blowing past me

on her way into the foyer. Moments later, the wind chimes and sleigh bells jingled with her escape.

The impromptu Q-and-A session ended several minutes later, and folks returned to the tea dispensers and cookie trays, eager for seconds. Aunt Clara pumped the music back up and dozens of lively conversations resumed. I took cookie orders until my receipt book was nearly full and the trays I'd set out were going for empty. Then, I scanned the scene for signs of Aunt Fran.

She hadn't returned, and at least half the guests were suddenly gone, including the Dunfrees and Bracie Gracie.

How much time had flown by?

I left the receipt book on the counter and slipped into the foyer for my winter coat and hat. With any luck, Dunfree and Bracie hadn't cornered Fran outside and irritated her into saying something they could later use against her.

I huddled low in my coat as I walked the snow-dusted planks of my wraparound porch in search of Aunt Fran. Angry winds snapped my cheeks and bit my nose. White waves crashed and rolled in the distance beneath a smooth and inky sky. The beach was void of people as far as I could see, so I gripped the handrail tightly and climbed down the steps.

I paused for a look back. My creepy gnome was gone. *Hopefully not in search of my best cow.* I shivered as a wave of gooseflesh crawled over the skin beneath my coat.

"Ahhh!" A sudden scream of terror rent the night and spun me on my toes.

I knew that voice.

"Aunt Fran!" I called, already in motion toward her gut-wrenching wail. "Aunt Fran!"

Had she fallen? Slipped on ice? Hit her head? Broken her hip? The gory possibilities worsened with every heartbeat. "Aunt Fran!"

The silhouette of someone crouched on the ground came into view beneath a tree I'd wrapped in twinkle lights. I recognized the flowing salt-and-pepper hair immediately and slid to a graceless stop at her side. "What happened? Are you hurt?"

She pushed herself off the snowy ground and stood trembling before me. She had tears in her eyes and my missing porch gnome in one shaking fist. The domed tip of his red hat had been broken off and his face was smeared in something red. "I saw it," she whispered. "I saw it in the snow—and I thought…I thought someone had—had vandalized it." The words came in fits and starts. "I didn't know. I didn't see him. Or anyone. I didn't think… I thought I was alone."

The rest of her message was lost to my ringing ears as I followed her gaze to the figure in the shadows near her feet.

Mayor Dunfree lay prone in the snow, his unseeing eyes open, and his forehead red with blood from an injury that could only have come from being hit with the gnome in Aunt Fran's hands.

CHAPTER TWO

Aunt Clara arrived on my heels in a flurry of distress. Nearly impossibly, but not surprisingly, she'd heard her sister's cry from inside and had run out in search of her. "What on earth happened?" she exclaimed as I pulled Aunt Fran away from Mayor Dunfree. "Are you hurt?"

Aunt Fran shook her head slowly, clearly in a daze and possibly in shock. "No."

Aunt Clara eyed us briefly with relief and confusion. A moment later, her gaze fell to the man at our feet. "Heavens!"

Fran trembled. "I didn't." She blinked an avalanche of shimmering teardrops free, then sucked in a shuddered breath. "He was already here. Alone. Except for this." She stretched the bloody gnome in her sister's direction.

Aunt Clara shrieked and swatted Fran's hand away, knocking the gnome hat-first into the snow.

We stared at it in the moonlight.

"Don't pick it up again," I advised. "We'll call the police and let them know about the gnome when they get here."

A low round of whispers lifted into the night, drawing our attention away from Mayor Dunfree. A small clutch of guests had gathered on the walkway near the bottom of my front steps.

"What do we do?" Aunt Clara whispered, pulling her sister against her.

"Whatever we can to help," I said.

I fumbled with my cell phone, searching the contacts for a very specific number. Aunt Fran had gotten herself into a pickle by picking up that gnome, and I doubted anyone but Detective Grady Hays would believe she was innocent after the public embarrassment Dunfree had caused her less than an hour ago.

"Hays," Grady answered. His voice boomed loud and strong through the receiver.

I tried to drag my thick, sticky tongue off the roof of my mouth and tell him everything, but only a small choking sound came out.

"Everly?" he asked. "What's wrong? Are you okay?"

I shook my head despite the fact he couldn't see me.

The little crowd on my walkway had grown and spilled into the snow, moving in my direction. A collective hush rolled over them when they recognized the figure at our feet. Some raced back into my home. Others clambered closer, straining for a better look and firing off questions faster than I could process their words.

"Everly," Grady demanded. The roar of an engine rose behind his voice.

I batted at my tear-filled eyes, still unable to speak.

The bystanders' questions kept coming. *What happened? Is he dead? Who did this? Did you do this? Did Fran? Why? Over a squabble? I don't understand.* Their anxious voices melded into the white noise of my pending breakdown.

"Are you hurt?" Grady demanded. The genuine concern in his tone freed my tongue.

"I think Mayor Dunfree is dead," I whispered. The words were bitter, too blunt, too unfair, too surreal.

"I'm almost there," Grady said. "I'll radio it in. Hold tight. Keep folks back, and don't touch anything."

My gaze dropped to the gnome in the snow as we disconnected. *If only Aunt Fran hadn't touched it.*

I counted my breaths, steadying my mind. Grady was on the way, but for now, I was in charge. I could do this. "Please step back," I said with as much authority as I could muster.

Beside me, Aunt Clara and Aunt Fran clung to one another, their rail-thin frames looking especially frail as they melted together for support.

The cries of emergency vehicles wound to life in the distance, racing closer until their carousels of ugly lights cast an eerie, heart-wrenching glow over the already awful scene.

The smattering of onlookers and barrage of questions had grown increasingly fervent and speculative with each passing second.

"Everly!" Grady appeared in the crowd, jogging confidently in my direction. "Are you okay?" he demanded, lifting his badge and waving the crowd back several steps.

"No," I whispered hoarsely, fighting the lump of emotion in my throat. I fell against his chest and wrapped my arms around his waist. "Not at all."

Grady planted his palms on my shoulders and pushed me away from him. His trained eyes scanned my body in search of injury. "Do you need to see an EMT?"

I shook my head and forced my spine to stiffen. There would be plenty of time for a proper breakdown later. At the moment, I needed to be a help, not a hindrance, and Grady needed information. "Mayor Dunfree hijacked Aunt Fran's *I'm-going-to-run-for-mayor* speech, and she came outside to cool off. When I noticed she hadn't come back in, I came to see if she was okay. I heard her scream, then found her here. With him." I nodded to the mayor. "He was already like that," I clarified. "Aunt Clara came next, then my guests filtered outside after her."

He cast his gaze over the broader scene outside my home, then turned a dissatisfied expression back to me. "Any idea what happened out here before you arrived?"

I shook my head and tried not to think about my frightened aunts or all the accusations yet to come.

"How about what happened to his head?"

That one I knew the answer to. I lifted a finger in the direction of the discarded gnome.

Grady moved his eyes in that direction, then grimaced. He rubbed his forehead as he crouched for a better look. "One of your aunt's?"

I didn't have to answer. Who else was painting and distributing gnomes ten days before Christmas?

He groaned. "Perfect."

I waited, unsure what to do next, and certain Grady didn't think the gnome's role in this was perfect at all.

He snapped a pair of blue plastic gloves over his hands and removed the festive figure from the snow. He rehoused him in a plastic bag marked *EVIDENCE*, then zipped it shut. "Did you touch this?"

"I didn't," I promised, "but…" My traitorous gaze flickered to my aunts. "Aunt Fran found it in the snow and picked it up."

Grady's jaw went slack before slamming shut. He expelled a gust of breath through gritted teeth, then let his eyelids close. When he reopened them, he'd switched seamlessly into cop mode. I was highly unlikely to get any personal favors or leeway while he was in cop mode, and I'd learned from experience that my odds of being threatened with obstruction had instantly quadrupled. "I'm going to interview the guests. You and your aunts should stick around. I'll drive them home."

I shuffled backward, poking a thumb over one shoulder as I moved, eager to put some distance between Grady and myself before I said more than I should. I didn't even know what that would be, only that cop-mode Grady was a little intimidating, and I had enough on my mind already. "I'll be right over here if you need me."

I hurried to the gazebo where my aunts had relocated once emergency personnel had begun to arrive. The ornate little structure, like the rest of my garden, picket fencing, trees, and shrubs, was bathed in the glow of twinkle lights. If not for the murder site behind me and gaudy flood of emergency lights, the space would have looked downright magical. "How are you holding up?" I asked. I wanted to comfort them both, but I'd only seen three murdered bodies in my life, and I'd been the one to find the last two. I wasn't sure how to be on the other end of this stick. "Is there anything I can get you?" I asked, shifting into hostess mode, the thing I knew best.

Aunt Fran blinked and heavy tears cascaded over her unnaturally pale cheeks, collecting and hanging like icicles along her chin before falling into her lap. "Who would do this?" she whispered. "Why?"

"I'm not sure yet," I admitted, though her question had been rhetorical.

Things like this weren't supposed to happen in Charm. Despite the two other murders this year, we were a kind, community-focused people. We weren't violent. Weren't killers. One of the previous murders was practically an accident, and the other had nothing to do with Charm at all. Neither the killer nor the victim had lived here. It was a crime of unfortunate location.

Whatever was happening now had to be the same. A fatal accident, perhaps, or an attack by a transient criminal. "Maybe he was robbed," I suggested. "Mayor Dunfree was an older man, strolling alone at night. It's Christmastime, and people in need will do crazy things when the pressure is on to fill the space under the tree." The theory was taking shape even as I spoke, and I liked it. "Maybe a well-meaning criminal just wanted his wallet, but Mayor Dunfree fought back and the attacker panicked. Fisticuffs ensued, and Dunfree lost." It was a stretch to think an out-of-towner in need of cash had stumbled upon my house at the moment Dunfree had wandered out, but I was willing to make that theory work if it meant one of the locals wasn't a killer.

I reran the idea in my mind, preparing to present it to Grady when he came to question Fran and I, officially. "Wait," I said, turning for a slow scan of the area. "Mayor Dunfree wasn't alone."

Fran mopped her eyes and nose with a handkerchief. "What?"

"Where is his wife?" I jerked onto my feet and sprinted away from the gazebo with purpose. What if she was hurt? Abducted? *Or the killer?*

The crowd had disbanded, taking many of the golf

carts that had previously lined my drive and the boardwalk with them. Presumably, the rest of the guests had been pushed inside, if the set of deputies standing sentinel at my door were any indication. I nearly tripped over my own feet stopping short of my front steps.

Mrs. Dunfree sat in a sobbing heap halfway up.

She was alive! Unharmed! And she was also with Grady, so even if she turned out to be the killer, I breathed a little easier.

Grady was crouched before her. "Tell me what happened." His voice was low and encouraging. His posture and expression were all business. "Take your time. Stick to the facts. I know it's hard to focus during a tragedy, but I'd appreciate whatever you can share."

She nodded and sniffled, swiping tears with the pads of her thumbs and fingertips. "I was waiting in the golf cart," she said. "Dudley stopped to take a call, and I told him I'd meet him in the cart. When he didn't follow, I went looking for him to remind him he has a wife who was freezing!" Her voice cracked, and she broke into sobs. "If he hadn't taken that stupid call, he would've been with me."

"Any idea who called?" Grady asked as I crept a little closer, hoping to hear her answer without ruining the conversation's momentum.

Grady looked over his shoulder to where I stood.

I raised my shoulders in case that look of his was some kind of question.

"Mrs. Dunfree," he said, turning back to the grieving woman, "why don't we get you out of the cold? I'm sure a deputy would be glad to escort you anywhere you'd like to go. Then, I'll follow up with you tomorrow."

She nodded, accepting his offered hand and rising unsteadily onto her feet.

The deputy I recognized as Tom peeled himself away from his post at my door and went to help Mrs. Dunfree into a waiting cruiser.

Aunt Fran and Aunt Clara passed Dunfree's widow on their way up the steps.

The EMT who followed them shot Grady an apologetic look. "I saw them huddled in the gazebo and thought they ought to get in out of the cold."

Grady shook the man's hand. "Thank you." He motioned my aunts inside. "Why don't you wait for me in Everly's private quarters?" he suggested.

In other words, *away from the crowd.*

I lifted my palms in a plea. "Aunt Fran didn't do this. I know it looks bad, but she wouldn't, and you know it."

Grady pinched the bridge of his nose. "What I know," he said, dropping both hands to his hips, "is that you had a café full of folks who heard Fran announce her intent to run against Dunfree in the election, and those same folks saw him interrupt and condescend all over her until she fled the scene. The next time anyone saw the two of them, he was dead, and she was hunkered over him with the possible murder weapon."

"Hey," I said, lifting a finger to point at him. "She wasn't hunkered."

He rolled his eyes, then pulled the phone from his pocket and handed it to me. "This isn't going to be an easy one to get out of, Everly. You can't ignore facts like these with the number of witnesses you have here. It's your word and Fran's against half the town."

"No one saw her do it," I said, accepting the phone. "Everything you have here is circumstantial evidence."

"You're a lawyer now?" he mused. One corner of his grumpy mouth twitched with an almost half smile.

"No." I smiled back, enjoying the fact I amused him, even at times like these, "but I've watched some on TV."

I lowered my attention from his steel-gray eyes to the phone, where the *Town Charmer*, Charm's anonymously run gossip blog, glowed the screen. A photo of Aunt Fran scowling at a self-important Mayor Dunfree erased my moment of good humor.

"'Holiday Gnomes: Whimsical Delight, or Eyesore and Tripping Hazard?'" I read the headline, my shoulders drooping lower. The article rehashed my aunts' earlier debate with the mayor, blow by blow. "This just covers a typical store owner and council member discussion," I said.

"Dunfree isn't a council member," Grady corrected. "He's the mayor."

"All the more reason he should've left this alone."

Grady tented his brows. "All the more reason for Fran to be angry. And we haven't even seen what kind of article will cover their public spat about her run for office. You know that's coming, and this blog gets everyone all worked up, not to mention it's been a couple of months since the gossips have had anything meaty to gnaw on. I hate to say it but *not* arresting her won't be easy."

I scoffed. "Be serious."

Grady leveled me with sharp eyes. "I'm dead serious. I have to follow procedures and the evidence. Right now, all the evidence is pointing at your great-aunt."

~

My aunts had waited while Grady and his deputies spoke with the remaining guests. I'd listened earnestly and to no avail for a clue about who might've been outside when Mayor Dunfree and his wife left the party, who else might be angry with him, or who'd written the anonymous blog post covering the mayor's behavior toward Aunt Fran. The gossip blog was a lesser, but ongoing curiosity to me. Nearly a year after having moved back to Charm after a long time away, I still had no idea who was behind the website, if that person worked alone or if they had help, and if they had help, how large was their crew?

I wiped my countertops for the thousandth time, threatening to wear grooves in the marble and waiting for Grady to return from dropping my aunts off at their home.

The chimes and bells above my door jingled into action, and I dropped my hands below the counter for the three-foot candy cane I'd kept handy, just in case. "Hello?"

"Everly!" My best friend, Amelia Butters, skidded into the café looking as utterly bewildered as I felt. "I heard what happened! Are you okay?"

"I'm fine." I released the giant peppermint stick and darted around the counter to meet her.

She launched herself at me, sliding on the melting snow and ice from her boots. She flung her arms around my neck. "Some of your guests came to Charming Reads after the police busted up the party. I can't believe this is happening again. And so close to your home!"

She was referring to the fact a dead man had been found in the surf just down the beach from my home last summer. A few months before that, a body had turned up on the boardwalk several yards from my mailbox. I'd found them both and had the residual nightmares to prove it.

Amelia owned Charming Reads, Charm's only bookstore, and she took the responsibility of being our community's literary overseer very seriously, lining up speakers, story times, and other literary and education-related events as often as possible. She was equal parts book and theater nerd, and I loved her for both.

"I suppose you still don't believe this house is haunted," she said. "Maybe it's cursed." She shivered.

I puffed my cheeks and stepped out of her embrace. "It's not haunted or cursed," I said. "You know how I can be sure? Because neither of those things are real." At least, that was what I told myself on a near-daily basis.

Amelia shrugged, as if to say *to each her own.* Amelia was a believer. "How's Fran? Was she really found standing over the body? Holding the murder weapon?"

"Yeah. By me."

Amelia pulled her petal-pink lips into a deep, unnatural frown. "Yikes." She unfastened her red vintage swing coat and slid the fashionable number off her shoulders, then hooked it over the back of the nearest chair with her bag and knitted hat. Her black dress pants accentuated her trim figure, and the shimmery silver blouse she wore illuminated her pretty face. She hopped on to a stool at the counter and rested her elbows on the meticulously cleaned marble. "What can I do?"

I turned to fix us a snack. "I don't know, but I'm glad you're here."

"I came the moment I locked up for the night," she said through a long yawn. "Sorry. The holiday hours are killing me. You wouldn't think that adding an hour or two to the start and finish of your day would wipe a person out, but it really does."

It wasn't just the extra hours at her shop that exhausted her; it was the season. Amelia had a creative mind and an intense love for Christmas. She went overboard on everything from Halloween until New Year's, attempting to make the time as special for everyone else as it was for her. I was slightly guilty of the same thing. I made seasonal cookies, specialty teas, holiday menus with coordinating decorations, gifts, cards… And I'd doubled down on my usual over-the-top efforts this year in an attempt to show everyone in Charm how glad I was to be home again.

I filled a mason jar with ice, then set the cubes afloat with tea and delivered it to her.

She lifted the drink to her nose and inhaled. "This smells amazing. What is it?"

"I'm calling it Santa's Southern Cinnamon. It's apple cinnamon tea with a little nutmeg and pumpkin pie spice."

She took a long sip before setting the cup on the counter. "I think the tea's delicious and the name is adorable."

I beamed. Those were the kinds of compliments I lived for. I poured a jar for myself, then set a tray of my family's secret recipe snickerdoodles on the counter between us.

"You should probably lock your door," she said. "All things considered."

Meaning: *since there's another killer on the loose.*

I snagged a pudgy cinnamon cookie from the top of the pile and sunk my teeth in. "I'm hoping Grady will stop by on his way home and fill me in on what he knows about the murder."

Amelia frowned. She didn't like it when I asked too many questions about dead people. She wasn't wrong to worry. My curiosity admittedly got the best of me from time to time.

I waited for words of warning or a plea to leave this case alone.

Instead, she pointed at my receipt pad, which was covered in frantic scribbles. "Are these all cookie orders?"

"Yep, and those are just the orders that were placed tonight," I said, selecting a second cookie. "I've got enough baking to keep me busy until spring." Sadly, it all needed to be done in the next nine days.

"What about your website videos?" she asked, pushing the pad away with a frown. "I checked today, and that video you made for the seven-layer bars isn't up yet."

"I've been busy prepping for tonight's party," I said. Though, it was only partially true. In reality I'd been worried about what people might think. I'd loved making tutorials while I was away at culinary school, back when I'd been required to keep a video log as part of my first-year grade. Students kept a blog of their favorite recipes and posted videos of themselves as they created them so the chefs could take their time scrutinizing our techniques. For most students, video blogging was a frustration, but I'd enjoyed the process and had a lot of fun with the results. I'd planned to continue after graduation, but I never graduated. I'd flown home in tears after a heartbreak and started a new life. Was it ridiculous that I missed the videos? Or that I wanted to start them again, but now featuring the Swan family recipes I used at Sun, Sand, and Tea?

"Get out of your head," Amelia said. "I can literally

see you getting in your own way right now." She dusted crumbs from her fingertips with a grin. "Do it. Put up the video. Share your gift. Spread your wings, Everly Swan."

I snorted.

She bobbed her head. "I accept your snort as agreement."

I lifted a third cookie from the pile, my mind still turning over the awful night's events. "What do you know about that group, Charmers for Change?" I asked.

"Not much. Aside from their occasional calls to action pinned to telephone poles all over town," she said.

Charmers for Change was a group of locals in support of Fran's policies to fund local arts and increase tourism. They also had a desire to appoint new voices to the town council and mayoral throne. It was easy to see why so many people assumed Aunt Fran was a part of their organization, but in truth, she had nothing to do with them. We didn't even know exactly who belonged to the cause, but their alignment to her well-voiced opinions had made her the unspoken face of their movement.

"Do you think the CFC could be behind what happened to Mayor Dunfree?" I asked.

Amelia stopped chewing and swallowed audibly. "I think the CFC wants a reassessment of town rules and regulations by the local government. They want hundred-year-old nonsense like ordinances against carrying an ice cream cone in your pocket or riding a horse into church erased from the books. Fresh eyes. New beginnings. That kind of thing. I don't think there's reason to think they're a violent group, and most importantly, I think *Detective Hays* will figure out what happened to the mayor. After all, that's his job." She gave me a stern look.

"I know," I said. "I just wish I knew at least one of their members so I could see what they think of all this."

Amelia rolled her bright blue eyes. She'd been my voice of reason when I'd dove headlong into the last two murder investigations, a voice I'd elected to ignore, much to my own peril.

"I saw his wife crying tonight, but spouses are always suspect in these things," I said. "Then, there's Bracie Gracie. He might've billed her as his future deputy, but a few months ago she'd planned to run for his seat."

Amelia shook her head. "Her name's Mary Grace Chatsworth. You've got to stop calling her Bracie. People will think it's a reflection on Fran, and she needs to look above reproach right now."

I frowned. "I *am* trying."

My phone buzzed with a message from Aunt Clara. "My aunts are home," I told Amelia after reading the message. "Grady should be here soon, if he's coming. He didn't say for certain either way." He rarely did.

Amelia nodded. "How's he doing with this? I know he likes your aunts. It's going to be awkward if he has to arrest one of them."

I made a sour face. "He's not arresting Aunt Fran. She didn't do it." Grady had done his best to shield my aunts from the whispers and curious looks while the other guests were still here, but it wouldn't take long for the embers of doubt to light a fire.

I shivered at the visual. My ancestors had literally fled a similar situation in Salem, Massachusetts, many centuries ago. The witch trials had been too heartbreaking for them to stick around and watch, so they'd run south, found our island, and set up a new home. That home soon became a village, and that village became Charm.

Folks had speculated over the years that my ancestors fled Salem to avoid being held at trial themselves. The notion still clung to our name. I would agree that we were somewhat odd, decidedly quirky, and possibly cursed, but we weren't witches. Though, we could use a little of that rumored magic right now.

CHAPTER THREE

I dragged myself out of bed at the first sign of daylight. The churning fear in my gut had kept me awake most of the night, worried that the entire island had come to the wrong conclusion about Aunt Fran and Mayor Dunfree's murder.

I stretched my weary muscles, then begrudgingly pushed my feet into waiting slippers. I missed the soothing feel of cool floorboards under my bare toes. The bizarre cold snap we were suffering through had made multiple layers of clothing and boots a requirement. No more sticky hot walks on the boardwalk in cutoff shorts, flip-flops, and tank tops. I had to get bundled up to visit the mailbox.

I shuffled to the kitchen in flannel jammies and set the coffee to brew. I thanked the home's history as a boardinghouse for my substantial second-floor living space and respectable kitchen. The cabinets and fixtures were all older than me, but the appliances were somewhat new and the counter space was plentiful.

A private staircase in the foyer provided passage to my second-story living quarters. The space was just as big and full of potential as the first floor, but more cosmetically neglected. My theory was that the previous owner had simply run out of money before putting the house on the market the moment I was looking to buy. As a result, parts of the first floor and the entirety of the second were in need of a handyman.

I'd been putting a little money and a lot of elbow grease into the place any chance I got. I'd already repainted the rooms, sealed the aged windows, and added personal touches throughout the upstairs, but there were still nearly a thousand square feet downstairs that could become an expansion to the café. The possible updates to my private quarters were limitless. In a home as old as mine, there were perpetual opportunities for sprucing. If the snow kept up beyond Christmas, it would be a great distraction from being held hostage to the cold.

I poured the coffee and moseyed downstairs to count cookies. Amelia and I had worked until midnight when she'd gone home to get some sleep, and then I had kept going. I'd completed enough inventory to begin scheduling deliveries, assuming the forecast cooperated.

I set my mug aside when the empty bottom came into view, then plucked a tiny tea bag from my grandma's advent calendar. The quilted, hanging portrait of a fancy white teapot had been in our family for generations, hand-stitched by an ancestor and slightly yellow from age and wear. Little pockets around the teapot contained mock tea bags with strings attached to paper tags with the numbers from one to twenty-five. I dragged my fingertip across the delicate blue snowflakes around the pot's middle, then tossed the faux tea bag into a little dish on the countertop. This dish was filling up fast. Only nine days left until Christmas.

I rolled my shoulders for several beats, then twisted at the waist a few times, attempting to release the tension in my bunched-up muscles. I'd implemented a morning stretching routine two weeks back when the temperatures had first dipped into freezing territory and the windchills had kept me indoors. I sometimes kept it up until I broke a sweat, adding a few sit-ups, push-ups, and general calisthenics to the agenda, but I didn't have all that in me today. Instead, I cut the whole thing short and poured another cup of coffee.

My little plastic fitness bracelet beeped at me.

Be more active.

"Easy for you to say," I complained. The bracelet didn't have to sleep or manage stress, holidays, cookie orders, and insane winter weather issues. "I can't go walk in this," I told it. "I'd probably slip, slide, and break something I need, like a hip or my head. You're going to have to be happy with the stretching." I dropped my arm to my side and shook my head, deflated. The bracelet was right. I did need to keep moving. I just didn't want to. The stress was too high.

My mind was already reeling with a super-sized to-do list and the sun had barely risen.

Maybe what I needed was yoga? That was what all my women's magazines said, and I definitely needed something. I'd already gained back four of the twelve pounds I'd lost making tracks around the island this year, and at this point I was shaping up to look more like Santa than a seaside iced tea maker.

I brought up a beginner's yoga video on my cell phone, carried it into the empty former ballroom, and propped it on a windowsill, then began the instructed breathing.

My mind wandered.

I reached for the ceiling on a deep inhale. Then the floor on a long exhale. The ceiling. The floor. The ceiling. The floor.

My phone.

I stopped the video.

Ten minutes later, I'd filled my favorite travel mug with liquid energy and bundled up to my nose against the frigid winds. I was an outside bird, and I needed to fly. The temperatures had risen slightly since the night before and the snow had stopped falling. I used a long-handled sand shovel to push the cold white tufts off my porch, steps, and walkway, then I headed to the carriage house to check on Blue. Blue was my fixer-upper golf cart. I'd bought her off a lawn where a hand-painted sign said she'd be "great for parts!" but she ran fine. I gave her a bath and painted her to match her sisters: my thrift store bicycle and upcycled wagon. Now, she was a beautiful shade of sky blue with the Sun, Sand, and Tea insignia on her hood and flower chains of pink and white petals painted along her sides.

I dropped my bag onto her passenger seat and patted the steering wheel. Blue didn't like the cold, but she had a silver duct tape star on her headrest that I thought made her invincible. Grady had put it there after someone had stabbed her as a warning to me, and it felt like his stamp of approval. The star meant a lot to him. He'd been a fast-rising powerhouse within the U.S. Marshals office before I met him. Then his wife died of cancer, and he became a grieving widower and single father to a preschooler all at once.

I climbed aboard in silent prayer and gave Blue a try. Tenacious and true, her little engine kicked into action. We motored out of the carriage house, victorious against the weather. Nothing stopped my baby. Not an island snowstorm. Not even the recent collision and extensive body work I'd be paying on until the new millennium.

I stopped at my mailbox, set upon a white post at the end of my picket fence, and climbed out. I'd bought Blue a new winter enclosure, the golf cart equivalent of a ski coat and mask, with hinged doors on Black Friday. The local golf cart retailer had installed the enclosure at a discount, and given the recent historic drop in temperatures, I was wildly thankful. Blue's new duds included a plastic cover that enclosed everything from the windshield to the side and back windows, plus two operational doors. The gift was for both of us because it kept the racing wind off my face, and I could smile while I drove again without freezing my lips to my teeth.

A pile of brightly colored envelopes spilled out from the mailbox when I opened the door. I beamed at the shimmering paper, festive stamps, and fancy handwriting on each. Holiday cards made me happy. Every archway in the café was already lined in them, and I loved that they kept coming. I flipped through the return addresses to be sure I had the senders on my list of cards to send. I set a card I hadn't expected on top of the others, so I wouldn't miss the sender when it was time to get my next batch of outgoing cards into the mail. Sending a card without getting one in return seemed like a bummer, and I wasn't in the business of being a downer.

I climbed back behind the wheel and motored on. The boardwalk was edged in a little wall of snow that the wind had blown and sculpted while I slept. Families were already out, cheerfully bundled and carrying sleds. They zipped down the normally seagrass-covered hills on orange plastic tubes and sleek rectangular sheets, then skimmed across the icy beach. Frothy white waves rolled steadily in as children added driftwood arms and sea glass eyes to the first snowmen Charm had seen in years.

There was nothing like the ocean in any weather, but the unusual scene before me seemed a lot like a gift. I'd missed far too many holidays while I was away at culinary school and chasing a cowboy on his rodeo circuit. Still, Wyatt might've broken my heart, but that act had led me home, and I owed him a debt of gratitude for it.

As fate would have it, Wyatt had taken a job at the local nature center in Charm during his off-season. I now spent more time dodging him than I'd ever spent chasing him.

Blue and I rolled off the boardwalk and cruised up Middletown Road, then made a left at the square. I trundled down Main Street and smiled at the view. Boughs of holly had been tied to every lamp post. Mistletoe hung from street signs, icicle lights dripped over rooflines, and happy holiday tunes piped through speakers high on telephone poles.

I angled into a snow-covered parking spot outside Blessed Bee, my great-aunts' shop, and took a moment to people watch. Shoppers with broad smiles and rosy cheeks hustled in and out of stores, their arms heavy with packages despite the early hour. Mouthwatering scents of rich buttery pancakes and warm sugary syrups puffed out from local cafés with each exiting customer.

Blessed Bee was just one in a row of pastel-colored houses on the main strip through town. The homes had long ago been converted into a delightful selection of cafés, shops, and second-floor apartments. Outside, Blessed Bee's bright yellow clapboard was bookended by matching homes. The blue shop on the left was an ice cream parlor, and the pink one on the right was Charming Reads, Amelia's amazing bookstore. Basically, my aunts' shop was prime real estate, and one of the most profitable shops in town.

I climbed out, careful not to step in a puddle or on slippery ice. From where I stood, I could see that Aunt Clara had added little Santa and elf hats to the painted honeybees flying errant patterns over their shop window. What Aunt Clara had in creativity, Aunt Fran mirrored with business sense. Together, they used the honey from their personal hives, plus dried flowers and herbs from their extensive gardens, to make uniquely fabulous, holistic potions like lip gloss, facial soap, and mouthwatering condiments.

While my aunts weren't magical, they were absolutely superstitious, and they loved to retell our family legends, which probably contributed to the somewhat fantastical opinions about our family that still occasionally circulated among the townspeople. My aunts believed it was our sacred duty to pass along the tales of "unwritten history," as they called it. I worried the practice equated to little more than really old gossip, but one day, I supposed, I'd be alone and want to carry on the tradition. I'd want to feel as if I was part of something bigger. For now, I had my aunts and they were enough.

One of my least favorite family legends suggested that Swan women were somehow cosmically tied to the island—a nice way of saying we were cursed. In other words, if we left, bad things happened. I could argue that I'd left, and I was fine, but that wasn't the whole story. My heart had been shattered, then stomped into dust. Clearly, I had fallen in love with the wrong man.

My second least favorite of my aunt's stories declared that Swan women were cursed in love. It was as farfetched as the other legend, but infinitely more unfair. If I believed, I would say it explained why no one could remember a man in any Swan woman's life who hadn't succumbed to an early and unexpected death, but I didn't want to believe. I'd originally considered Wyatt's still-beating heart as proof the love curse was a lie, but that had only drudged up the possibility he'd never actually loved me, and that just ticked me off. Also, he'd left more than one rodeo in an ambulance during those days, and lately he seemed to be in the best shape of his life. As if my love had been actively trying to kill him.

I moved slowly onto the sidewalk, partially so I wouldn't fall, but also because I'd parked beside a white BMW with giant *Swan for Mayor* stickers covering the hood, roof, and doors. I recognized the car as belonging to Janie Crouch, Aunt Fran's unofficial campaign manager. The stickers were new. I rubbernecked the stickers all the way to the door, then stopped short again. Aunt Clara's goofy collection of hand-painted Christmas gnomes were missing from outside the store.

The door swung open before I reached it, and Aunt Clara ushered me inside. "What are you doing standing out there? You'll catch a cold."

"That's an old wives' tale," I told her, turning to give her a hug.

"Why take the chance?" she asked, smiling brightly back. "Who wants a cold?"

I couldn't argue with that.

The interior's pale yellow walls and bright white trim reminded me of the towering sunflowers that grew in my aunts' garden each summer. They'd stained the wide-planked floor a deep shade of green and painted the ceiling to look like the sky. A few little painted bees flew there as well.

I pulled my hat off and unbuttoned my coat.

Aunt Clara burrowed deeper into her heavy wool cardigan. "This weather is out of control," she complained. "If it doesn't warm up soon, I'll freeze in my own skin."

"It's nearly thirty-five now," I told her. "It's been this cold before."

"Not with the snow," she said. "The snow makes it colder."

I frowned. "Well, at least you have your sweater and some hot tea." I nodded to the steaming mug near the register.

"It's a toddy," she said. "Purely medicinal."

Aunt Fran strode out of the back room, arms heavy with stock. "Everly! Good morning." She adjusted the load against her chest and began to refill her stocking stuffer display with tiny lotions and soaps. "Were the roads bad?"

"No." I shook my head, then relieved her of half

the load and lined the boxes onto shelves. "The sun is out, and the snow is melting." I shot a cautious look in her direction, then abruptly changed the subject. "You didn't call to tell me how it went with Grady last night."

"He's a nice young man," Aunt Clara said, coming to join us with her hot toddy.

"Honest too," Aunt Fran added flatly. "He says I need to think of something that will help my case because right now everything points to me as Dunfree's killer."

I offered a sad smile. Aunt Fran was playing it cool this morning, but she was clearly affected by all that had happened. She hadn't called the mayor by his actual name in years. "Grady told me that too."

Aunt Clara hummed softly as she worked on her toddy. "I suppose we should light this place up before we're the last shop on the block to welcome shoppers."

I gave the store a long look. It was a bit dimmer inside than usual, though the sunlight reflecting off snow had done a good job of illuminating the space. "Were you thinking of not opening today?" I gave the pair a closer inspection. They looked fine on the surface, but that was all a mask. In addition to Aunt Clara's brandy-laced toddy for breakfast, Aunt Fran's too-tight smile was starting to look more maniacal by the minute. "You're not okay!" I accused. "Why are you pretending with me?"

Aunt Clara moved around the shop's perimeter hitting switches and plugging in cords until the room was alight with fluorescence and holiday charm. “We don’t want to worry you, dear.”

Aunt Fran huffed. “It’s your first Christmas home, and it’s absolute rubbish that something as ghastly as this has to ruin it.”

I smiled at my silly, protective great-aunts and at the scene before me. The shop’s crown molding danced with chasing lights. The counters and shelves were heavy with themed decor, from tiny faux-snow covered villages to stacks of holiday books and strings of paper snowflakes galore. Blessed Bee was a winter wonderland, and I loved it. “My Christmas isn’t ruined,” I promised. “Far from it, and I won’t let yours be either.”

Aunt Fran reached for my hand. “Have I told you lately how glad we are that you’re home?”

I set the last tube of bee balm lip gloss on the shelf, then squeezed her waiting hand. “Where else would I be?”

Aunt Clara headed our way, slightly lighter on her feet. Her bright smile reminded me of the missing gnome collection that had made her so happy before. “What happened to your gnome garden?” I asked. “Did you move them inside somewhere?”

My aunts exchanged a look.

“What?” I asked. “Is it because of what happened last night?” *Because one was used as a murder weapon?* Maybe it was wise to move them out of sight for a while.

“No,” Aunt Fran said. “They were gone when we got here this morning.”

Aunt Clara pressed a palm to her collarbone.

"Gone?" I parroted, unsure what to make of the simple word. "Stolen?" Who would steal a bunch of festively attired garden gnomes? "Why?" It wasn't as if the thief could put them out at his or her place, or even sell them. Everyone in Charm knew exactly who the gnomes belonged to. "Have you called the police?"

"Of course not," Fran said crankily. "I think the police have bigger problems right now, and who cares about the loss of a few garden gnomes? Except us, I mean. Complaining seems frivolous in light of everything else."

"It's not complaining," I said. "It's making a report, and letting the police know there was another gnome-related crime last night beside the big one. The two could be connected somehow."

Clara batted too-wide eyes, and I went to hug her.

The bell over the front door rattled, and a woman I recognized immediately as Janie Crouch blustered inside. Janie stomped bits of snow from her boots and pulled her wrap off in a fit of pique.

Janie was roughly my age, fresh from L.A., and endlessly in search of a cause. Aunt Fran's run for office had become her purpose du jour, which I appreciated significantly more than her blatant and ongoing interest in Grady Hays.

Janie pulled thick brown hair free from the collar of her sweater and sighed. "They're taking down the signs," she said, her bright blue eyes troubled. "I'd say I can't believe it, but that would be a lie. Oh, hello, Everly."

I raised one hand hip high and wiggled my fingers. "Hey." I had more questions about the missing gnomes, but that would apparently have to wait. "What signs?"

Aunt Fran met Janie at the store's center and rubbed her back as they made their way to the counter.

Aunt Clara seemed to stiffen a bit at my side, but turned her face away when I shot her a questioning look. Something else I'd have to circle back to.

Janie frowned. "There's a man taking down every CFC flyer posted on the telephone poles. He says the council ordered them all removed. I guess there's a 'no flyers on telephone poles' policy."

My aunts and I nodded.

"It was nearly impossible to route folks to a yard sale before GPS," I said.

Janie groaned. "This is exactly the kind of thing the CFC wants to change. It's why they support Fran so devotedly. Dunfree's regime wastes time worrying about some outdated mandate on flyers when it could be looking for ways to improve life here."

"Flyers are allowed," I said, feeling nonsensically defensive. "Notices are welcome. They just need to go on the community board."

Janie gave me a disbelieving look. "Exactly."

I tried to find her point.

The community board was a giant corkboard near Main Street and Middletown Road. The council had long ago deemed it the singular designated space for notices, and they kept it both behind glass and under lock and key. Charmers checked it regularly in nicer weather, and the *Town Charmer* blog often featured the events posted there. It certainly wasn't anything to get upset about.

Janie leaned in my direction. "Anything posted on the community board has to first be approved by the council. How is that fair? You know they censor what you see, right? Imagine all the things that have been refused a spot on the board." She paused dramatically, eyebrows high. "I don't even think there's a universe where the council would approve a CFC flyer, or any other propaganda that goes against their ridiculous rules."

I bit my lip. She had a point. The council would never add a CFC flyer to the public board, and that wasn't right. It was censorship. How many flyers had been vetoed over the years? What had I missed?

Janie slumped against the counter. "I hate to see the CFC be silenced. So far, they're our biggest allies and an excellent mouthpiece for reminding Charmers why we need change. There shouldn't be rules against posting signs. If the council denies this, where does the censorship end?"

I mulled that over, feeling a little like part of the problem. I *liked* some of our rules, the flyer one included. I didn't want to see tattered, weather-beaten remnants of forgotten signs clinging to the poles up and down our streets. The community board solved that problem. It limited the number of signs posted and it required their removal after fourteen days. It was easy to see what was coming up or going on around town without the clutter or the eyesores. I couldn't be sure about the censorship allegation without looking into it, which I didn't have time to do.

"I noticed your car out front," I said, smiling at Janie. "The 'Swan for Mayor' signs sure are… something."

"Thanks." Janie beamed. "I ordered them on the internet and applied them last night. I was on my way in here to show Clara and Fran when I saw the guy at the telephone pole and went to introduce myself. I'd kind of hoped he was a CFC member putting the flyers up, not a Charm employee taking them down." She lifted and dropped her hands then smiled warmly at me. "Hey, I'm sorry I missed your party last night," she said. "I had every intention of coming, but the hoopla at the lighthouse ran over, and by the time I was finally on my way, your party had been broken up."

"It's fine," I said. "How'd it go with the lighthouse?" I'd hated to overlap events, but finding a "good" time for most people so close to Christmas was tough, and mine was an open house. Folks could come as go as it fit their schedule. I'd planned to keep the festivities going until the last person left. *Or someone died*, I thought miserably.

She groaned. "We hardly raised any money, and there's no way the Historical Society can make any of the necessary repairs with the funds they have available. They should probably invest in warning signs to keep eager tourists at bay until the proper maintenance can be completed."

"Agreed," Aunt Fran said. "Safety needs to be a priority. I know they don't like the idea of posting signs around historic features or anywhere that disrupts the views, but we have to think of people first. Aesthetics later."

Aunt Clara refilled her cup from a carafe on the counter, then took a minute to inhale the steam. "It's hard to fundraise any time of year, but it's especially tough around the holidays. Most folks are already overspending on friends and family."

Janie nodded solemnly. "I'd rather hoped that the holiday spirit would inspire some generosity, but I suppose you're right. Just because I don't have any family doesn't mean everyone else isn't out shopping until they drop."

My aunts closed in on Janie with one of their healing hugs.

I felt a well-deserved stab of guilt when a few jealous thoughts rubbed their way to the surface. My aunts loved Janie, and why shouldn't they? She was profoundly beautiful, intelligent, independent, and dedicated. She had the right hair and clothes, and she embodied every deep-rooted LA stereotype I could imagine, short of having been an aspiring performer of some kind. She was an anomaly in Charm, and so far, a good one. Doubly lucky for us, she'd worked in PR and marketing, so her interest in Aunt Fran's campaign was priceless.

The real truth was that I'd become overprotective of my relationships after losing Grandma unexpectedly. No one could will their loved ones to stay or live forever just by holding on extra tight.

Janie wiggled free from my aunts and batted emotion-filled eyes. "Thank you. Sorry. I suppose my need to fix things has gotten out of control. I came here to relax and figure myself out, but I see all these causes and issues that need support, and I can't stop myself." She smiled. "I guess I have learned somethings about myself. I'm a doer and a fixer," she said proudly and with a giggle.

Aunt Fran smiled warmly at her. "You absolutely are. Your enthusiasm alone has kept me on course multiple times when I've wanted to bow out of this election. Now that I've made the announcement, I'll be counting on you to keep me straight. Assuming I'm not wrongfully convicted for murder."

Aunt Clara clutched at her sister, pulling her securely against her side. "You have nothing to fear, and we're behind you whatever comes."

Janie nodded in agreement. "You'll be absolved of every suspicion soon. I'm sure of it. People just aren't thinking clearly right now. They're all probably still in shock. They haven't had time to be sensible about it."

Aunt Fran looked almost hopeful at the other women's encouragement.

Their confidence was admirable, but I'd never

known a crowd to be sensible, especially when something dramatic was unfolding. Aunt Fran was right to worry. Grady had said so himself, and he never exaggerated. "I think I'll see if I can find Grady," I said. "It would be nice to know what he knows before I open Sun, Sand, and Tea. See if anything else turned up overnight. Maybe a witness or some piece of evidence that will help set things straight."

Aunt Clara nodded. "That would be lovely, but maybe let him handle things from here this time," she suggested.

I pursed my lips. She sounded like Amelia. It was true that I'd gotten myself into a couple of jams while following leads on other cases, but I had learned a thing or two. I wouldn't wind up in a killer's crosshairs again so easily. "Don't worry about me," I said sweetly. "I'll help Grady figure this out and everything will be right again soon."

Janie's eyes went wide. "Well, at least be careful, if not for you, then for your aunts." There was pain behind her words, and I remembered that as small as my family was, at least I still had Aunt Fran and Aunt Clara. Janie was alone. "Family's everything," she said. "You three need to take care of yourselves for each other. And on a more practical note, anything you find that could help Fran will likely be considered suspect by the public, both due to your relationship with her and your relationship with the detective."

I pulled my chin back. "I don't have a relationship with Grady."

"But you're friends," she said, eyes twinkling. "Do you know if he's interested in anyone in town?"

My jaw tightened. "Not that he's mentioned."

She smiled. "He's such a reclusive bad boy. What do you guys talk about? Is he into music? Movies? Cars?"

I had a sneaking suspicion she really meant *gorgeous leggy brunettes*, and I didn't want to know the answer.

"Hold that thought." Janie pulled her phone from her pocket, still smiling. "Oh, hey. I've got notifications set up for that gossip blog, and there's been an update."

My aunts moved in tight to Janie's sides, eyes and lips moving slightly as Janie scrolled through the article.

I followed their lead, navigating to the *Town Charmer* on my phone. With a little luck another crime, related to the murder, had just occurred because Aunt Fran had three witnesses who could verify her whereabouts for the last hour. Would that be enough to eliminate Fran as a suspect?

The page loaded, and I read the headline aloud. "Fran Swan: A Gnome de Plume?" The smaller line beneath added *Or should we call her Killer?* The tongue-in-cheek essay went on to suggest all the ways the anonymous author thought were better suited to address Aunt Fran. *Bee Keeper, Honey Collector, Shop Owner, Snazzy Dresser…* "Good grief."

The headline and subscript weren't exactly encouraging, but the blog post wasn't awful. No new evidence had been offered, and the author seemed to think the idea of Aunt Fran as a murderer was as ridiculous as I did. Unfortunately, the comments were rolling in hot and snarky, all under aliases, of course. The rudest responses were probably from Mary Grace Chatsworth. It would be just like her to try to eliminate Aunt Fran as her competition by kicking her while she was down.

Janie inhaled deeply, audibly. "I've got this. Marketing and public relations are what I do." She kissed my aunts' cheeks, smiled brightly at me, and made a beeline for the door.

"This will be fine," I promised.

Aunt Fran shook her head. "One of the names that blog writer called me was CFC Leader."

"I know." I'd seen it, and it had bothered me too. Aunt Fran might've put herself out there as proponent of change, but she wasn't a member of the group. We didn't even know who they were.

Yet another fact *I* intended to change.

Aunt Fran hoped to change the way Charmers approached things like tourism, art, and wildlife. She believed they all needed to be embraced. That tourists were a great thing. Art was meant for more than once a year during the summer festival, and our maritime forest and wild horses should be honored and studied. Fran thought it was time Charm stopped trying to keep a lid on our amazing community and start looking for ways to see it grow—including becoming more welcoming to outsiders.

I tucked my phone away and backed toward the door with resolve. "I'll talk to Grady about this blog post and about the stolen gnomes," I said to my aunts. "Whoever took the statues might've also had something to do with what happened to the mayor." It was a long shot, but there hadn't been many crimes in Charm since the last murder, and when multiple things had gone wrong last time, those crimes had all been related. "It's worth asking," I added when they opened their mouths to protest. We couldn't afford to discount any unusual happenings, and a herd of stolen holiday gnomes definitely counted as unusual. "I'll call if I learn anything," I promised. "You guys do the same, okay?"

They exchanged a hesitant look before nodding, and I made my escape into the chilly morning air.

Janie's *Swan for Mayor* mobile was gone when I stepped outside.

Getting information from Grady would be challenging, especially if he thought I was meddling, which I wasn't. I only wanted to tell him about the gnomes, and if he happened to have things to tell me too, then that was just how conversations worked. Even if he refused to share tit for tat, he was fun to look at, smelled good, and I liked his voice. It made hunting him down feel a lot less like a chore. Basically, my day was off to a nice start.

Until I stepped off the curb.

The breath caught in my throat as a solitary gnome came into view, on his back in the puddle forming outside Blue's new winter door. A thick black X had been gouged into the ceramic of each eye, and the back half of his head was missing. There was no denying that this curl-toed statue was a nothing less than a warning.

CHAPTER FOUR

I scooped the creepy, broken gnome into my gloved hands and tossed him onto Blue's passenger seat before reversing hastily into the road. The gnome rocked gently beside me, unlikely to roll away, thanks to his busted head. Still, I put my hand out when we stopped short to avoid a jaywalker.

The police station was on Bay Street, just across the island from my home on Ocean Drive. While I enjoyed daily views of the sunrise over the ocean, local law enforcement had gorgeous evening views of the sunset on the bay. The police department shared a parking lot with the nature center, a place I knew well. Though I hadn't been inside the police department until last spring when I was wrongfully accused of murder, the nature center had been a second home to me during my childhood. I'd had a deep interest in the island's vast ecosystems during middle school, and despite my paralyzing fear of bees, I'd helped my aunts through untold numbers of American honeybee preservation presentations in high school.

My great-aunts still frequented the nature center, sharing their passion for and leading classes on the plight of the American honeybee, which faced a host of environmental problems. That same passion had recently won them the starring roles in a documentary to be filmed on the island next spring. I could only imagine what the current town council would have to say about such unprecedented shenanigans. A film crew? In Charm? Surely there were numerous and very important forms to be completed for that, and an established wait period for the council to convene and consider before making their official denial of the request. I was sure they'd look for a way to stop it, though I didn't see how they could.

I slowed a bit, suddenly recalling something I tried consistently to forget: Wyatt worked at the nature center. I'd have to park near the police station door and hurry inside to avoid being spotted.

The lengths I went to avoid Wyatt were probably a little silly and overdramatic, but he'd broken my heart in ways I didn't know hearts could break, and my pride was still tender from the experience. The whole ordeal had been less than a year ago, and sharing my tiny island with him sometimes felt like too much, too soon.

I pressed Blue's gas pedal with purpose as I motored down Main Street toward Middletown, the road that acted as a kind of belt, cinching the island in the middle between the ocean and the bay. Blue's new tires gripped the wet street beneath the melting slush like a team of champs. I'd agonized about spending the extra money on new tires when I bought Blue's winter enclosure, but I was infinitely thankful I had. The new, deeper tread did wonders to hold me in place where my aged, worn tires would have sent me off the road at every turn. I supposed learning to drive in unfavorable conditions was something else I'd gained from my time away from home. Culinary school in Kentucky had come with plenty of snow.

I slowed at the sight of Grady's truck parked along the road's edge. The hazard lights of the mammoth black pickup were blinking, but Grady wasn't behind the wheel. A chill of worry rocked down my spine.

I slid Blue into the space ahead of him and opened my door. I couldn't imagine anyone getting the drop on Grady, but if someone had, I didn't want to run into him on the other side of the truck. I took a tentative step in the direction of a low whirring sound, then stopped.

"Ready?" Grady asked in his low, authoritative voice.

"Yes!" An older female called from behind the expensive enclosure of a high-end golf cart that had slid off the road.

Grady wasn't hurt.

I smiled at my silliness. Of course he was fine. I'd overreacted. Projected my fears and issues onto someone else.

He counted to three as I hurried toward him, then added, "Go!"

The woman behind the wheel of the expensive cart made a determined face, and the tires began to spin. She had apparently slid off the road and gotten stuck there. Grady pressed his shoulder to the cart's back end and shoved. The sound of spinning tires on frozen grass and snow zipped through the air.

His eyes caught mine, and he relaxed his stance. The tires stopped spinning, and the woman's shoulders dropped away from her ears.

I waved to her as I passed. "Hey," I said to Grady, admiring his dark jeans, black leather coat, and matching black knit hat. Even without the steed and Stetson, Grady embodied everything I loved about cowboys. He was respectful, honorable, hardworking, and true. At the moment, he was this older woman's hero. He'd been mine on a few occasions too. "Need a hand?"

Grady's serious mouth twitched, likely fighting a smile as he repositioned his boots in the snow. "Yep."

I pressed my gloved palms to the opposite side of the little cart and pushed when Grady gave the signal.

The woman hit the gas and rocketed forward with a scream. She slowed when all four tires found purchase on the slushy asphalt, then smiled over her shoulder and waved.

Grady chuckled as she drove slowly away.

"Who was that? I didn't recognize her," I said, dusting my gloves together.

"Visiting family for Christmas," he said. "She's from Arizona."

"Ah." I laughed. "So, it's not just locals who are struggling with our unexpected weather. How about you?" I asked. "Enjoying the ice and snow?"

"Actually, yes," he said. "We took Denver sledding on the beach this morning before the snow began to melt. Not many people can say they've done that, and he loved it. Reminded him of home."

By *we* Grady meant himself and his beautiful, blond au pair, Denise. I'd originally mistaken Denise for Grady's inappropriately young wife, but nowadays, I suspected she was actually an undercover assassin assigned to protect him and his son. Either I had a good imagination, or I was incredibly intuitive, but something about Denise had always screamed *more than a live-in caregiver* to me.

"I love snow," I said. "It's nice to see a few people have taken the initiative to get out and enjoy it. Charm may never see weather like this again in our lifetimes."

"It's thrown your town for a loop," he said. "Schools are closed. Half the shops haven't opened yet, and everyone's struggling to get around."

I felt my brows furrow as a new fear crept into my mind. "I hope this won't stop the Holiday Shuffle."

Grady wrinkled his nose at me. "The what?"

"The Holiday Shuffle," I repeated, shooting him a disbelieving look. "It's our annual progressive dinner. Do you know what that is?"

He crossed his arms. "Not unless the meal is forward thinking or comes from a can with that blue logo."

I sighed. "Not Progresso. Progress*ive*. Every year, the island divides into groups and visits multiple homes and businesses for different parts of a holiday meal. People volunteer months in advance to be one of the hosts. Then, we post our names, addresses, and menus on the community board so people planning to attend can pick and choose which places to stop for each portion of the dinner. The *Town Charmer* has a running log in their sidebar if you don't have time to stop at the community board."

Grady tilted his head. "So, I look at all the menus and decide on a route?"

"Yes! And the routes can be different for each person. Some homes open for cocktails and hors d'oeuvres, other begin with coffee, tea, and finger foods. The second stop is always soups and salads. Third stop is a main dish and sides. Fourth stop is for desserts and coffees or nightcaps."

"You volunteered?" Grady guessed.

"Of course, but I'll join in with everyone else once my portion is over. Each stop is only slated for an hour, otherwise the whole thing would take forever."

"Four stops is four hours," Grady said.

I smiled. "True, and it's so much fun. You have to come. It'll be a great way to get to know folks on a casual level. Visit their homes and stores, exchange some small talk, get a full stomach, and maybe a little tipsy."

He grinned. "Are you planning to get tipsy, Swan?"

I laughed. "No, but Charm has been doing the Holiday Shuffle for generations, and it's brought us closer as a community. Try it. Bring Denise and Denver. It'll be fun." Though the trips between each stop could be a nightmare if the weather didn't straighten up.

Grady gave the busy sidewalks around us a long look. "Maybe."

"Great." I clapped my gloves together.

He pulled his attention back to me. "Were you just passing by, or were you looking for me when you stopped to help with the golf cart?"

My smile fell at the reminder of why I'd gone in search of him. "I hoped to run into you, actually."

Grady waited, his patient eyes searching mine.

I cleared my throat as a residual pang of panic surfaced. "I thought I'd see if you have any viable leads on what really happened to Mayor Dunfree."

He exhaled long and slow, but didn't answer. "Anything else?"

"Someone stole all the gnomes outside Blessed Bee," I said, saving the worst for last.

His gaze shot in the direction of my aunts' store. "When?"

I lifted a shoulder, unsure. "They were gone when my aunts arrived this morning. Apparently, my aunts didn't call it in because they didn't want to bother you while you're tending to the murder investigation."

He turned a bemused expression on me. "Didn't stop you."

"That's because I think the crimes might be related." I marched back to Blue.

Grady followed me to her passenger door. "You should get a car. Better yet, get a truck. Something sturdy and substantial. Golf carts are cute rolling around here all summer, but they're meant for a golf course, not driving in the snow."

"They're cheap, energy efficient, and low emissions," I said, retrieving the gnome and suppressing memories of a recent accident that had nearly reduced Blue and I both to scrap. "Look. I found this in the snow outside my driver's side door when I left Blessed Bee this morning."

I handed Grady the broken gnome, and he swore under his breath.

"That's what I thought too," I admitted. "Have you checked the gnome from last night for fingerprints?"

Grady walked away, heading for his truck in a silent fury. I followed.

He pulled a black duffel bag from behind the passenger seat and dug inside until he found an evidence bag to stuff the gnome into. "There was only one set of prints on the murder weapon," he said, pushing the bagged gnome into the duffel and turning steady gray eyes on me. "Fran's."

"Circumstantial," I said, channeling every television judge I'd ever seen. "It's cold. Everyone else was wearing gloves. Fran went out without hers because she wanted to cool off."

"After a fight with the victim," he said.

I let my eyelids close briefly. I hadn't realized how much I'd been counting on the lab to recover new evidence from the murder-gnome. I needed something to point the blame away from Aunt Fran.

Grady's truck door thumped shut, and I reopened my eyes.

He'd braced his hands over his hips and locked a regretful look on me. He clenched and released his jaw as if whatever he was about to say wouldn't be easy and he knew I wouldn't like it. I tensed in anticipation.

"Look," he began softly. His phone buzzed in his coat pocket, interrupting him.

I released a nervous breath and craned my neck to look at his phone screen. I hated to be nosy, but I wanted to know if it was about the murder, and Grady was especially stingy with facts about his cases.

Senator Olivia Denver. I rocked back onto my heels. That call was personal, not business, and definitely none of mine. Senator Denver was Grady's former mother-in-law. Grandma to his son, who'd been named after her. It wasn't an uncommon practice in the South, using a mother's maiden name for a child or grandchild's first name. Senator Denver missed her grandson so much, she planned to leave the senate and move to Charm where she could see him as often as she liked. So far, Grady had seemed less than enthusiastic about the whole plan.

He rejected the call with the swipe of his thumb, then gripped his forehead a moment before refocusing on me. "What was I saying?"

"You okay?" I asked stepping a bit closer. "Do you want to come over? Have some tea?"

He shook his head. Negative. "I'm fine. Just a little worried about Denver. It's his first Christmas in a new place. He's been through a lot of change these last couple years, and I'm afraid I'm screwing him up."

I could tell it cost him to tell me that, so I reached for his hand and gave it a squeeze with my glove. To my utter surprise, Grady squeezed back. Before he let go and the rush of warm fuzzy feelings ended, I added the thing I'd meant to say before I'd reached for him. "Denver is amazing. He's happy and healthy, well cared for, and full of joy despite all the changes and an unthinkable loss." My throat tightened with sadness at the thought of any child losing a parent. I knew firsthand the hole that absence left, even with the best of substitutes in place. "All that good stuff? That's all you, Hays," I said. "You've got this. You're doing an A-plus job, and the fact you're still worried about him just proves what a lucky little guy he is."

A look of genuine pleasure spread over Grady's face until his perfect dimple sunk in. There might've even been a bit of a flush to his cheeks, but the biting wind made it hard to tell. "Thanks," he said, his voice lower and more gravelly than it had been a moment before. "I appreciate that. More than you know."

I smiled. Grady needed to find at least one good friend in Charm. Someone he could confide in on a regular basis or he was going to have an early stroke from all the pressure he put himself under. I was hoping to get the job, but didn't want to push. "You know what Denver might like?" I asked, hit with a sudden gem of an idea.

Grady raised his brows and released my hand slowly. "What's that?"

"The Giving Tree," I said, stuffing my hand into my pocket to savor the hum of electricity still clinging to it beneath the glove. "Have you seen it?" I asked. The Giving Tree was a towering evergreen growing outside the nature center and hard to miss. The ancient pine was estimated to be at least two hundred years old, and it was part of another long-running tradition on our island. People hung cards with their needs listed inside or the names of those they thought could use some holiday help or cheer. "Maybe Denver would like to take a name from the tree and be a Santa for them," I suggested. "When I was his age, I started asking a lot of questions about where the gifts really came from, so my grandma set me down with a proper lady's tea and told me she had a secret. Grandma told me that there wasn't *a* Santa. She said there were lots of Santas, and that it was every Santa's job to make another person's life special. She explained that most parents chose to be Santas for their kids because they love them so much, but that we could be Santas for strangers or neighbors or friends. That was the year she started taking me to the Giving Tree."

My heart grew a little heavier as I repeated the story, an ever-present itch of grief scratching my eyes and nose. I longed to see and hold my grandma so much sometimes that I was sure the pain would stop my heart. Instead, I sent up a silent note of thanks for all the years I'd had with her and all the memories I could now share with others. I brushed my gloved fingertips against the corners of my eyes.

"Holidays are hard," Grady said, emotion carved deep in his brow.

"Yeah." I knocked away a bead of guilt for my own pain when he'd lost a wife to cancer. I hoped to never know the kind of loss he and his son had experienced. I was sure my weakling heart couldn't take it. "You can bring him by my place after the tree for hot cocoa and cookies," I added. "I'm open until seven tonight."

"Another day," Grady said. "Amy's mom arrives today."

"Ah." Senator Denver. "Is she staying with you?"

He sucked his teeth and looked into the distance. "No. She bought the Northrop Manor a few weeks ago and sent a crew to prepare it for her."

I blinked. The Northrop Manor made my cavernous old Victorian look like a tiny hut. "There must be thirty rooms in that place, and two guest homes on the property. I thought the historical society planned to buy it and turn it into a museum of island history."

"They did," he said. "She outbid them. Now, the guest homes will house her staff and security."

I guffawed. "She knows this is present-day Charm, North Carolina, and not Victorian England, right? No one has a house staff or personal security."

"She likes to make a statement," he said. "She tried to assign a man to our home after the wedding, but I drew a line."

"You said your mother-in-law hired Denise," I said, watching his expression for signs I'd overstepped. "Maybe she's your protective detail."

He pursed his lips, but didn't answer.

I was being nosy again.

I stepped back casually, pretending to enjoy the sights around us instead of dying to know if he thought Denise was a trained spy for his mother-in-law or a hired assassin body guard.

"Have you told Fran about Olivia yet?" Grady asked. "Does she know Olivia plans to run for mayor?"

I wrinkled my nose. Grady had told me as much months ago, but I'd chosen to ignore the uncomfortable truth and hope it would go away. "Leaving D.C. for Charm is a big decision. I thought she might reevaluate and change her mind."

"Right," he said.

"Hey, what were you going to tell me earlier?" I asked, recalling the solemn expression he'd worn before his mother-in-law had called.

The expression returned before I finished speaking. The hands-on-hips, no-nonsense pose wasn't far behind.

"Go on," I pushed.

"I'm getting a lot of pressure from Mayor Dunfree's family to make an arrest."

My jaw went slack. "Pressure to arrest Aunt Fran?"

"She had means and motive," he said. "And I don't have any other suspects or evidence that leads me anywhere but back to Fran. The mayor's family knows it, and they're demanding action."

I scoffed. "You haven't had time to investigate. It's too soon to demand action. He just died last night!"

Grady lifted his palms to slow my rant. "I'm sure they just want closure," he said. "Justice."

I frowned. "Have you spoken to Mary Grace Chatsworth? Maybe she knows someone who had a reason to want Mayor Dunfree dead, or maybe she didn't want to be deputy mayor. Maybe *she* decided to take him out of the equation and run for mayor like she'd originally planned."

My internal temperature rose. I could understand the Dunfrees wanting closure, but not at the expense of a thorough investigation. "He was a cranky small-town mayor, for goodness sake," I continued. "I'm sure lots of people had a beef with him." I snapped my fingers. "We should talk to the council and see who's taken issue with him lately. Better yet, I'll ask Fran. She's on the council. She'll know if there's anything to know. You should talk to Mary Grace."

Grady's stare grew cold. "You're not investigating this," he ordered.

I put up three fingers like a Girl Scout. "It's not investigating. It's a conversation with my beloved aunt. Nothing more." *Unless Fran knew something worth looking into.*

"I mean it," he pressed. "You're too close to it this

time. Save yourself, your aunts, and everyone who cares about you a lot of worry and butt out."

I jerked my chin back. "Rude."

His lips twitched, fighting a small, reluctant smile.

"By the time you finish talking with Mary Grace, the lab should have news about the new gnome," I said. "Maybe this one will have prints."

"The last one had prints," he said.

I narrowed my eyes. "Prints that aren't Aunt Fran's," I clarified. "And don't forget about all those missing gnomes from outside Blessed Bee." I thought about that for a moment. "If you count the broken-headed guy you zipped into your duffel bag, that's three gnome-related crimes in twenty-four hours. That has to be significant. At least promise you'll look into Mary Grace and the gnomes."

Grady pressed a fingertip to the pulsing vein in his temple. "Mary Grace is already on my list of folks to meet with today," he said. "Why don't you open the tea shop and let me know what Fran says? Don't talk to anyone else about this. I'll handle it."

I nodded without giving a verbal agreement. I wanted to make him happy and leave things alone, but I couldn't allow my innocent great-aunt to go to jail for murder. "I can't let you arrest Fran," I said, "and I won't let her spend a minute of the holidays behind bars just because the pushy dead mayor has a pushy, still-kicking family who'd rather see you do *something* than do the right thing."

"Everly," Grady breathed my name long and slow,

accentuating each syllable. "I know you want to help, but you're going to have to let this play out. I have to follow procedures and protocols on this the same way I would with any other case, and you're going to have to let me. People are already talking, and I can't let my professionalism come into question. The islanders have to know I'll always do the right thing, no matter what."

"What are people saying?" I asked.

"That I should've brought Fran in last night, for starters," he answered. "That there's something between you and me that's causing me to turn a blind eye."

I bristled. "That's ridiculous. I would never try to influence you against doing the right thing. And I really hate that people think you would go along with such nonsense. For any reason."

Grady's lips quirked at one side, and he relaxed his stance.

I felt my temper cool. "What?"

Sunlight reflected off the clear gray of his eyes. "You don't seem too upset about the town's other implication."

I wrinkled my brow and feigned innocence. "What do you mean?"

"Folks seem to think there's something going on between you and me," he clarified.

"Isn't there?" I asked, feeling suddenly, inexplicably light. I turned away to hide my wide smile and headed for Blue. I cast a teasing look over my shoulder as I went.

Grady smiled after me, making no move to follow. “You’re just going to leave right now?”

“I’ve got to open for lunch,” I said. “You’ve got to talk to Mary Grace and check on the new gnome.”

Grady dragged a heavy hand through his hair and headed for his truck. “Watch your step, Swan.” There was a real warning in his tone, despite the teasing gleam in his eye.

I pulled onto the street, smile widening, and noticed a number of folks staring openly. I wasn’t sure how much of my exchange with Grady they’d seen or heard, but I flattened my expression anyway. Clearly the town didn’t need any more fodder for gossip.

CHAPTER FIVE

I took it easy along the slush-covered streets, avoiding jaywalkers and icy puddles. When I reached the broad earthen pathway linking Ocean Drive to the boardwalk, I hung a right, then slid a little on the frosty wooden planks before settling into a steady *thump-thump* rhythm over the weathered boards.

A familiar red bundle with blond hair and a wagon of books caught my eye up ahead. I smiled and waved. When Amelia didn't notice me, I honked.

She wrenched upright, eyes wide as I slowed to a stop a few feet away. A broad smile broke over her pretty face as she took in me and Blue. "Hey!"

"Good morning!" I called, popping open the door and levering myself out from behind the wheel. "Look at you," I said. "Braving the cold in your quest to keep Charm reading regardless of weather."

She stacked a pile of books from her wagon onto the shelf of her Little Library and arranged the titles alphabetically. "What can I say? It's my passion."

Amelia had set up a number of Little Libraries throughout the island. Some looked like giant bird-houses or massive tomes, but most were created from repurposed furniture pieces like curio cabinets and stout chests of drawers. She'd gutted the interiors, replaced the wooden doors and drawers with clear plexiglass fronts, and painted each unit in a different theme. My favorite was the one before us. Not only was it closest to my house, Amelia had painted a seas`cape on it, complete with sun, sand, and surf, a variety of colorful fishes, sand pails, and flip-flops.

"Anything good today?" I asked, teasing just a little. Of course everything she stocked was good.

Amelia waved a palm in front of the books like a game show hostess. "Absolutely. I've restocked all the favorite feel-good holiday classics."

"Excellent." I steepled my gloved fingers and scanned the newly added titles. I already had three of her books on my nightstand in need of returning. The Little Libraries worked on a take one/leave one honor system, and I frequently both took and left. "Do you have *Wuthering Heights*?" I asked, not seeing it among my choices.

Amelia wrinkled her nose at me. "That is not a feel-good holiday classic."

"Sure it is," I said. "I read it every Christmas." And it was inarguably a classic.

Amelia let her head fall back. She stared at the sky a long beat before returning her attention to me. "You realize that book is awful."

"What are you talking about?" I laughed. "It's a love story."

"No. It's about a selfish girl and her stalker who are awful to one another until she dies and haunts him, and he likes it." She reached into the Little Library and pulled out a small red book. "Here. Try this instead."

I read the title. "*The Greatest Gift*." I scanned my mental catalog of holiday reads but couldn't place this one.

"It's the short story that the movie *It's a Wonderful Life* was based on. Try it. You'll like it."

I gave the thin hardcover a skeptical look, my thoughts already on the moors with Catherine and Heathcliff. "*Wuthering Heights* is a powerful story," I said, circling back to defend my favorite star-crossed couple. "I think the idea of a love that endures all, one that is all consuming and eternal is"—fantastic, swoon-worthy, inconceivable—"interesting. You'd understand if you were cursed in love."

Amelia drew her lips to one side. "All right. I'll give you that, but I still think it's creepy."

I wasn't sure how I felt about her letting the *cursed in love* bit slide.

She straightened the remaining books, then closed the Little Library door and adjusted the tiny wreath she'd hung over the front window. "You should come to Charming Reads tomorrow night. We're doing a holiday party for the book club. We each read our favorite Christmas title, and we're going to share what we love most about our selected stories, open-mic style. Maybe you'll find a few fellow Heathcliff fans."

"Maybe," I said, though it was more likely her bookstore would be filled with fans of Dickens and Dr. Seuss. Much as I loved the Grinch, he'd never stolen my heart or made me believe love could conquer major obstacles...like three-hundred-year-old curses, for example. Not that I believed in curses.

"Are you planning to open for lunch today?" she asked, adjusting her knitted scarf and hat against the wind.

"Yeah." In light of the murder in my garden last night, I probably shouldn't, but as a woman hoping to prove her great-aunt's innocence, opening the café seemed like a smart move. "I'm hoping to loosen some lips with tea and cookies," I said, only partly kidding. It had occurred to me that the killer might drop by, posing as a customer, to see if anyone saw or heard anything they shouldn't have, or that I might overhear something I could use to help Aunt Fran. Either way, closing today would be a missed opportunity.

"Well, I've got to get back to Charming Reads," she said. "Dad's manning the register while I restock the Little Libraries, but I still have to create my menu for the progressive dinner. I thought serving desserts, coffee, and cocktails would be easy until I used the internet to look for ideas. Do you know how many holiday dessert ideas are out there?"

"A lot?" I guessed.

She closed her eyes in despair. "So many."

I patted her shoulder. I hadn't made my selections yet either, though I'd chosen the hors d'oeuvre portion of the evening to showcase a few café favorites and my mad culinary skills. If all went as planned, everyone would become permanently enchanted with my recipes, then come back regularly for more. "Let me know if you need help choosing desserts," I said. "I'm happy to assist, especially if there will be taste testing involved."

"Noted," Amelia said, gripping her book wagon's handle in one mittened hand. "I'll go online when I get back and try to narrow my choices." Her brow puckered. "That reminds me. How's it going with the videos for the Holiday How-To section of your website? I thought I might find a video there this morning after our talk last night. I know you didn't sleep."

My traitorous gaze darted away. "I couldn't concentrate last night, and my mind's still swimming."

Amelia hiked her brows. "So, no progress? Any idea on when you'll get to it?"

"Not really," I said, happy to tell the truth. "Right now, I need to find a way to help Aunt Fran."

"Is that what you're doing?" she asked. "Because it sounds like you're procrastinating."

I pressed a palm to my chest and headed back to Blue, buying myself time to think of something to say other than *Bingo!*

"I thought you were going to start with a video you've already finished," she called after me.

"Something from your culinary school days should only take a minute to add to your website."

That was true, but my plans had changed after I'd watched several of the old videos. I'd looked so much different then. Younger. Thinner. I'd made the videos before I wore a double-digit dress size and had to lie down to zip my pants. "I thought it would be better to make new videos," I said. "I've changed too much to use the old ones. People might not recognize me."

Amelia seemed to consider my excuse for a minute. "I suppose," Amelia conceded. "You've definitely changed."

I curved a protective arm over my middle, fighting a bout of self-consciousness and hating myself for it.

She nodded, appraising me until I squirmed. "You're clearly happier now. That definitely shows."

I dropped my arm back to my side, suddenly perplexed. "It does?"

"Sure, plus you look a little older, more mature and confident." She tipped her head over one shoulder. "I guess you're right. Better to use videos of you today than ones from when you were still figuring things out."

I bit back a goofy smile and felt my chest inflate with pride. "I'll try to make some progress soon."

"Perfect," Amelia said. "I'll be watching your website. Remember there are only nine days until Christmas."

"Okay, but editing takes time," I warned. Putting

the videos together so they played seamlessly without stretches of silence or awkward snafus wasn't easy, and they needed the right filters and music to make them fun. "It's an artistic process, and my mind's on Aunt Fran. I might be having artist's block."

"That can be tough," Amelia said too sweetly and in obvious jest. "Are you sure you're not having a chicken block."

I hopped behind Blue's wheel and shut the door. "I'm not a chicken," I called through the plastic windshield.

Amelia crooked her arms and flapped her elbows as I motored passed.

I plugged in all the Christmas lights at Sun, Sand, and Tea, then the tree. I adjusted the volume on my little boom box until the crooning sounds of Bing Crosby demanded we *Let it Snow! Let it Snow! Let it Snow!*

My spirits lightened. It was hard not to be enthusiastic when the tea shop was decked out in its finest holiday garb, and everything smelled of warm cinnamon, vanilla, and sugar.

All I needed was the perfect menu.

I grabbed a stick of green chalk from behind the counter and stared at my giant blackboard, outlined in twinkle lights and jolly velvet ribbons. The tea list wouldn't need to be changed. I'd made the batches fresh for last night's party, so they were in good standing with my strict twenty-four-hour rule for freshness. Tonight, however, I'd be making more.

I tapped the chalk against my palm, then went to inspect the contents of my fridge for inspiration. Cranberries, meats and cheeses, pasta, crescent rolls, and veggies. Thanks to the party's sudden and dramatic end, I had a multitude of leftovers to work with, and a spark of creativity zipped through me.

After a few moments, I climbed onto my folding stool and set my chalk against the slate. I scripted the new menu in an elaborate curlicue print.

Baked Ham and Cheese Pinwheels
Cranberry and Brie Bites
Caprese Salad
Antipasto Salad
Crab and Artichoke Dip

Satisfied, I set the green chalk aside and selected a stick of muted pink for the dessert list. I printed *Swan Holiday Cookies, Pastries, and Sweets* as prettily as possible, then added *Get them before they're gone!* Because those recipes were going back in the vault on New Year's Day, and they were staying there until next Thanksgiving.

My cell phone's alarm buzzed and vibrated on the counter. *Eleven o'clock! Opening time!*

I unlocked the front door and flipped my new window sign from *Closed* to *C'mon in, y'all!* Amelia's dad, Mr. Butters, had painted it for me as a café warming gift and delivered it after Charm's summer arts festival. I'd never seen anything so perfectly southern, and I loved it.

Guests trickled in and out all day, but the café was never truly full. The phone, on the other hand, barely stopped ringing. If I didn't stop taking cookie orders soon, I'd have to hire a staff to complete them. I spun through the room between calls, delivering plates of rich, butter-scented creations until my stomach was nearly as loud as the music. My heart swelled with every guest's compliment, refill, and request for more. This was what it felt like to be exactly where I belonged, doing exactly what I'd been destined to do.

I took advantage of a lull in the chaos to toss a few frozen shrimp and scallops into a bowl of cold water for defrosting. It had occurred to me late last night that Lou, my resident seagull, might not know how to hunt in this weather, and I couldn't let the poor guy starve. My aunts thought Lou was the reincarnated soul of a wealthy businessman who'd commissioned my home for his mistress nearly two hundred years ago, then died here decades later after losing her and going full-blown nutty. Reincarnation was another thing I didn't actively believe in, but passively, it concerned me. How could I let a guy who'd been through all that go hungry?

The idea was no less far-fetched than the notion his wife had drowned herself out back after discovering Lou (the guy, not the gull) with his young mistress, Maggie, or the idea that Maggie had thrown herself from the widow's walk after seeing the destruction she'd caused. My aunts couldn't decide which of the women had been allegedly reincarnated as my white cat, a downside to "unwritten history," I supposed, but I'd liked the name Maggie, so I went with that.

As if on cue, Maggie appeared on the snowy deck outside, lazily grooming her face and paws while overseeing the beach as if it were her job.

I slid the deck door open and tiptoed out, careful to close it behind me before freezing any of my patrons. "Hey, Maggie," I said sweetly. "I haven't seen you in a while." I patted her head and scratched behind her ear before resting the tray of shrimp and scallops on a snow-covered patio table for Lou.

The big gull landed roughly on the handrail beside me, wings expanded, feathers ruffled. He looked twice the size he had been when I met him.

"Hello," I said with a breathless smile. "You really come out of nowhere, don't you?"

He cocked his head and locked a beady black eye on the tray.

Maggie gave Lou and his dinner a long look, then seemed to decide better of pursuing the crustaceans and went back to her grooming herself and feigning disinterest in the meal.

"I keep fresh bowls of kibble and water inside for you," I reminded her, "where it's warm."

She ignored me. Maggie preferred her freedom and became quite the feline Houdini whenever I tried to make her a house cat.

"Hungry?" I asked, stepping back to give Lou room. A hearty blast of wind sent a shiver down my spine, and I wrapped my arms around myself for warmth. I'd need a coat if I spent another moment outside. I slid the patio door open once more and crept back through, this time with Maggie on my heels.

I scooped her up immediately and moved as quickly and inconspicuously as possibly through the café and into the foyer where I unlocked the door to my private stairway and ducked inside. "I can't have a cat in the café," I told her. "You'll have to stay up here to get warm and catch up on your naps." I dropped her before her food and water dishes, then patted her head. "I'll be back as soon as I can," I promised.

She watched with luminous green eyes as I waved goodbye, then darted back down the steps. I closed the door behind me at the bottom and relocked it, only partially certain she'd be there when I returned. Maggie had an uncanny way of vanishing and reappearing like vapor.

I stepped across the threshold to my shop and slowed at the sight of a tall, dark, and inviting silhouette near my patio doors. The long lean lines of him, coupled with the Stetson turned my knees to jelly. *A cowboy.* Images from the covers of my favorite romance books crowded into my mind. A closer look turned my stomach into knots.

Wyatt.

I scurried around the counter and busied myself cleaning and ignoring him. There were still a few people finishing their tea and snacks. I didn't want them to see anything that could later be misconstrued in any way for the sake of gossip. Very few islanders were unaware of my former relationship with Wyatt, and too many were showing a keen interest in my friendship with Grady. I was starting to feel like the unwitting star of a fairly boring reality show.

He began to move in my direction, and the steady sound of his measured footfalls set my stupid heart aflutter.

"E," he said, removing his hat and upturning it on the counter. He boarded a bar stool before me and smiled.

"Wyatt," I said. "What can I get you?"

"How about some tea for starters?"

I filled a jar with ice, careful to look anywhere but directly into the blue eyes that had been my undoing once before. "Anything to eat?" I asked, sliding the jar beneath my Old-Fashioned Sweet Tea dispenser.

Wyatt tipped his head toward the deck. "His lunch looks pretty good."

I followed his gaze to Lou before sliding the tea across the counter. "Cold shrimp and scallops?"

Wyatt lifted the jar in cheers. "I love shrimp and scallops, and I love your grandmama's Old-Fashioned Sweet Tea. You remembered." He winked.

"I remember lots of things," I said, meaning nothing in particular but letting him think on the implication. "Do you really want shrimp and scallops?"

Wyatt leaned back to rub his washboard stomach

through a fitted thermal shirt. "Nah. You choose. You know I'm always happy with whatever you make."

I turned away to grab a plate and roll my eyes privately. "Well, I run a café now. Normal people place orders instead of leaving everything up to me."

He chuckled. "As if you'd ever take an order from me."

I paused to smile at him. "Touché." I grabbed a loaf of fresh-baked bread and tossed it onto the counter.

Wyatt hiked a thumb in the direction of the deck. "You know you don't have to worry about him, right?"

"Who?" My gaze jumped toward the sliding doors. "Lou?"

Wyatt watched me carefully, a small smile lifting his stubble-covered cheeks. "I know you think he's going to freeze out there, but he'll be fine."

I paused. I'd forgotten that Wyatt was more than a rodeo-hopeful. He was an animal lover and student of nature as well. It was one of the things that had drawn me to him.

"See the way he fluffs himself up?" Wyatt pointed toward the windows across the café where Lou had become a virtual volleyball of feathers on the handrail outside. "There are pockets of air between his feathers that keep him warm. His body heat stays in, and the feathers are waterproof too, so they repel the precipitation."

I smiled back, thankful for the information. "That's good to know."

"Yeah. Plus, see how he's sitting on his feet?" Wyatt

pressed on, apparently unable to stop himself. "You can't see them because he's using his feathers to keep them warm too. Even if he didn't, his feet have very few blood vessels. It would take a lot to freeze them." He dragged his gaze back to me. "Your little friend out there is designed for survival."

I selected a bread knife, then gave Wyatt an appreciative nod. "Thanks, I guess I do worry."

"Wouldn't be you if you didn't," he said. "It's nice that you feed him. He'd be okay without it, but he uses lots of energy to stay warm, so the extra calories don't hurt."

I cut two thick slices from the bread loaf, then liberally buttered them both.

Wyatt took notice and sat up straight. "Are you making grilled cheese?"

I grinned.

Wyatt and I had been so poor when we'd first left Charm together that we'd practically lived on grilled cheese and instant noodles. Over time, I'd learned to add things to the sandwiches that made them feel more personal and more like my own. He'd cheerfully tried every new combination I'd put in front of him, and we'd joked that I could sell a grilled cheese cookbook for money one day if he never made it in rodeo.

I bit my lip, hating the way I fell so easily back in sync with the man who'd broken my heart. I was supposed to be avoiding him.

I turned away and got to work. He'd done the right thing by dumping me, I reminded myself. I'd wanted him, and he'd wanted the rodeo. It would've been cruel for him to keep me around knowing how much that was true. Maybe, I realized, flipping the golden-brown sandwich, I wasn't avoiding him just because I was angry with him. Maybe I'd been avoiding him because I didn't like feeling like a cast-off sock.

"That looks amazing," he said, leaning on his elbows across the counter. "Have any pickles or potato chips in this fancy-pants café?"

I plated the sandwich with a pickle spear and bag of kettle-cooked chips. "Voila."

Wyatt moaned in satisfaction as he stared at the simple meal. "This is perfect."

"Almost," I said, turning to ladle some homemade chicken soup from the small Crock-Pot under the counter. "For that impressive response, you get to share my lunch." I set the bowl beside his plate, and he collapsed back on his stool.

"You're a goddess."

"Eat." I ladled a second bowl of soup for myself, feeling a little ashamed of all my attempts at avoiding him. "How are things at the nature center?"

"Good." His eyes widened. "There's so much to tell people, and so much more I want to know." He relayed the details of his research and anecdotes from the classes he held about our island's wild mustangs with the enthusiasm of a kid who'd discovered unicorns. He brushed a napkin over his lips when the sandwich and chips were gone. "How's Fran doing?"

I supposed I should have known he'd heard about that too. Everyone in town probably had by now. "She's okay. She's tough, and she believes things usually work out the way they were meant to."

"And how about you?" he asked, concern dripping from the words.

"Frustrated." I sighed.

"Understandable," he said. "Anything I can do?"

"Not that I can think of." Though, I still needed to ask Fran if she could think of anyone with an aggressive grievance. "I'm going to figure out what really happened to Mayor Dunfree. Janie's on top of everything else."

He nodded. "That's the new girl. The brunette from LA, right?"

"That's the one." I ignored the ridiculous pang of jealousy. Janie was outgoing, gorgeous, and pretty hard to miss. Of course he would know her.

"You don't like her," he said, pushing his empty soup bowl in the direction of his crumb-covered plate. "Why?"

Because I'm childish and petty? "I like her," I said. "I'm just trying to think of a way to clear Fran's name. People are talking, and I need to nip that in the bud. Otherwise, her reputation won't recover, even after her name's cleared. She'll never be mayor, and the lingering suspicions could hurt her business or worse, damage our legacy, and that would probably kill her. Figuratively, I mean."

Wyatt offered a sad smile. "You'll figure this out."

I puffed a sigh of doubt into my bangs. “You’re the first person who hasn’t told me to leave it alone.”

He laughed. “Would it matter if I had?”

“No,” I admitted, “but I appreciate the support.”

He looked up at me from beneath his thick lashes and offered an impish smile. “Anytime. Returning the favor.”

I nodded. I’d followed him everywhere on tour. Believed he could win it all every time.

Wyatt dropped a twenty on the counter and stretched onto his feet. “Thanks for lunch. It was amazing as usual, but it’s time for me to chase the mustangs.”

I took the twenty to the register to make change, but before I could ring him up, he tipped his hat and was gone.

CHAPTER SIX

The afternoon moved slowly once the lunch guests cleared. I worked on editing my new holiday cookie-making video, never quite satisfied with the results but knowing it was as good as it would get.

When the seashell wind chimes and jingle bells sounded just after four, I was so thankful for the excuse to walk away from my laptop, I was prepared to offer whoever had come into the café a free meal.

Lanita, Mr. and Mrs. Waters's niece, bustled inside with a shiver and a smile. "I'm so glad you're open. There aren't any carts or cars parked outside, so I wasn't sure."

I lifted one palm. "Everyone seems to be shopping. They're probably eating in town. Closer to the action."

"True," she agreed.

I hurried into position behind the counter and beamed. "The good news is, you've got me all to yourself and I'm itching to serve. What can I get you?"

"Cookies," she said, stripping off her black wool

pea coat and matching scarf. "I have three separate orders to place, plus a personal, soul-deep need for more of your peppermint fudge."

"Perfect!" I grabbed a knife and went after the fudge first. "I can help with all of that."

"I need separate bills for each order," she said, sliding a rumpled sheet of paper in my direction. Three sets of random holiday cookie names were written on the lines.

I stared blankly at the sheet. On another day, I might not have been so surprised, but on the heels of Fran's crisis, the threat-gnome, and Wyatt, the list caught me off guard. "These aren't for you and the Waters?"

"No. They're afternoon Pick-Me-Ups," she said. "I told you, Charmers are loving the idea of deliveries instead of braving the cold. I've been driving around town all morning, picking up packages, delivering lunches, taking people from here to there. Your only cabbie is swamped, so I'm making myself useful."

"Ingenuity at its finest," I said. "Impressive." I hadn't given any thought to how all the shoppers I'd seen had gotten into town when the number of cars and golf carts on the road had been so few.

I delivered Lanita's fudge first, then took the lists to my cookie bins to fulfill the other orders while she recorded the details in her glittery pink notebook. "There you go," I said a few minutes later, setting the bags before her, each with a receipt stapled to the top. "Your fudge is on the house."

"Thanks!" She dug in her purse for a wallet, then handed me a thin stack of cash. Her phone buzzed and she turned it over with a smile. "College friends," she said. "I took pictures of the snowy beach last night, and my roommates are going crazy."

I returned the change from her orders before peeking at the photo on her phone. The beach had been beautiful this morning, but the photos she'd taken last night were completely enchanting. The combination of snow, sand, and frothy white waves under moonlight was downright surreal. "These are fantastic," I said. "May I?"

She handed the phone to me, and I scrolled through the images. "You have a real talent." *I still cut off half my head in selfies.*

Lanita smiled. "Thanks, but I can't take the credit. Mother Nature did all the work for me." She polished off the last bite of her peppermint fudge and fluttered her eyelids. "Amazing."

"Oh!" I hurried to the pile of holiday cards waiting to go out with the morning mail, then ferried a small red envelope back to her. "This is for your aunt. Would you mind delivering it for me? It's a thank-you for the peppermint stick."

She tucked the envelope into her pocket. "No problem. She'll love it, and we can call it a trade for the fudge."

I laughed, then bagged another piece for the road while she bundled up. Her phone caught my attention again, and something about the images she'd shown me niggled in my mind. "Were you outside taking those pictures when Mayor Dunfree was killed?"

"Mm-hmm." She zipped her coat and settled a large messenger bag across her body. Three white takeout bags poked through the open top. "I heard him angry-whispering at someone when I went out, so I headed the other way to give them privacy. I'd assumed he was arguing with his wife, but people are saying he was on the phone."

I'd heard that too. "Mrs. Dunfree told Grady she'd walked to the golf cart alone while her husband took a phone call. Can you remember anything else?"

Lanita frowned. "Not really. The next thing I knew, I heard a woman scream, and I ran back from the beach. I caught sight of you as I reached the top of the hill. You were already telling people to stay back. Help was on the way. I couldn't believe it was the mayor on the ground when it was a woman who'd screamed."

"My aunt screamed when she saw him," I said.

Lanita sighed. "Everything happened so fast. I went inside to tell my aunt and uncle what was happening, and by the time we came back out, the night was flooded with emergency lights."

I couldn't argue with her assessment of the timeline. Things had unfolded quickly.

I chewed my lip as a new thought came to mind. "I wonder who he was talking to," I said quietly. What if Mrs. Dunfree was lying about the call? Or what if she'd taken advantage of her husband's distraction?

"Who knows," she said. "My mom says he was a

total misogynist. When I was applying to colleges, she told me about the mayor here, who refused to be a reference for her when she was being considered for Stanford. *Stanford*," she repeated for emphasis. "Mom worked at the town hall with him all through high school, but he wouldn't write a simple reference. He told her she should be realistic. She was going to quit her future job to stay home with the kids eventually, so why take the seat away from a man who'd use the training all his life?" Lanita looked ill. "Can you even imagine someone saying that to you?"

"No," I said honestly.

"Needless to say," Lanita said, "we aren't big Dunfree supporters in my family."

"Understandable," I said, drumming my fingers on the counter. Real grudges were hard to let go. I tried to imagine Mayor Dunfree outside, pacing in the shadows, engrossed in a heated call. Had his misogyny persisted? Had someone called him out on it? "Could the mayor have been so wrapped up in the argument that he never saw the killer coming? Could the person on the phone be the same one who killed him?" Maybe calling the mayor was a tricky way to make him think the caller was somewhere else, when in truth he or she was right behind him with my porch gnome!

Lanita looked at her watch. "I don't know, and this sounds like it's about to get interesting, but I've got to deliver these orders. Will you keep me posted if you find any answers?"

I nodded in agreement, but I didn't mean it. As

I knew well, people who got caught up in amateur investigations often got hurt, and I liked Lanita. Plus, her aunt and uncle would never forgive me if anything bad happened to her. "Drive safely," I said, fumbling for my cell phone.

Grady hadn't said anything about Mayor Dunfree's cell phone when I had spoken to him earlier. Had he found it? Did he know who the mayor had been talking to that night? I dialed Grady and waited impatiently for the call to connect.

"Hays," Grady answered.

"Hey, it's Everly," I said dumbly. I'd rushed into dialing without making a plan to explain why I was so interested in the mayor's last phone call. "I was just wondering if you happened to find Mayor Dunfree's cell phone last night." I closed my eyes and waited.

"No," Grady said slowly. "Why? Did you?"

My lids sprang open. "No, but I was just going out to feed the birds in the garden and thought I'd take a look by the light of day for you."

"My guys were there at dawn. The phone's not there."

"Okay," I said sweetly. "I just thought if someone accidentally kicked it out of sight or if it was buried in snow during all the commotion, I might see it while I was out there."

Grady sighed. "Please don't look for it. If you come across a cell phone in the garden, give me a call, but don't get involved in this intentionally. I'll come by and take another look after I finish my interviews."

"Sounds good," I told him. "I guess I'll just feed the birds then."

"Uh-huh," he groaned.

I imagined him pinching the bridge of his nose or popping antacids.

"Have you had a chance to talk to Fran?" he asked.

"Not yet." I grabbed my coat and a bag of birdseed from the foyer closet. "I'm sure Blessed Bee has been swamped, so I'm inviting her and Aunt Clara over for dinner."

"Great. I'll be there when I can."

I headed for the front door with a smile on my lips. "Sounds good." I disconnected and dashed into my gardens to search for a cell phone. I kicked tiny windblown drifts of snow and checked along the ground under every bush, shrub, and frozen plant. Grady was right, there was no phone to be found, and that could only mean one thing.

The killer had taken it with him.

A blade of fear cut through my bravado, and I ran back toward the house, flinging birdseed over the snow as I fled. I paused briefly to fill the feeder near the gate, then took the porch steps two at a time.

I jerked to a stop behind the counter and pressed my palms to my knees, then sucked in deep, calming breaths. I really was out of shape, and an enormous chicken.

When I righted myself, my open laptop stared back at me. *Speaking of chicken*, I thought. The video I'd been editing was paused on the screen. All I had to do was press a button and the video would be added to my website under the Holiday How-To tab I'd created especially for videos just like it.

I'd spent hours in early November selecting the perfect cookie recipe, *my grandma's delectable Seven-Layer Bars*, the right mixing bowls, *red and green with mitten and stocking stencils*, an apron with the word *Believe* embroidered over the chest and the backdrop of *my beloved café*, complete with bright ocean views beyond the windows. I'd spent time each night creating the script, perfecting the lighting, and performing countless dry runs until I was sure I was ready to record. Now, it was time to show the world all my hard work, but I couldn't convince myself to post the video.

People online were mean, and I didn't have room for negativity in my life. I was making something good and positive for myself. Why would I jeopardize it by giving haters a chance to see me baking and leave nasty comments? If I deleted the comments, I'd look like a baby. If I left them, the negativity could influence other people's opinions of my café and products.

Maybe I'd set it up so comments weren't allowed.

What would that say about me?

I shut the laptop.

I had too many other things to do at the moment. There wasn't time to press the button anyway. I dialed my aunts instead.

"Thanks for calling Blessed Bee, where we're buzzing for the holidays," Aunt Clara answered.

"Hey," I said. "Are you busy?"

"Never too busy for you," she cooed. "Did you have a chance to tell Detective Hays about my missing gnomes? I've been thinking about what you said all day, and you're right. We should've called him right away."

"I did, and he's looking into it," I said. "While he and I were talking, I realized I have a few questions for Aunt Fran, and Grady said I should ask them. Any chance you guys are free for dinner?"

"I think so," Aunt Clara said. "Just a minute." A scraping sound swept through the receiver, muffling the white noise of shoppers and holiday music on her end of the line. "Fran?" Aunt Clara's familiar, albeit muted, voice warbled. "Everly wants to know if we're free for dinner."

There was a loud scuffling sound through the receiver, and I pulled it away from my ear.

"Hello?" Aunt Fran yelled.

"Hi." I cringed. "You're really loud."

"We're sharing the phone, darling," Clara clarified. "We're making sure you can hear us both."

I shook my head at the empty café. "Push the speaker option instead. You don't have to yell."

They broke into a side conversation about whether or not the phone had a speaker button.

I waited. Some days I wished I had a sister to grow old with, and other days I was thankful not to. I wasn't sure which sort of day this was. "Hello?" I asked. "Dinner?"

"We're free," Aunt Fran said, only slightly quieter and probably still not on speaker. "Did you talk to Detective Hays?"

"She did," Aunt Clara hissed. "She already told us that."

Fran grunted. "She hasn't told me. I just got here."

I rubbed my forehead. "See you at seven?"

This was definitely one of the days I could get onboard with growing old alone.

"We'll be there," Aunt Fran confirmed. "Can I bring anything?"

I looked around my café and smiled. "I've got dinner covered, but can you bring the name of someone who might've had a beef with the mayor lately?"

"Ha," Aunt Fran said. "I'll bring a list."

CHAPTER SEVEN

I watched the day slip away as I served the dinner crowd and prepared for my aunts to arrive. Blessed Bee closed promptly at seven each night, which gave me plenty of time to wrap things up at Sun, Sand, and Tea while I prepped our private meal. The logistics would be especially simple because I planned to use café leftovers as side dishes and hors d'oeuvres.

Choosing the main dish was trickier. I flipped through multiple Swan family cookbooks in search of inspiration before landing on the perfect dish. In honor of the cold snap, which hadn't let up the way the weather channel predicted, I decided on my grandma's favorite: chicken potpie. I browned the chicken between bouts of serving and cleaning up after guests, then mixed the ingredients and poured everything into a glass baking dish. I kicked it up a notch with fat cubes of my best sourdough bread and smiled at the pretty results. I slid the dish into the oven, already set at 350 degrees and waited for the rich, buttery scents of the hundred-year-old recipe to fill my lungs, café, and heart.

Not surprisingly, business ground to a halt at half-past six. There wasn't much to do at the seaside after dark this time of year. In town, however, most restaurants and shops would be going strong for another couple of hours. My thoughts wandered in the stillness, and my gaze drifted to the night beyond my windows. Outside the patio doors, a silver moon rose over the water, its rippled image fluttering on the dark surface below. The view was enchanting, distracting, and darn near magical. I considered going onto the deck to be closer to it. I wanted to breathe in the crisp sea air.

Unfortunately, I had work to do.

I reopened my laptop and stared at the how-to video, still waiting for me to add it to my website. Not quite ready to push the button, I opened a new window and brought up the *Town Charmer* blog. Maybe there was an update, and I could use the information to guide my questions for Aunt Fran tonight.

The new feature article showcased menus for the upcoming Holiday Shuffle. Was it strange that our mayor had been murdered, but the annual progressive dinner was the top news story on our gossip site? Maybe. It could have been that the annual shuffle was more current and pressing, but I suspected the blogger simply hadn't gotten any new material.

I poured a jar of tea and settled in to review the available menus. First, I chose my path for the night based on what was being served and where, then I focused on what would be served at the other cocktails and hors d'oeuvres locations. Whatever I served needed to blow everyone else's selections away. The bottom line of the article was both bold and underlined. Anyone who didn't submit their menus immediately would be removed from the list of stops.

Jeez. No pressure or anything. It wasn't as if I didn't have a business to run, my great-aunt's name to clear, and a how-to-bake video to upload.

I left a comment to assure everyone I was just having trouble choosing what to make after reading all their incredible selections, and I promised to get my menu together as soon as possible.

The pressure left me slouching against the counter. Whatever I made had to be perfect. I wasn't just another home on the list of stops that night, I was a café owner. I needed to make an impression that would bring people back to Sun, Sand, and Tea. The food had to be an example of my abilities. A showcase. Especially for those who would be stopping in for the first time. If I didn't impress, the negative word of mouth could ruin me.

The wind chimes and jingle bells sounded again, and I checked the little clock on my laptop. It was already after seven. Closing time. I heaved a sigh of relief as I realized the new arrivals had to be my aunts.

I hurried in their direction, beginning to babble before I caught sight of them. "I'm so glad you're here. I've been going crazy since I spoke with Gra—"

I slammed my mouth shut at the sight of the woman before me. The bells hadn't announced my aunts. They'd welcomed Senator Olivia Denver. I'd only seen her in online photos and news articles, but I'd recognize her anywhere. Auburn hair. Piercing blue eyes. The expression and posture of someone who could break a person with their words, their bare hands, or their stare. I didn't let the black designer pantsuit, heels, or handbag fool me. There was a soldier beneath that fancy facade.

"Pardon me," I said, regaining myself and forcing a congenial expression. Immediately on edge. "I'm expecting my great-aunts for dinner, and I was certain you were them."

She looked me over, head to toe, with the same blank expression Grady used to evaluate criminals. "Are you open?" she asked, lifting one gloved finger to point at the door behind her. "The sign said to come inside."

"Yes. Of course." I hopped into action, turning back in the direction I'd come. "Right this way." I led her across the foyer and into the café. "Welcome to Sun, Sand, and Tea. Today's menu is on the blackboard." I slid behind the counter to put some space between us and hoped to look professional while I hid. "I keep twenty iced tea selections on tap. Every recipe I make here has been passed down through my family's cookbooks, but I put a personal twist on most." I bit the insides of my cheeks to stop myself from talking. I was acting strangely. Saying too much. *Why am*

I so nervous? I knew the answer immediately. I'd seen the way Grady avoided her, dodged her calls, groaned at the mention of her name. If she made him uncomfortable, then I was in big trouble. "Can I pour you a glass of tea while you decide on something to eat?"

Senator Denver watched me with the tolerant curiosity of someone forced to attend a play they hadn't particularly wanted to see. She approached slowly, taking in the details of the room before folding her long black coat over a chair and setting her bag on the counter. "Apple cinnamon, please."

I grabbed a jar and filled it with ice while she selected a stool. "Are you enjoying the weather?"

"No."

"Been out shopping?" I asked, setting the jar beneath her chosen dispenser. "Enjoying your visit?"

She tipped her head slightly as I passed her the tea. "I'm sorry, are you pretending not to know me?"

"Have we met?" I asked, suddenly fearful I'd somehow forgotten having experienced this unnerving exchange before.

"No." She turned the jar in her hands, locking me in her careful stare. "But I'm sure you know me, and I know you, Everly Swan."

I went rigid at the sound of my name on her sharp tongue.

"Twenty-nine years old," she went on. "Born and raised in Charm by your grandmother after the loss of your parents. You left the island to attend culinary school in Lexington and travel with a rodeo cowboy, but returned to Charm early this year following a breakup and the loss of your grandmother. My condolences on all your losses." She lifted the tea for a small sip, then nodded. "This is very good."

I tried to look less shell-shocked than I felt. "How do you know all of that about me?" I asked. Had she used her government connections to hack into my computer? The thought struck a new horror through me. *Did she read my emails? My saved files? Know the things I searched for?*

Because I had absolutely searched for her.

Senator Olivia Denver wasn't like most politicians. She'd retired from the military at forty-two before landing in politics and rising with unprecedented speed to the top. She'd met her husband while he was under her command in Germany. They'd had one child, Grady's late wife, Amy, while they were both still in the service. Mr. Denver had taken a position with the CIA following his time in the armed forces, and after a couple decades doing whatever CIA operatives do, he went missing from Langley shortly after Amy's death. The speculation surrounding his disappearance was dramatic and varied. Most suspected suicide. They assumed he'd been unable to deal with the loss of his only daughter to cancer and had offed himself. Others suspected he'd been abducted or simply hadn't returned from a secret mission. There were no real answers, and I didn't have a guess, but as far as I could tell, there had never been a funeral.

Senator Denver narrowed her arresting blue eyes

slightly. "It's my business to know who my son-in-law is involved with," she said flatly.

My hackles rose instantly. I wasn't involved with anyone, and if I was, it wouldn't be any of her business. I took sudden offense to the air of superiority she wore like a crown, the way she looked at me as if I was something to be studied, and the way she made me feel like a child called to the principal's office. I wanted to bite back, but I suspected that was what she wanted as well. I decided to go with sweet southern ignorance instead and allowed my natural drawl to hang thick over every word. "I don't know what you mean."

A genuine look of amusement passed over her features before she tamped it down tight. "Cute, but you're much too clever for that act," she said. "I know you ranked at the top of your graduating high school class and were set to do the same in college until circumstances changed your path. You have a lifelong history of excelling at anything you've tried, and it's followed you into business. You've earned equestrian awards for dressage and show jumping. Became a certified lifeguard before you could drive. And you have been a major player in the capture of two murderers in the past eight months. All before your thirtieth birthday."

I forced my sticky tongue off the roof of my uncomfortably dry mouth. "I've been fortunate."

"Some might say blessed."

I snorted at that, the tension instantly blown

away. “Not many,” I said with a sly grin. In fact, most would have used another word to describe me or any Swan woman. The senator’s mistake was a welcomed reminder. She hadn’t found the story of my life written somewhere and studied it. She did some research and guessed the rest. Poorly. Like an ordinary human and not some superior political goddess. I smiled warmly. “Can I get you something to eat? Have you had dinner?”

“And you’re unflappable,” she said. “I’ll add that to my list.”

“Great.” I smiled wider. “How about a sampler platter on the house?” I asked. “You’re clearly having some kind of day.”

When she didn’t protest, I got to work. I prepped and plated a trio of baked-ham-and-cheese pinwheels in minutes, then arranged a small caprese salad to the side. “Try these and let me know if you can add ‘darn good chef’ to that list of accomplishments.”

Her lips twitched, possibly fighting a smile, and she reached for a pinwheel.

I turned to set up a plate of cookies and chunked fudge. When I turned back, the pinwheels were nearly gone, and so was the tea.

She dusted a napkin across her thin lips. “There were no groceries at my house when I arrived today. I’ve had staff setting everything up so I could move in and get on with my life, and no one thought to stock the kitchen.”

I refilled her empty tea jar and returned it. “Molly’s

Market is a great place to pick up food staples and anything else you need to get by on the daily. Mr. and Mrs. Waters named the business after their daughter. They're a very nice family and a great resource for information on Charm. So, if you're ever out and have a question, Molly's is a great place to stop."

"I will. Thank you." The senator sipped her tea and let her lids flutter softly. "Very. Very. Good."

My heart kicked and jumped at the compliment, sending a rush of heat to my cheeks. I was a shameless sucker for applause, especially when it came in the kitchen. "I'm glad you like it."

Senator Denver pursed her lips as she pressed the tines of her fork into the caprese salad. "My grandson wasn't home, or I'd be having dinner with him. Apparently, his au pair took him to the Wright Brothers First Flight Celebration in Kitty Hawk instead of waiting to see me on my first night in town."

"I'm sorry to hear that," I said, noting the hurt in her voice. I'd completely forgotten that event was tonight. Grady had told me how excited Denver was to show him the flyer last week. "He's going to be a junior ranger today," I said. "He was really looking forward to it, and I'm sure they won't be late. Maybe you can catch them for dessert." I clasped my hands before me to keep myself from grabbing my phone to check Denise's Instagram.

Senator Denver slid a bite of basil, mozzarella, and tomato between her lips and watched me as she chewed.

"If you like it," I said, fumbling to fill the silence once again, "I can send some home with you for tomorrow. I'm not open for breakfast, but I'll be here again at lunchtime if you haven't had a chance to make it to the market by then."

She dotted her lips with a napkin, not responding to my offer. "What do you know about my grandson and his au pair?"

I considered her question for a moment, unsure how to answer without giving away too much. "I know she's really good with Denver."

The senator sat impossibly taller. "She should be. She was fully vetted and handpicked from more than thirty viable applicants, *by me*. Denise is more than qualified to rear, nurture, educate, and protect my grandson." She forked another bit of salad and paused, letting it hover over her plate. "She's fully capable of meeting all of their needs."

I didn't like the way she'd let the words *all* and *their* linger on her tongue, as if Denise was somehow intended to fill in for Amy's absence in Grady's life as well. I felt the corners of my mouth pull down. My gaze snapped to meet the senator's. She had meant exactly that. *Ew.* Did Denise know how far the parameters of her job description were meant to stretch? Did Grady? Had she ever filled that role for him?

The senator smiled. "It's interesting that you're willing to admit you know my grandson and his au pair, but you lie about knowing my son-in-law. Why would you do that?"

I pulled my shoulders back and pushed a curious smile into place. “I never said I didn’t know him.” She’d accused me of being involved with Grady. I’d told her I didn’t know what she meant, and I still didn’t. It was strange that she’s even suggested Grady was involved with me when he lived with the equivalent of a tall, blond underwear model whose literal job was to meet his every need.

My stomach knotted, and my chest tightened. Where were my aunts?

Just then, the seashell wind chimes and jingle bells sounded. The familiar trill and flutter of my great-aunts’ voices and laughter were balm to my jagged nerves and panging heart. I hurried to greet them in the foyer before they could be caught in a conversation unintended for my guest’s ears.

“Hello!” I hugged them one by one and kissed their cheeks.

They each fell back in confusion, clearly hearing the distress in my voice, or perhaps seeing the intense crazy on my face. “I’m so glad you came. Dinner’s almost ready. I just have one guest left in the café.” I made exaggerated pointing motions and repeated wide-eyed looks at the wall between us and Senator Denver. “I’ll get the tea.”

Aunt Clara and Aunt Fran exchanged a peculiar look.

“Tea sounds lovely,” Aunt Clara said.

Aunt Fran motioned me onward.

I ducked back into place behind the counter and

watched with bated breath as my aunts homed in on the senator. I swapped her newly emptied plate for one with a selection of sweets.

Aunt Fran was the first to speak. "Well, hello there," she said with a cautious smile. Her gaze darted pointedly over Senator Denver's nearly empty plate and tea jar. "How did our great-niece do on the tea and salad?"

Senator Denver extended a hand. "Everything was top notch, as expected. I'm Olivia Denver. It's lovely to meet the aunts of such a talented young woman."

Aunt Clara nearly floated from pleasure at the senator's praises.

Aunt Fran accepted the handshake. "I'm Fran Swan, and this is my sister Clara."

"Wonderful to meet you," Aunt Clara cooed.

The senator smiled. "Well, Fran Swan, I suppose we'll be getting to know one another very well soon."

Aunt Fran hiked a brow and cast a glance at me. "Is that right?"

Heat rushed across my cheeks once more. "This is *Senator* Olivia Denver. Detective Hays's mother-in-law and Denver's grandma."

Aunt Fran whipped her face back in my guest's direction, confusion plainly evident. "And why will we be getting to know one another?"

Senator Denver's lips curled into a mischievous grin. Her gaze flickered in my direction before landing back on Fran. I hadn't told Fran about her intended run for mayor, and she knew it.

I checked the exits, deciding if I could make it past Aunt Fran if I tried, or if it would be best to jump off the balcony.

"I believe I'm one of your competitors in the upcoming mayoral race," Senator Denver said jovially, "assuming my son-in-law doesn't put you in jail."

I sucked air, and my aunts gaped.

Senator Denver barked out a laugh. "Kidding," she said. "Of course I know you're innocent, and Grady's too good at his job to make a mistake of that magnitude."

Aunt Fran swallowed long and slow. "Of course."

Aunt Clara looked like she'd been struck with a stick.

"Wait." Aunt Fran's expression morphed slowly from shock into a deep frown. "Did you say you're planning to run for mayor? Since when?" Her voice hitched in disbelief. "You don't even live here." She turned her confused expression on me. "She doesn't live here."

I lifted a palm and grimaced. It seemed there was more I hadn't told her. "Senator Denver bought the Northrop Manor."

Aunt Clara's mouth fell open. "Heavens."

Aunt Fran scowled at me before retuning her gaze to the senator. "Well, welcome to Charm," she deadpanned.

"Thanks." Senator Denver lifted her tea and finished it off. "It's an interesting place."

Aunt Clara cleared her throat and smiled, eager to

dissipate the tension. "We're big fans of your son-in-law. He's been great for our town, and he's saved our Everly's life. More than once," she added with a droop of her lips. "They've become quite close."

The oven dinged, and I spun away to tend to it, wishing I'd locked the door a few minutes sooner and turned off the café lights until my aunts arrived.

"I've heard," Senator Denver said. "The au pair likes her, though I hear she's a handful."

Electricity charged the air, and I peeked over my shoulder at the pair of women facing off behind me.

"Darn right," Aunt Fran said, narrowing her eyes on the senator. "Everly's a pistol."

I smiled at the beam of pride that burst over her face as she spoke.

The senator nodded. "I can see where she gets it."

"Honey, you haven't seen anything yet," Aunt Fran said with a wicked smile.

Senator Denver barked a laugh.

Suddenly, the tension and uncertainty I'd felt upon their meeting was strangely comfortable, as if each crabby old lady had found a part of her tribe.

Aunt Clara hummed her way behind the counter and poured two jars of tea. "Can I get you a refill, Senator Denver?"

"No, thank you," the senator said. "Please, call me Olivia." She opened her purse and set a twenty beside her plate. "Everything was delicious, Everly."

My mouth opened, but no words came out.

She slid on her coat and tied the belt at her waist,

then extended her hand to Aunt Fran once more. "I like you," she said, a mix of surprise and contentment in her careful eyes.

"Who wouldn't?" Fran wondered.

The dearly departed Mayor Dunfree came to mind, but I kept that to myself.

Fran gave their joined hands a firm pump. "I like you too. Shame we're going to be competing against each other soon."

"I wouldn't call what happens in November a competition," Senator Denver stated matter-of-factly. "Annihilation or devastation maybe. No one would blame you if you backed out now."

Aunt Clara sighed as the tension crackled once more. "Great. Now there are two of them," she whispered in my direction.

I set the steaming potpie on the nearest table, then waved an oven mitt. "I know you've just had a bite, Senator, but you're welcome to stay for dinner. Finish your desserts. Get to know my aunts." I waited for her to tell me to call her Olivia like she'd told my aunts to do.

She didn't.

Aunt Clara clasped her palms. "Won't you?"

"I'm afraid not, but I'd love to take these sweets to Denver, if you don't mind." Senator Denver lifted the little plate of cookies and fudge I'd set for her. "Maybe you're right and I can catch him once he's finished being a junior ranger."

"Of course." I tucked my oven mitts under one

arm and went hunting for a pastry transport. I pulled out a small white bag and then settled the treats inside. "Don't be a stranger," I said, handing her the bag and returning her twenty. "On the house. Welcome to Charm from Sun, Sand, and Tea."

An accepting smile budded on her lips, but before I could pass her the items, a thunderous crash exploded on my porch.

I screamed.

Fran and Clara reached for one another.

Senator Denver produced a handgun from somewhere beneath her stylish coat and headed toward the front door, all in the space of a heartbeat. She moved silently, confidently, exactly like the well-trained general she'd once been.

"Holy cow!" I yipped, snapping out of my stupor and flying from behind the counter to follow her. "She has a gun!" I told my aunts, who were busy impersonating wide-eyed statues. "She can't have a gun in here!" I ran after the senator. "No guns!"

Icy wind stole my breath as I bolted through the foyer. I stopped short at the threshold to my porch.

Senator Denver stood at the base of the steps, still wielding her weapon, scanning the darkened area with keen, trained eyes.

I stared, horrified, at the pile of busted gnome bits shattered at my feet.

CHAPTER EIGHT

A flash of approaching headlights drew the senator's attention, and I ducked back inside to call Grady before his mother-in-law shot someone or was abducted by a gnome-wielding maniac.

The headlights blinked out, and I peeked into the night, keeping an eye on the truck and Senator Denver as the call connected.

"Everly," he groaned through the speaker at my ear. "Why is my mother-in-law at your house with a gun?" The truck door opened, and the fog-induced panic of my brain cleared.

I knew that truck.

Grady climbed down from the cab and marched in the senator's direction.

"There's been another gnome-related incident," I said into the phone, grabbing my coat and rushing outside.

"Wait for us," Aunt Clara called, the patter of hurried steps following me onto the broad wraparound porch.

Grady dragged his stare from my aunts and me to his mother-in-law. "What happened?"

She holstered her sidearm and took her time answering. "Hello to you too, Grady."

He shifted his weight, impatient. "Hello, Olivia. It's nice to see you again. Now, what the hell happened?"

She rolled her eyes. "Someone broke some garden statues," she said, raising a disinterested hand in the direction of my front door. "There was a loud crash, and I came to check it out. Whoever the vandal was is long gone or hiding. Who can tell out here? There aren't any lights outside the property."

I gave the world around us a sweeping look. Rows of icicle lights twinkled and swung from the eaves and dormers of my stately historic home. A similar web draped the trees along my property line in a luminous lacey backdrop against the velvety sky. Beyond that, we were at the seaside. Where did she propose the extra lights should be?

"I suppose breaking garden statues in the winter is some bizarre form of island mischief," she said. "Bizarre seems to come standard issue around here."

Grady rubbed his face. "Was anyone hurt?"

"No," I said quickly, eager to break up the tension and get Grady on task. Someone was trying to scare me, and the attempts were escalating. "We were inside when it happened. Come look," I said, waving him in my direction. "The statues were gnomes. Someone smashed at least four of them on my porch."

Grady jogged up my porch steps, lips pursed. He dropped into a squat and used a pen to push the pieces of busted ceramics around. "I have to ask, for argument's sake. Is there any chance the gnome stuff is a separate problem?"

I crossed my arms, not liking where this was going. "No one would be stalking me with these murder-gnomes, except the murderer."

Aunt Clara gasped behind me, probably preparing to object to the term *murder-gnomes*, but I kept my eyes on Grady.

He furrowed his brow and pressed on. "Could the murder weapon have been an item of convenience, while the gnome thing is unrelated to the mayor and coincidentally going on at the same time?"

"No," I said defensively. "This is another warning."

He worked his jaw. "I have to look at this from every angle. It's not an accusation. Have you argued with anyone lately? Maybe someone's holding a grudge for something you've already let go?" He turned his gaze on my aunts. "How about you?"

I gaped. "People love us."

Senator Denver drifted gracefully up the porch steps. "She's right. I've looked into the Swans, and they're very well respected." She quirked a brow. "The whole family has a strange monarchy feel."

Grady rubbed his forehead, managing to look more exasperated than I felt, which was saying something. I blamed his mother-in-law. "The Swans helped found the town. They've been part of Charm's history from the beginning. People here like that. History. Continuity."

A quiet sob turned me on my toes. Aunt Clara pressed a frilly white handkerchief to her nose. "I don't understand why my gnomes have to be a part of all this. I've spent weeks selecting and painting them, giving them unique and individual personalities. They were supposed to be whimsical accents to our enchanting town, but now look." She released another shuddered sob, muffling it carefully with her hanky. "Some lunatic has dragged my hard work into his crime spree and perverted my plans. This awful person has stolen, smashed, and destroyed my works of art and even used them for harm. Who would want one now?" she squeaked. "I might as well be giving the black plague for Christmas."

I gave her what I hoped was an understanding and compassionate look. She really had worked hard on her gnomes. I still had no idea *why*, but she had, and she was right. No one would want one of her gnomes now. If she had any left, maybe she could put them out at Halloween.

"Whoever did this was probably the same person who killed Mayor Dunfree," I said. "I know it sounds like a stretch, but there's no way all of these gnome crimes are unrelated."

Grady rose on a long exhale. He braced his palms over his hips and gave us each a long look. "You're probably right."

My heart skipped, whether in victory from his easy

agreement or in terror for the same reason, I couldn't be sure. Adrenaline jolted through my veins as another fantastic point came to mind. "Aunt Fran was inside with us when this happened," I said. "If Dunfree's killer broke these gnomes, then the killer isn't Fran."

Grady left us on the porch and made a trip to his truck. He returned with his black duffel bag and began shoveling the broken gnomes into evidence bags using a pair of legal pads as a broom and dustpan. The muscle in his jaw jumped with every repetitive clench of his teeth.

"How about some hot cocoa?" I offered the women. "No need for us to stand out here in the cold, cramping the detective's process. We should go inside and let him work. Detective Hays can join us when he's ready."

My aunts slipped through the front door without another word.

Grady rolled his eyes up to me, brows furrowed.

His mother-in-law's gaze moved slowly from me to Grady and back. "No, thank you. I'm leaving," she said. "Besides, I've already eaten, and your dinner is getting cold."

As if on cue, a small silver SUV pulled up beside Grady's truck. Lanita popped out and waved. "Someone call for a Pick-Me-Up?"

Senator Denver sighed. "Here," she called. "Coming." She ducked into my home and returned a moment later with the small white pastry bag and her purse. "This is ridiculous," she muttered, leaving us behind on the porch. She shot an ugly look over her shoulder at Grady. "I don't see why I couldn't bring my driver and escorts with me."

Grady shook his head. "Because it's pathological," he said. "You don't need all that. No one needs all that. And I still need your statement."

"I'll give it when you get home," she said. "I'm taking some cookies to my grandson. I'll stay until you return."

"Great," Grady mumbled.

I watched silently until Lanita drove away before turning back to Grady. "Are you hungry? I made a potpie."

"No. It looks like you've gained another stalker, and now I've got to find out who it is before you get hurt again." He grabbed a flashlight from the duffel and headed dutifully into my gardens.

"Come see me when you finish," I called after him.

He kept walking.

By the time I hung up my coat and entered the café, my aunts had set the table for three and dished out the potpie.

"Hey," I said, my hands in the air. "I didn't invite you to dinner so you could serve me. Sit down. Let me do that." I inhaled the rich, buttery aroma and my stomach gurgled.

Aunt Clara ferried drinks in my direction. She lowered a tray with three ice-filled jars and a pitcher of tea onto the table. "Nonsense. We love to do things for you."

Aunt Fran followed with a heaping plate of cookies and fudge. "You've been serving people all day. Have a seat. Eat up, and let's talk."

Conceding, I nearly collapsed onto my chair. It was pointless to argue with my aunts, and I was too hungry to hold my ground. I took a few bites of moan-worthy chicken and veggies before delving into my questions for Fran. "Did you have time to make a list of people with recent grievances against the mayor?" I asked.

She grimaced. "I tried. I called Maven, the town hall receptionist, to see what we could come up with, but it wasn't much. There were a few open complaints on the mayor's desk and several made with the town council, but nothing stood out as murder-worthy. I thought there would be more. Dunfree was a pain, and he rubbed a lot of people the wrong way by denying that woman a paper lantern vigil for her son this summer."

"I remember," I said. *Vividly.*

"I warned him about that," Fran said. "I did everything I could to sway the council on the issue, to make an exception, but no one wanted to upset Dunfree, and he was a stickler for adherence to the rules. Even stupid ones." She poured a glass of tea and sipped, her red cheeks slowly losing their color as her temper cooled. "Every situation is different. We have to treat each instance as it comes. That's supposed to be what the council is for, to make decisions on relative issues as they arise, not to blindly uphold every rule at all costs. Who does it serve? Not the people. It's nonsense."

Aunt Clara patted her sister's hand.

Aunt Fran raised woeful eyes to mine. "The entire council, myself included, is nothing more than his puppet, and it breaks my heart when we could be so much more."

"Were," Clara said, dipping the tines of her fork into the bowl before her. "You were his puppets."

I blinked. Harsh, but accurate. Dunfree was gone. Whatever had been true before wasn't anymore, or didn't have to be. "Who's in charge now?" I asked. "We don't have a deputy mayor, so who took over?" Had Mary Grace moved in somehow? Had his wife?

"Chairman Vanders stepped up," Fran said.

I puzzled over the name. "Who?"

"He's been head of the council for a decade," she said. "He moved out here after Hurricane Katrina displaced him from New Orleans. He owns the bike and kayak rental company on the bay."

"Interesting." I speared a stack of golden-brown sourdough cubes with my fork. "He didn't even have to run for office. That's a convenient way to move up."

"I suppose," Fran said, her eyes widened in understanding. "You think Chairman Vanders could have killed him?"

I lifted a shoulder noncommittally. "You know him better than I do. Did he ever talk about wanting to be in charge?"

Fran shook her head. "He never said anything like that at the council meetings. He talked more about cars, sports scores, and his most recent dates than actual council business."

The description of Chairman Vanders reminded me of Lanita's family's experience with the mayor. "Was Dunfree a misogynist?" I asked. "Did he treat women poorly? Or as if they were less-than?"

Aunt Fran gave a coy smirk. "Dunfree thought everyone was less-than."

Aunt Clara fidgeted. "He liked to make comments about us being spinsters. When I was younger, he worried about how I'd take care of myself without a husband. I think he was just being kind. It was a man's world then."

"It's a man's world now," Aunt Fran snapped. "We're working on it, but change is slow. Especially here. We didn't get women on the council until 2001." She leaned back in her chair, eyebrows high.

"You're kidding," I said. How had I never noticed the inequality?

"Very few women ran for the positions until then. We all knew it was a boys' club and figured we could get more done without them. It was as if they'd taught us not to try, all without saying as much."

I blinked, processing how simply, quietly, things happened right under our noses.

"And Dunfree wasn't being kind back then," she told Aunt Clara, "he was hitting on you. Anytime he and his wife were on the outs, he went trolling for a mistress to make him feel virile. He was offering to keep you on the side."

Aunt Clara's face gleamed red. Her mouth opened and shut like a fish out of water.

I pushed her tea closer to her hand. "So, he was a misogynist." Maybe it was nothing more than an unfortunate personality defect. Or maybe it had played a role in his death.

"What about Dunfree's marriage?" I asked, sweeping my gaze from aunt to aunt. They must've heard plenty of gossip at Blessed Bee. I overheard my share of things at the café. Hazard of the job. "Any chance he and his wife were on the rocks? Maybe getting a divorce or dealing with an affair? Sounds like that wouldn't be out of the question."

My aunts looked at me as if I'd asked them the color of the mayor's underwear.

"How on earth would we know something like that?" Aunt Clara asked.

"Never mind." Maybe I was the only one who heard more than she should. "Then what about Dunfree's speech? When did Mary Grace change her mind about running for mayor?"

Fran set her fork beside her empty bowl and selected a slice of fudge. "That was all news to me, but I'm sure he had an angle. He always had an angle. Usually a self-serving one."

"Convincing Mary Grace to partner with him eliminated one of his competitors," I said. "That seems smart, I guess." Though I still wasn't sure why she'd agreed to it.

Clara leaned forward, dotting the corners of her

mouth with a napkin. Her long silver-and-blond hair draped across her shoulders in a braid. "Well, he was sick, you know. He probably expected to need help, and she was probably sympathetic to that."

I went for a second serving of potpie with a humorless laugh. "It's as if you don't know Mary Grace at all." She was as surely in it for her personal gain as Dunfree had been, which was what made the partnership all the more unbelievable. "I didn't know he was sick. What kind of sick?" I asked. "Something serious?" *Something fatal?*

Aunt Fran frowned at her sister. "That was just a rumor. No one knows for sure if he was ill. I don't even know where the story started. You can't put any stock in it."

"Sure I can," I said, digging into my bowl with gusto. "If whatever was wrong with him was serious enough, he might not have been expecting to finish another term. Which means, he could've offered Mary Grace a position as deputy so he could groom her to take over in his absence. Make sure she'd handle everything exactly as he had. Then he'd still have control of Charm from the hereafter."

Aunt Clara signed the cross.

"Maybe Mary Grace resented the position he'd put her in," I said, "and knowing he was on his way out anyway, she might've helped him along."

Aunt Fran sipped her tea and watched me. I could practically see the wheels of thought turning behind her smart brown eyes. "That won't explain who he was arguing with on the phone. Mary Grace was here with him."

"Was she?" I asked. "I lost track of her after the obnoxious sabotage of your announcement. Mary Grace could've easily slipped outside and waited for him to leave. I didn't see her after the murder either. Did you?"

My aunts traded looks, heads wagging in the negative.

"And we can't be sure that whoever was on the phone was the killer. Just like we can't be sure they weren't," I said. "Not until we find the missing phone and track down who he spoke to last night. Mary Grace could've called him from the shadows and lured him into an argument for distraction's sake, then snuck up and gnomed him."

Aunt Fran laughed.

Aunt Clara cringed. "Don't say it like that. It sounds awful, and my gnome had nothing to do with it. The gnome was innocent."

I bit into my lip to stop the brewing laughter.

Aunt Fran shifted on her seat and frowned. "For being innocent, it certainly showed him *gnome* mercy."

I choked back a laugh, wiping the sting from my tear-filled eyes.

Aunt Clara blanched. "Stop," she whispered.

"You're right," Fran said, setting her napkin on the table. "I'm sorry. We'll figure this out. Don't worry. The culprit won't go *ungnome* for long."

"Ah!" Aunt Clara gasped. "Fran! Really."

The giggle I'd tried to swallow burst free.

Aunt Clara's eyes stretched impossibly wider as she watched me lose myself in laughter.

I shook my head apologetically. "No. It's not funny. I'm so sorry. I really will figure out who did this," I said, sobering up.

"Thank you," Clara said, back stiff and shoulders squared.

My lips wiggled into a fresh grin. "It's just that at the moment, there's *gnome* way of knowing."

Aunt Fran crumbled into laughter and I followed.

Aunt Clara left the table.

CHAPTER NINE

I passed the night in fits and turns, my mind never quite able to relax despite the absolute silence. Grady hadn't stopped in after checking the garden like I'd suggested. Instead, he'd been gone when I walked my aunts out, and I'd been left wondering why. Had he found the phone? Had he found something else? What? Where had he gone without saying goodbye? How was I going to clear Aunt Fran's name? And what on earth was I supposed to serve for the Holiday Shuffle?

I dressed in my softest jeans and favorite T-shirt at the first sign of daybreak, then pulled a hooded sweatshirt over my head. I'd had the Sun, Sand, and Tea logo printed on the back of several sky-blue shirts this summer, and the shop had thrown in the pullover at a discount I couldn't pass up. I was especially thankful for the purchase as I slogged away from my toasty bed and through my cavernous, drafty old home. Suddenly, I couldn't remember what it was like to be truly warm. I missed the searing southern sun on my brow, the humidity pulling sweat from my pores and wrapping me in its sticky cocoon.

I plugged in my Christmas tree on my way to make coffee and lit the strands of twinkle lights across my hearth as well. Clusters of chubby white pillar candles bookended the mantle where my stockings had been hung with care. The three tan-and-cream numbers had been made by a local artist and adorned with seaside accents from sand dollars to starfish and had seahorses on the toes. Names were embroidered across the cuffs and underlined in tiny footprints to match the owner. *Everly* with barefoot tracks in the sand, *Maggie* with a row of kitty prints, and *Lou* with one sturdy set of webbed gull tracks. Unlike the more colorful displays in my café, my personal holiday decor was a muted palette of creams and tans with accents in pale blue or silver.

I shoved a mug under the coffee maker and jammed my bare feet into faux-fur-lined boots from the mat near the door while I waited for the coffee to brew. Maggie's bowls were empty, though I hadn't seen her come or go. In fact, she'd been gone, as expected, when I'd returned to check on her yesterday. I added fresh food and water to her dishes, then sampled my steaming coffee, attempting to warm myself from the inside out.

I'd checked the house for signs of Maggie's secret passage before. I'd never found anything, but I was sure it was there. Somewhere. A crack or crevice small enough to go unseen by my eye, but large enough for her to squash her fluffy white body through. I'd been torn at the time. I couldn't bring myself to stop her from coming and going at will, but leaving the passage open could lead to who-knew-what following her inside one day. Wherever the secret door was, I prayed regularly that it was too small for an alligator.

My little bracelet beeped as I lifted the mug to my lips once more. The words *be more active* flashed across the small rectangular screen.

I pressed the heel of my hand against a dull thump developing over my temple and went in search of aspirin. Fatigue headaches had become a frequent companion of mine since my return to Charm. Between owning and operating the café on my own, reacclimating to the community, and dealing with the previous two unhinged murderers, my sleep patterns were a mess. I probably needed to consider getting some part-time help at Sun, Sand, and Tea before tourist season began in the spring.

I pushed the idea out of my mind as I rifled through my medicine cabinet for the painkillers. Two tablets and a swig of black coffee later, my eyes were opening beyond a squint.

By the time my mug was empty, the aspirin had kicked in, and a smile had followed. Crazy as my life had become these last few months, it was certainly never boring, and I loved everything about my new seaside home and business. I fixed a second cup of liquid enthusiasm and savored the taste of the satin heat on my tongue, the tendrils of bitter steam warming and teasing my nose.

My gaze drifted from the snow-laced view outside my window to the postcard-worthy scene all around me. The beautiful old home I'd once only dreamed of entering was now my personal, peaceful sanctuary. I fingered the row of glittery cards lining my window. Taping them to the woodwork had become one of my favorite evening activities. I loved finding them in the mailbox and opening them like gifts. Somehow, seeing the cards here, addressed to me at this address, made my sheer abundance seem almost unfair. Not just my abundance of things, but of love, joy, and hope. My thoughts drifted to the needs hanging patiently, hopefully, on the Giving Tree, and I knew I needed to visit soon.

My phone buzzed on the counter beside Mr. Coffee, and Grady's number appeared on the screen. I swiped to the new text message with a mix of hope and fear. Then, I remembered I was irritated with him for vanishing on me.

Sorry about last night.

I read the words twice. Was he sorry he'd left without saying goodbye? Sorry I didn't get to see him as promised, or maybe sorry he didn't get to see me?

Did he know I'd taken a warm mug of tea out to look for him before I realized he was already gone? Did he know I'd snuggled into bed frustrated and a little hurt, with visions of gnomes smashing in my head?

The real question I should've been asking myself was why I overthought everything when it came to Grady. Nine months ago, I hadn't even known him. Now his calls and texts were vitally important. They had the power to make or break my day and to send shock waves of anxiety and anticipation tiptoeing across my stomach.

It wasn't healthy, and I didn't like it.

Before I could respond to him, the screen lit again: Raincheck?

I chewed my bottom lip as I typed my response: We'll see.

I finished my second cup of coffee and wadded my wild mass of dark waves into a ponytail, then headed downstairs to check on Lou. I had a deck outside my second-floor living room, but Lou liked to sit on the railing outside my café. Closer to the beach, I supposed. Quicker access to food.

I delivered a hearty tray of deboned fish fillets to the deck, called "breakfast" into the sky, then headed into my former ballroom. I propped my phone against the wall of windows and willed myself to get some exercise. I needed to counter some of the holiday cookie damage to my waistline. Plus, the movement would appease my bossy bracelet.

I selected a beginner Zumba video and rocked my head back and forth over my shoulders. I kicked my faux-fur boots into the corner and marched around, warming up my muscles. I'd heard good things about Zumba. It was supposed to be fun, unlike step aerobics, which had nearly cost me my life when I tripped and fell over the step. I bumbled through the salsa-esque warm-up, my hips doing things they didn't understand and my brain trying frantically to command my limbs not to hurt one another. The reflection of my broadening silhouette in the windows kept me going to the warm-up's end. The girl on screen encouraged a water break, never a good sign, then smiled, pumped her fist and the music's tempo warped into double-time. It was hard to tell if the singer was speaking English as I got my hustle on. More likely the roaring in my ears was distorting the words.

When the peppy woman circled an arm overhead and yelled, "Again!" I bent forward at the waist and gripped my knees. "Uncle," I panted, straightening with effort and weaving a drunken path toward the phone. "Stop," I commanded, mashing a fingertip against the screen to still and silence the video.

I toppled onto the floor near the window and waited for my breaths to even out. "That was a horrible idea," I told the ceiling.

I peeled my head and shoulders off the ground when my pulse returned to normal, mentally marking all dance-based videos off my list of potential indoor exercise. I was a walking, horseback riding, or water sports kind of girl. I excelled at simple, repetitive movements. I needed to get outside.

Maggie leaped onto the windowsill and stared at me. The judgmental look in her luminous green eyes suggested she'd seen the whole thing. My choreographed seizure, as it were.

"We shall never speak of this again," I told her, rolling onto my side, then pushing up to my knees. "No one needs to know."

She trotted behind me into the café.

"You've got fresh food and water upstairs," I told her.

She pranced past me, presumably headed up for breakfast, and I opened my laptop. My video was still on screen waiting to be launched.

I inhaled deeply, tired of worrying about what people thought about me, about my appearance, about things that didn't matter. I closed one eye and pressed the button.

The little bar stretched across my screen, marking the upload progress. *Ten percent. Twenty. Fifty.*

I regretted it instantly and briefly considered chucking the laptop into the Atlantic, but it was too late.

One hundred percent.

My head dropped forward. Well, at least Amelia would be happy. An instructional video on making the Swan Family's Seven-Layer Bars now appeared beneath the Holiday How-To tab on my website. My goofy smile was frozen, lips parted, eyes wide. A big white triangle lay on its side beneath my chin, waiting to be selected. Waiting to animate me.

My stomach clenched in terror. What if no one watched it? What if everyone did? What if everyone watched it and they all hated it?

I wasn't sure which result would be most humiliating, or if I wanted to know.

Instead, I pulled another tea bag off my advent calendar and grabbed a stack of cookie orders, then got to work. Eight days until Christmas and zero progress made on clearing Aunt Fran's name. I had problems, and nothing took me away from my problems like baking. I arranged the necessary ingredients across my workspace and preheated the oven. Staying busy was the key to sanity.

According to the clock on my stove, I had four hours before opening time at Sun, Sand, and Tea, and I intended to complete as many cookies as possible before then. A personal challenge. Once the café opened, I'd schedule the pickups and deliveries.

I put the first round of snickerdoodles in the oven, then checked the *Town Charmer* blog for updates on Mayor Dunfree's murder. I found another article about the Holiday Shuffle instead. Apparently, Senator Denver had added Northrop Manor to the list of stops and the town was chomping at the bit to get a look inside the formerly exclusive residence. Sheer curiosity pushed me to click her link.

I scrolled through her menu, jaw lowering further with each astoundingly gourmet item. Clearly, she planned to schmooze the locals into loving her. I considered this a moment. Joining the Holiday Shuffle was a smart move for a newcomer. A good way to meet a lot of people all at once…

Of course! She was laying the groundwork for her

campaign! Who in their right mind wouldn't want be a guest at Northrop Manor for Christmas? Eating things like prosciutto, mango, and parmesan salad or pork tenderloin crostini with organic cranberry-pepper jelly? Charmers would go and they'd remember her. They'd like her without even knowing her.

Worse, she was going to show me up at my own game. I was the café owner, but she'd probably asked her personal team of celebrity chefs to prepare the fanciest recipes they knew. I imagined Gordon Ramsey and Rachael Ray working in the Northrop kitchen, while Senator Denver pretended it was all her doing.

How could I compete with that?

I turned back to the messy countertop and whipped together a batch of thumbprint cookie dough while I mulled over my options. I needed to serve the perfect cocktails and hors d'oeuvres. My portion of the Shuffle came first, and I wanted people stuffed so full of my authentic southern recipes that they'd barely have room for her schmancy main course. When the oven timer dinged, I swapped the trays. Snickerdoodles out. Thumbprints in. I reset the timer and inhaled the mood-lifting scents around me. The café smelled like some of my best dreams.

I wiped down the counters as I waited for the cookies to cool. Something prickled in my mind. The senator's thinly veiled attempt to get into Charm's good graces reminded me of Mary Grace, another virtual outsider suddenly trying to take control of island politics. What was it with people? Worse, I suspected the senator would stop at nothing to get what she wanted, and I knew Mary Grace wouldn't. My gaze shifted to the oven.

Maybe it was time I made a special tray of cookies for Mary Grace and asked her how she was doing after the sudden and tragic loss of her campaign partner. Was there a universe where she'd open up to me and be candid? Could my cookies build that bridge?

My phone buzzed, and Grady's face appeared on the screen. A call this time instead of a text.

"Hello?" I answered eagerly, suddenly dying to know if he'd spoken to Mary Grace, and if so, how she had responded. "Grady?" I pressed when he didn't answer quickly. "Is everything okay?"

"Yeah, sorry." The silence returned, and I wondered if he'd changed his mind about talking to me. "I know you aren't open yet, but I wondered if I could come by for a few minutes while it's still quiet."

"Of course," I answered instinctually. "Anytime."

My chest constricted once the words were out. I looked down at my disheveled self. I hadn't showered, put on makeup, or brushed my hair, and I was wearing sweatpants and a hoodie that I'd recently laid on the floor in and sweated all over. "Can you give me thirty minutes?"

"See you then." Grady disconnected before I had a chance to say goodbye.

I checked my watch, willed the thumbprints to finish baking, then sprinted upstairs the moment the oven timer dinged. Twenty-three minutes wasn't much, but I could move mountains with the right motivation, and Grady Hays was a powerful incentive.

~

My hair was still wet when Grady arrived, but at least I'd washed and conditioned the crazy mop, so it smelled like coconuts. I'd twisted it all into a knot on top of my head and hoped it looked intentionally messy, like the cover models on fashion magazines, instead of what it really was: wet because I hadn't had time to dry it. And unruly because my hair was a curse I could believe in. I'd spent the extra minutes on my makeup, spreading concealer over the dark crescents beneath my eyes and choosing an outfit that accentuated my good curves and drew attention away from my bad ones. I decided on faded jeans, white tennis shoes, and a fitted satin tank top with a loose cashmere cardigan. I didn't want to look as if I was trying to impress him. I was at work after all.

Grady, on the other hand, had clearly not tried to impress me. In fact, he looked like he hadn't been home since I'd seen him outside my place last night.

"Whoa," I said, tugging the beleaguered detective inside. "Did you sleep?"

"No." He rubbed both palms against drooping eyes, then fixed an all-knowing look on me. "Did you?"

I pressed my lips tight. *Touché.*

"Well, at least let me feed you," I said. "Food helps,

and I've got a pot of coffee ready. How do scrambled eggs sound?"

Grady nodded, and I led him to the row of seats at my counter. I patted one on my way around to the business side. "I'm expecting a usual day here," I said, pouring him some coffee. "I'll be serving tea and other delicious items until seven tonight. What's on your agenda?" I slid the mug before him.

His hands seemed to wrap around the cup on instinct. His thumbs beat a rhythm along the rim. "I get to meet with the mayor's family again," he said, emphasis on the final word and not looking at all happy about it.

"Why?" I asked. "Do you have new information for them?"

He shook his head. "No."

I pulled a carton of brown eggs from the refrigerator and cracked a half dozen into a bowl. I stirred and seasoned them gently before adding a dollop of sour cream to the mix and whipping it hard.

"Your aunt Clara confirmed the gnomes were hers," he said. "All of them. The ones smashed on your porch. The one used to kill the mayor. The one left for you outside Blue."

My whipping hand slowed. That wasn't new information. "And?"

Grady looked up at me, swirling his mostly empty mug. "I don't know, but it's not good, and what's with her and those gnomes anyway? Are they some kind of weird island tradition? Are they a Swan thing?"

"I don't know what you mean by a *Swan thing*," I said, "and what do you mean it's not good?"

He finished the coffee and set the mug aside. "All the evidence points to your Aunt Clara," he said, catching me in a pointed gaze. "Your other aunt, *the accused*, is her roommate and business partner with complete access to those gnomes, and none of them, aside from the murder weapon, have any prints on them. Nothing to prove anyone else handled them."

I refilled his mug with one eyebrow cocked. "So? That's all the more reason to know these crimes weren't committed by my aunts. There wouldn't have been a need to wipe their prints off. Aunt Clara's prints should have been all over the gnomes because she painted them. Aunt Fran's could've been on there from helping her sister arrange the little garden she was making outside their shop. Why would anyone wipe their prints off something they readily admit belongs to them?"

"They wouldn't," he said.

"Right," I agreed. "It's counterproductive."

Grady blew across the surface of his refill. "Still, Fran's prints were on the murder weapon."

"And mine and Aunt Clara's should have been," I said. "We all held and admired that thing when Aunt Clara delivered him to me, but when you sent it to the lab, after the murder, only Aunt Fran's prints were there."

Grady watched me closely. "There's no way to remove your prints and Clara's without disturbing Fran's."

I nodded. "Aunt Fran's prints are there because she went outside to cool off. She didn't take her coat or gloves, and she picked the gnome up when she saw him in the snow," I said, hoping he was beginning to see.

Grady made a low, guttural sound and hunched further over his mug. "The mayor's family wants blood. His wife is outraged that I haven't arrested Fran. She's been at the station all morning, demanding justice and painting a vivid story for anyone who will listen."

"Let me guess," I said, scrambling the eggs in a pan. "Aunt Fran was a woman scorned, humiliated, and sent fleeing her own party. The murder was an act of passion."

He sighed, so I must've been on the mark.

The expression on his handsome face became stricken. Grady clearly didn't want to believe my aunt was a killer, but he worked by the book, followed the facts, and at the moment, the facts were breaking his heart.

My anger quelled. "We'll figure this out," I said. "Hold the Dunfrees off as long as you can, and we'll find something to clear Fran's name. I think we already have a solid argument about the fingerprints. That should at least exclude Fran from the suspect pool."

Grady shook his head. "It's circumstantial. You can wipe something off, then pick it up again."

I frowned. "Do you have any other possible suspects yet?" I asked. "Did you find the cell phone?

Have you spoken with Mary Grace? I'd really like to know why she decided to run with the mayor as his deputy instead of against him."

Grady lifted a finger. "No to the phone, and I'm working on the rest." He reached for me with the hand he'd lifted between us, and I stilled to let him. "I've got this, Swan. *I'll* figure it out."

My breath caught at the rush of electricity coursing between our joined hands. Unfortunately, his blatant emphasis on the word *I'll* felt uncomfortably pointed and a little like *butt out*. I wriggled free of his grasp and refocused on the eggs. "Did you know Mayor Dunfree was a misogynist?" I asked. "Lanita told me and my aunts confirmed it."

Grady frowned. "His wife indicated as much. She didn't seem to mind."

I tried and failed to understand how a woman married to a misogynist wouldn't mind. Lanita minded and she didn't even know the mayor personally. Her mom minded and she hadn't spoken to him, presumably, in years. "What do you think of it?" I asked, setting a lid on the skillet and jamming four slices of homemade bread into the toaster with unnecessary oomph.

"What do I think of misogyny?" Grady laughed. "I think it's antiquated bull that has been proven fallible at every turn and seems to be on the decline, thankfully."

I laughed approvingly. "I hadn't expected such a thorough answer, but I'll take it."

Grady's smile turned sad. "Amy," he said by way of explanation. "She was strong. Someone I aspired to be like. And you've met her mother."

I nodded.

"As for this investigation," he said, "you've got to let it go this time. Trust me to handle it. Alone. Okay?"

"Mm-hmm," I hummed, noncommittally. I hated to lie, but it was unfair of him to put me on the spot.

"Everly," he challenged, his voice turning me to face him. His shoulders were square as he pinned me in place with his cool, gray eyes.

"She's my family," I said, hating the whine in my voice. "I can't stand by and do nothing."

"You can," he said, "and you will."

I bristled. "You're only one person," I grouched, plating the finished eggs and setting the plates on the counter between us. "You're Charm's only detective, and you can't do this on your own."

"I absolutely can, and I will," he said. "And for the record, Charm has a fully trained and capable police force to back me if I need them."

"Ha!" I barked, reaching for the toast as it popped up. "I went to school with half those guys. They're all well-meaning, and I'm sure they make lovely upholders of the peace, but they aren't detectives. I'm honestly surprised they can find their uniforms to get dressed every morning. You need help. Just admit it." I stacked the toast on a plate for us to share.

"I don't need help," he argued, aggressively forking up the eggs, "and while we're being so honest, it's irritating that you constantly think I do. You have to know by now that every time you get involved, it only serves to divide my attention, slow my process, and delay the arrest. Plus, you put yourself in danger."

"But the killer gets caught," I said, smugly digging a fork into the eggs on my plate.

Grady glared at me.

"Why didn't you come in last night?" I asked. "After you finished looking in the garden."

He released a sigh and went back to his food, more calmly. "Denise called. Olivia was making her nuts, and she needed my intervention, so I headed home from here. I thought about coming in to let you know, but Denise seemed pretty upset, and I can't afford to let Olivia scare her away. We need her."

I bit my tongue against the words piling on it. I highly doubted Denise would be fired since she'd been so carefully chosen for Denver…and Grady. I felt my mouth pull down at the sides. "You want to talk about it?" I asked, turning for the toast as it popped up.

"Not really." He cast me a self-deprecating smile. "Same old. Olivia thinks Denver should have a bigger home, more things, live in the city. Arlington, specifically. She thinks I've moved him to Timbuktu, and she can't even see how great this place has been for a hurting kid." Emotion flashed in his eyes, and for a moment I thought he might've been talking about himself too.

I puzzled over the notion that his mother-in-law thought he needed a bigger house and more things. In my experience, stuff always complicated life. I had a huge house, for example, and I loved it, but the house didn't return my love. Happiness required family and friends, a sense of purpose and belonging. Those were the things that mattered most. "What kind of house does she think will make him happy? A big manor like Northrop? How does she expect you to pay for something like that on a Charm detective's salary?"

Grady snagged a slice of toast off the stack and chewed it slowly. "She wants me back with the Marshals service, to assist on a personal agenda. As for the money, I have it. Amy's life insurance police was...substantial."

"Oh." My eyes widened. Grady was opening up to me. He trusted me, and I had so many questions. I held back a moment, giving him time to tell me more *if he wanted.* I hoped he did.

Grady offered a bitter smile. "Her mother took out a policy on each of us the moment she learned Amy was pregnant. I was named as the beneficiary, but Olivia maintains a constant and ongoing opinion about how I spend the money, or don't," he added, lips curving slightly. "The insurance was meant to support Denver and Amy or I in the event one of us passed away, but my policy has always felt more like a bounty on my head than insurance."

Suddenly, some things about Grady made more sense. For starters, I'd wondered how he'd afforded to build a stable so soon after he'd moved to Charm. The finished structure was easily worth as much as the simple home he'd chosen for himself, Denise, and Denver. The three horses that had come to live there had baffled me as well. Now, I understood. Grady had money, he just didn't want to spend it. I couldn't blame him. He'd received it under unthinkable circumstances, and he didn't need it to live happily. He'd alluded to as much at the summer arts festival. He'd told me he'd spent his whole life saving instead of spending, and it was a hard habit to break. I'd assumed he'd meant being a poor young man verses an established older one. The comment had gone directly over my head, but he'd been trying to tell me more about himself even then.

I smiled for a moment, enjoying the weight of that truth. The heroic and secretive Grady Hays wanted me to know him. The pleasure was squashed when my thoughts jerked into another direction. *Life insurance.*

"Grady?" I asked, hating to ruin the moment, if that's what we were having. "Do you think Mrs. Dunfree had an insurance policy on her husband? It could be a possible motive, and if Mrs. Dunfree killed him or had him killed, it would explain why she's pushing you to arrest Aunt Fran. People get crazy about money."

Grady bobbed his head slowly as he stole one of my slices of toast and bit into it with a scowl. "You're not kidding."

CHAPTER TEN

By seven, the café had been empty for more than an hour, so I didn't feel guilty for closing up a few minutes early. I grabbed my coat, purse, and the cheery red holiday book Amelia had given me, then headed outside for some fresh air. I'd return the book to the Little Library so another reader could take a crack at it before Christmas. I hadn't opened it, but I was on chapter twelve of my personal copy of *Wuthering Heights*.

It took a little extra patience and coaxing to get Blue's engine humming in the cold, but she rolled out of the carriage house like a champ a few moments later. We stopped at the little metal box on a sturdy wooden post at the end of my driveway. I swapped the small stack of outgoing holiday cards in my purse for the pile of newly delivered ones in my mailbox and smiled. Today had been a good day.

I guided Blue onto the boardwalk and trundled along with Amelia's copy of *The Greatest Gift* on my lap. It was a picture-perfect night with snow lingering on the beach and over the tall grasses. The crisp snap of winter was in the air. Moonlight glittered on the dark water and about a million visible stars flashed and winked overhead. The simple rush and pull of the tide were enough to settle my worried mind. I used the peaceful moments to pretend my great-aunt wasn't going to be arrested for murder.

I brushed snow off the Little Library's roof when I arrived. A note taped to the plexiglass window caught my eye before I set the little book inside. According to the flyer, tonight was the book club's holiday party at Charming Reads. I climbed back behind the wheel, book in hand, and changed trajectory. I'd return the book to Amelia herself instead, and maybe have a snack and visit with my fellow bookish Charmers while I was there.

I hummed a cheery Christmas melody all the way through town. I breathed in the moments, committing our town's snow-covered streets to memory, then stole the last available parking spot outside the string of adorable little shops. With the book and my purse in tow, I left Blue behind and made my way onto the sidewalk teeming with shoppers. I admired each festive window display as I passed, enjoyed the warm scents of hot chocolates in passersby's hands and the mouthwatering aromas wafting from nearby vendor carts selling kettle corn and warm candied nuts.

I arrived at my destination several minutes later,

after making a pit stop at one of those carts and stashing the roasted pecans in my coat pocket. Charming Reads was packed with shoppers and adorable with a capital *A*. Amelia had chosen the store's name as a nod to our town, but inside, she'd taken the charm to a whole new level, liberally applying her lifelong love of fairy tales to every nook and cranny. The walls were lined in ornate cherry bookshelves and topped with custom wooden arches. Each arch showcased a different detail from a beloved childhood story. An enchanted rose caught beneath a glass dome, a pair of blue birds taking flight with a ribbon stretched between their beaks, a wand that hovered above a bucket and mop. The children's section had hand-carved tables and chairs, all shaped as toadstools. Their brightly colored tops were polka dotted and rarely without a book. The whole place was delightful, and tonight it was doused in clever holiday decor to rival Disneyland at Christmas.

I scanned the semicircle of chairs, horseshoed before a speaker's stand and mic. A sign on the podium proclaimed *Holiday Book Club Tonight!* along with the event time and other details in slightly smaller print. Several women had already made a trip to the refreshments table and chosen their spots among the crescent of fold-out seating. I went to mix a cup of coffee and peppermint mocha creamer to go with my nuts.

Amelia beamed at the sight of me. "Everly!" She hurried in my direction with a distinctly false smile.

I looked over my shoulder for signs of trouble

and found none. Apparently, the distressed look was about me.

She pulled up short a few inches away and handed me a stack of bookmarks. “Look at these,” she whispered.

The bookmarks were simple, black and white with large red initials down the center. *C.F.C.* And beneath those, *Charmers for Change.*

Amelia’s expression was caught somewhere between awe and panic. “The CFC has made their way into my store,” she said, still whispering. “I don’t know who left these, so I still have no idea who belongs to this group, but obviously someone made them. They just appeared near the register out of thin air about ten minutes ago.”

I lifted them into the light for a better look.

Amelia grabbed my hand and pushed the bookmarks back down between us. Her tight smile was back. “It’s not that I have a problem with change, or Charm, or anything at all, but my store is neutral ground. I can’t be associated with any one group or appear to be taking a stand like this. I’m Switzerland.”

“Got it,” I said, handing them back to her. “Care if I keep one?”

She looked around before slipping one into my hand. “Put it in your pocket,” she whispered.

I obeyed with a smile. “It’s just a bookmark.”

Amelia raised her brows beneath her bangs. “They aren’t *just* anything. Revolutions always start small.”

I laughed.

She hurried back to the register, where a trio of customers had formed a line, and tossed the rest of the bookmarks into the trash.

I stirred my coffee and went to find a seat.

Janie came into view, sloughing off her coat at one of the folding chairs. I took the seat beside hers. "I didn't know you were part of the book club."

She startled. "Oh." One hand pressed to her chest, she smiled. "I try to get involved everywhere I can. I'm hoping to stop being the 'new girl' at some point this year. I figure if people start seeing me everywhere, I won't seem so novel."

"Good plan," I said, "but I have to warn you, I've heard folks refer to the mailman as being a newcomer, and he arrived when I was in high school."

"Great." She chuckled. "It's like trying to join a private club or a really large clan."

I laughed and sipped my coffee.

"It's one of the reasons I spend so much time with your aunts," she said softly.

I turned on my brightest smile and hoped she hadn't noticed how unreasonably childish I was when it came to sharing Aunt Clara and Aunt Fran. "They enjoy having you, and you aren't just spending time with them, you've been helping Aunt Fran with her campaign plans. We all appreciate that more than you know."

Janie wrinkled her nose. "Thanks. Is it weird that I still feel like an interloper most of the time?" She gave a soft smile and lowered her gaze to her fingertips, curved around a small disposable cup. "My parents split up when I was young. Their marriage just kind of imploded after a family tragedy, and my childhood became the collateral damage."

"I'm so sorry," I said on instinct, unsure why she'd chosen to open up to me. Was she that lonely? How had I never noticed? Maybe the fact she tried so hard to fit in should've been a tip-off.

"You came here to start over," I said. "You get to build your own family."

"Yeah." She blinked slightly unfocused eyes, lost in thoughts that were clearly breaking her heart.

"We're all about family here," I said. "Blood related or not. Move here, and you get a great seaside town with awesome views and food, plus a fantastic group of friends and neighbors." I tried to imagine Senator Denver in the equation but couldn't. She felt more like the force adjusted to, not the one who did the adjusting. Janie was different, softer, willing. She'd be happy here in time.

She stole a look at me. "I came here once as a child. Have I ever told you?"

She hadn't. Honestly, aside from dodging questions about Grady's romantic availability, I'd only exchanged general small talk and details about Aunt Fran's future campaign with Janie before now.

"It was the last trip my family made together," she said, a bit wistfully. "I've always imagined coming back here. So, when I got the notice that I'd been downsized, I packed my bags and headed this way."

"Well, I'm glad you're here," I said, surprised to mean it.

Janie's eyebrows rose. "You are?"

"Absolutely."

A smile spread over her lips. "Thanks."

I sipped my coffee as Amelia began to corral the readers toward the empty seats around me. "I wish I could do more to help with the campaign plans," I admitted, "but running the café takes a lot out of me."

"Well, yeah," Janie said. "You're a one-woman show over there. Get some help, why don't you?"

I laughed. "I'm thinking about it."

"Good." She set her cup on the floor and crossed her legs smoothly, folding her hands over her knee. "You know, I heard my first story about Mayor Dunfree and the council on the day I moved in. My landlord told me all about the hoopla I'd missed following a beach wedding this summer." She paused, waiting for a reaction, perhaps.

I felt my stomach rock with the onslaught of related memories. "Dunfree denied the paper lanterns," I said.

"He was more concerned with upholding some stupid rules than uplifting a hurting woman." She looked heartbroken at the thought. "That was crazy, right?"

"Yeah." But that was Mayor Dunfree. I wasn't sure how beloved he had ever really been, but the paper lantern decision had been his fall from grace. The ruling had somewhat divided the island. It had given

Aunt Fran the motivation she needed to stop complaining about local politics and do something about them. I suspected it had also been the catalyst for the creation of the allusive CFC, which had seemed to come out of nowhere shortly afterward.

Janie swiveled suddenly to face me, her cunning expression bright with enthusiasm. "When rumors started about a woman on the council who'd turned against the pack, one who planned to run against Mayor Dunfree, I knew I had to try to help her."

"Well, you are definitely making a difference," I said. "Thank you."

She nodded. "How about you? Have you learned any more about Dunfree's death?" Her eyebrows were up again, and I hesitated to answer.

"Not really," I said. "How's your PR intervention going?"

"I'm glad you asked." Janie pulled her bag onto her lap and fished out a handful of tiny discs. "I made some fun buttons," she said, hooking one onto the strap of my purse hanging across the back of my chair.

I twisted for a better look at the little thing. "No more ugly ducklings," I read. "It's time to vote for a Swan." I debated over explaining the obvious problem. In that story, the duckling was actually a swan. In the end, I let it go. "Cute," I said.

"Thanks." Janie set her bag back on the floor, and it yawned open at the top. Something black and white with red letters caught my attention just inside. "Make any bookmarks?" I asked, suddenly wondering if the CFC bookmarks Amelia had discovered by her register had come from Janie. And if she knew more about the group than she'd let on.

She furrowed her brow. "No, just buttons. Why? Do you think Fran wants bookmarks? I could probably get some printed up this week."

I waved a hand to slow her down before she abandoned book club to design bookmarks. "The buttons are perfect."

She turned forward again, after a long curious look, but thankfully let the conversation drop. "Right now, I'm working on a list of potential campaign promises and rally events for the next eleven months. I'm open to ideas if you have any."

I smiled, glad to be included. "I'll think about it."

Janie smiled back. "I think Fran should start with a big New Year's Eve party. We can theme the night around new beginnings and push the concept of ringing in a year of change. I'd like to rent the hall beside the lighthouse and kill two birds with one party. We can raise money for Fran's campaign and pledge to repair the steps there so folks can continue to safely enjoy that piece of the island's history. What do you think?"

"I think you spend a lot of time planning for Aunt Fran's campaign."

"It's fun," she said, "and both Fran's win and the lighthouse's repair are worthy goals. Did you know one of your ancestors was once the lighthouse keeper?"

I hadn't, but it didn't surprise me. The island was

small and Swans had been here from the beginning. I supposed that after three hundred years, a Swan had probably worked every job on the island.

"We can use that to our advantage," Janie said, lost in thought once more. "We'll get a slogan like, *Swans have a history of lighting the way*, or something like that."

Speaking of lights, the dim one in my head flickered on, a little late as usual. "Is that the reason you went to the lighthouse fundraiser before my Christmas party?" I asked. "You were scoping out the rental hall for Aunt Fran's New Year's Eve party and getting information on the lighthouse's needs and history."

She touched a finger to the tip of her nose.

"Smart."

Feedback from the speakers at the podium drew our attention forward. Amelia tapped the mic and smiled. "Welcome! I'm glad that so many of you could make it despite the weather. Thank you for that, and for being part of my book club. Book club is always one of my favorite nights of the month. I can't wait to hear what each of you read and why it's important to you at Christmas, but I know many of you are a bit shy, so I will start."

And just like that, book club was underway.

A number of brave women approached the mic when Amelia finished, and each was met with enthusiastic nods and laughter from their fellow readers. Most of the women in the chairs seemed to have read every book that was introduced as another woman's favorite. I'd read those books, too, but no one had chosen *Wuthering Heights*.

The door opened for the hundredth time that hour, just as the book club broke for refreshments, and Grady walked in.

I waved, and my smile grew at the sight of Denver on his shoulders.

Janie nudged me with her elbow before I could stand to greet them. "What's the real deal with you and the detective?"

"We're friends," I said, my traitorous heart fluttering. "Why?"

Janie stood and gathered her things with a sly grin. "He's cute, and folks seem to think you're a couple. Is it awful that I'm glad he's single?" She gave Grady a more thorough evaluation. "He's got that brooding bad boy vibe every woman secretly dreams about and a badge and uniform to go with it."

I fought the urge to wipe her chin. "Grady doesn't wear a uniform."

Her eyebrows rose, and I suspected she might be picturing him without his current ensemble. She cleared her throat, then dragged her gaze back to me. "Any chance he's given you some insight into the case against Fran? I'd love a little leverage I could run with. I'm not sure how far the buttons will go to change public perception."

"I'll keep you posted if I hear anything," I said, moving away to get my hands on the tiny cowboy.

"Denver!" I called, going in for a tummy tickle while he was helpless to run.

"Ah!" He squirmed and kicked and giggled until his face was red and he'd stopped producing sounds.

I stepped back and laughed while he regained his breath.

"We're here for story time," Grady said. "Mr. Butters is retelling *Jack and the Beanstalk* tonight. Denver heard there would be swords involved."

"There are," a low voice called from behind me.

I spun to find Amelia's dad wielding a half-dozen cardboard sword shapes. Some curved. Some straight. All painted silver from tip to wrist guard, their handles wrapped in thick black yarn.

Denver wiggled down and made a run for Mr. Butters. "Hooray!"

I turned back to Grady. "That's one enthusiastic reader you've got there."

Grady stuffed his hands into his pockets and smiled proudly at me. "He gets it, honestly. I wanted to be here for book club, but Denver and I took your advice and made a trip to the Giving Tree."

"Is that right?" I asked, hoping to sound cool and confident. In reality, my breath caught in my throat, and for a moment, I felt Grandma beside me telling me I'd done a good thing by sharing our story with them. "Did you get a child's name?"

Grady looked away briefly. "I took a few envelopes from the tree. A couple families in need of some pretty basic home and self-care items. Kids in need of the same. Denver thought they'd all like a new book too."

I nodded, fighting the lump of pride in my chest. "That's great."

Grady cleared his throat. "So what did you read this month?" His gaze drifted to the little red book in my grip.

I turned the cover to face him. "Amelia gave this to me because she didn't approve of my choice. What about you?"

His lips quirked in a lazy half smile as he reached behind him and pulled a well-worn paperback from his pocket. "It's not really a Christmas story," he said, "but I read it every winter."

I stared at the tattered copy of *Wuthering Heights*. "You don't think it's about a selfish girl and her stalker who are awful to one another until she dies and haunts him, and he likes it?" I asked, recalling each of Amelia's harsh words.

He narrowed his eyes, clearly confused. "I've never thought of them that way. I was drawn to the story in middle school. The darkness around the characters drew me in. They were nothing like my family or any family I knew, and Heathcliff amused me because he did whatever he wanted, consequences be darned. I liked that when Heathcliff was angry, he behaved angrily. I was always expected to show self-control."

Based on the cool exterior and subdued personality Grady had now, it was easy enough to imagine he'd been practicing for a lifetime.

"Wouldn't it be nice to just do or say whatever you wanted when you wanted to do or say it?" he asked, heat flashing in his pale gray eyes.

I longed to ask him what he would do or say if he could. What was he holding out on? And why?

Grady's gaze lifted suddenly over my shoulder and his smile returned. "I think I'm being summonsed."

I turned to find Denver standing on a chair in the children's section waving his cardboard sword in our direction.

"Go," I said. "Enjoy."

Grady touched my sleeve lightly as he passed, then hurried to his son in big, heavy steps calling, "Fe, fi, fo, fum!"

I envied them both for the sweet moment.

Outside the shop, Aunt Fran and Janie spoke under the twinkle lights.

I dropped Amelia's book in the Little Libraries' return bin, then went to hug my aunt.

"Everly," Janie said, immediately pleading, "I was just telling Fran about an interview offer I've received and how important it is for her to accept it."

I cast a skeptical look at both of them. It was the first they'd disagreed on anything as far as I knew. "What offer?"

Janie turned her phone to face me.

An email from the *Town Charmer* blog centered the screen, the site's logo positioned where a signature should have gone.

Aunt Fran peeked over my shoulder as I read.

"An interview with an anonymous gossip blogger seems like a wholly unwise decision to me," she said. "Whoever is on the other end of that email could twist my responses before putting them online and do a lot of damage. I say no way."

I read the entire message twice, looking for hidden clues about the sender's identity. There weren't any. Even the email address was utterly nonspecific: Charmer@TownCharmer.com.

"Please trust me," Janie pressed, "You don't want Mary Grace or Mrs. Dunfree to be interviewed first. Then, their truth will be out there and not yours. The first interview sets a tone. You want to be seen as the leader in this, not the one running behind doing damage control."

Aunt Fran shook her head. "Let someone else go first. I can always accept the interview later when I know which fires I have to address and am prepared to do so. I won't go in blindly on this."

"All right." Janie rocked back on her heels. "Say your piece when you're ready, but remember, you're the change Charmers want to see in their town. They're looking to you for answers right now."

Her speech sounded a lot like the Charmers for Change movement, and I wondered again if Janie knew more about the group than she'd let on. I worked the idea around in my thick, overly clogged brain and was interrupted by a completely different concern. "Where's Aunt Clara?" I looked down the sidewalk in both directions, but there wasn't any sign of her. I hadn't seen one of my aunts without the other in years, maybe never.

"Painting more gnomes," Aunt Fran said dryly.

"What?" I turned in the direction of their shop next door. "At Blessed Bee?"

Fran dipped her chin in confirmation. "I don't know what's going on with her lately. She's either obsessed or lost her mind. The last thing we need is more gnomes in this town."

"I'll go check on her," I said, agreeing wholeheartedly about the gnomes. I'd seen enough of them in the past forty-eight hours to last a lifetime.

Janie squared her shoulders. "Before you go and we move away from the topic of PR and campaign strategies, I think you should be careful when you're in public with Detective Hays," she said. "People are always watching here, and they see what they want to see." She lifted her gaze to the bookstore window. An illuminated fishbowl from where we stood. "Like it or not, your actions are going to affect Fran's image right now. Those looking to find fault with Fran will try to use you to do it if they can't find reason with Fran. I should probably be the group liaison with Detective Hays now, especially if it means meeting publicly."

I had to force my gaping mouth shut, unsure when it had fallen open. Janie was going to use this investigation as an opportunity to make friends with Grady. Based on our earlier conversation about him, she clearly hoped for more than friendship. I kissed Aunt Fran's soft cheek, unsure how to respond to Janie. I had no claim to Grady or anyone else on the planet, and everyone had a right to be happy. "Keep warm," I said. Besides, Janie was probably right, assuming people would think the worst. Maybe say I influenced Grady to turn the other cheek for Aunt Fran's sake, or that he would do that for me. Grady had warned me about the same thing already. I didn't like it, and I wanted to check on Aunt Clara. "Good night."

"Good night," the women echoed.

I huffed a cloud of ice crystals as I passed Janie's *Swan for Mayor* sedan on my way to Blessed Bee. *One problem at a time*, I told myself. And at the moment, I wanted to know why on earth Aunt Clara was painting more gnomes.

My phone dinged before I reached the shop door. There was a notification that my website had been updated. I swiped the screen to see the details.

I'd elected to send the automated notifications to my phone as an experiment when I'd first established the Sun, Sand, and Tea website. I'd wanted to know what the messages would look like to others who followed my site. The problem was that I'd already received a notice about the update I had made this morning, and I hadn't made any changes since then.

I clicked the link and followed it through to my site, eager to see what had changed.

"Oh no," I whispered, my heart hammering brutally against my ribs.

The screen was black and covered in small, white letters. No more beachy background, no cute southern sayings. Just white on black and thousands of tiny letters running across the screen in endless rows, looping off one side and returning midword on the other. I scrolled until the very last line, written in red.

> *I will leave Mayor Dunfree's murder alone. I will leave Mayor Dunfree's murder alone. I will leave Mayor Dunfree's murder alone. I will leave Mayor Dunfree's murder alone. I will leave Mayor Dunfree's murder alone. I will leave Mayor Dunfree's murder alone. I will leave Mayor Dunfree's murder alone. I will leave Mayor Dunfree's murder alone.*
>
> **Or I will be *very* sorry.**

CHAPTER ELEVEN

Everly?" Aunt Clara's voice registered through the whooshing in my ears. "Oh dear." She tugged my coat sleeve with purpose, causing me to stumble forward, out of my stupor and into Blessed Bee. "Come now."

The dead bolt snapped behind me, and the flurry of frigid wind that had been tossing hair into my stinging eyes ceased.

"You'll catch a chill standing outside like that," Aunt Clara said. This time, she curved a narrow arm around my back and ushered me forward, through the dimly lit store and into the bright backroom. "When I saw you standing out there, I thought Fran had returned. She's out with Janie again. Planning for the campaign and whatnot, but she's supposed to be back soon."

"I saw them," I said, my voice gravelly. "On the sidewalk outside Charming Reads." Right before I learned that a killer had eviscerated my website.

Swapping out all my hours of hard work for a devastating threat.

Aunt Clara poured me a cup of tea from the pink carafe on the table. The sharp scent of peppermint swirled into the air as Aunt Clara set the cup before me. "Want to tell me what's wrong? You look like you've seen a ghost."

I took the seat across from her and raised my eyes to meet her gaze. The fine hairs on my arms stood at attention beneath my coat. "Something like that," I whispered, my mind reeling. How had someone gained access to my website? When? I'd been on this morning uploading the instructional video. Everything had been fine then, hadn't it? How long was the delay between the content change online and the email notification? A few minutes? Hours?

"Was it one of our ancestors?" Aunt Clara asked, her elbows on the table between us, eyes wide.

"What?" I scrambled backward over our exchange. *She'd said I looked as if I'd seen a ghost.* "Oh! No." I wagged my head. "Nothing like that. It's my website." I woke my phone's screen with a swipe of my thumb, then turned the device to face her. "Someone hacked into my website and changed everything. Now it's just...this."

Aunt Clara lifted the fragile-looking spectacles hanging from the chain around her neck and hooked the frameless half-glasses over her snub nose. She took the phone from my hand and lifted it closer to her face for a proper inspection. "Mayor Dunfree's killer is a computer hacker? That's great news!"

I choked on the swig of tea I'd taken as she examined my website. The piping hot liquid scorched its way down my throat, burning my nose and making my eyes water. "Why is that good news?" I croaked, mopping tea off my chin and coat.

"Fran can barely use a computer," she said, "and it's a clue, isn't it?" Her confident expression wavered. "I would think that something like this significantly narrows the suspect pool. How many people can do this to a website?"

I considered the question a moment. My site-building skills were amateur at best, but I'd created a site I was proud of. Things were user-friendly these days. People of all ages managed blogs on every topic under the sun. I'd seen kids with gaming and scouting websites and octogenarians with blogs on everything from travel and religion to pets and woodworking. "Anyone," I said, the ugly realization setting in. "Most people have a site or blog and know exactly how to change one. Plus," I started, then bit hard into my lower lip. I'd never followed through with creating a proper username and password. I'd started with something easy to remember so I could focus on getting the site up and running. After that, I was supposed to change things for my protection. "My username and password are still USERNAME and PASSWORD," I admitted with a deep cringe.

"Everly!" She made a scornful noise. "We talked about that."

"I know," I moaned.

"You make Fran and I change our log-ins annually, and you never let me choose anything I can remember."

I groaned louder. "I know."

"You give us fits over it," she continued, "and you left your site like *that*? What were you thinking?"

I rocked my head over one shoulder, feeling like the first-rate idiot I was. "I got busy and forgot. Plus, who would hack into an iced tea shop's website?"

Aunt Clara leveled me with a disbelieving stare. "Well, that's the question, isn't it?"

I took another long drink of my tea, enjoying the smooth, warm sensation as it heated me inside and took the chill away from my skin. The peppermint was stronger than her usual recipe. I tried and failed to place the change.

"Feeling better?" she asked, watching me as I puzzled.

"Yeah, thanks." I slid my coat off and ran my fingers through my hair. "I was on my way here to see how you're doing." I forced a tight smile. "How are you doing?"

Aunt Clara raised a gnome from the partially painted collection on the table. "I'm fine. What did Detective Hays say about your website?"

"I haven't told him. I just found out before you pulled me inside, and I'm processing," I said.

She gave me a sharp sideways look, then chose a worn, red-handled paintbrush from the row before her and dipped the bristles into a blob of thick black paint. "Well, go ahead. Call now," she said. "I've got boots to paint."

I scanned the scene between us seriously for the first time. Her paints, palettes, and brushes were scattered over the table, now covered in a white cloth. The usual handmade and handed-down cover had been folded neatly and set on the cupboard across the room. The cloth beneath my hands was probably just as old, but splattered with a rainbow of accidental spills. A gnome army centered the workspace. The figure in her grip was unpainted except from his rosy cheeks and creepy black eyes. His friends stood in rows, soldiers awaiting their turn under the brush.

"Are you calling?" Aunt Clara pressed, brush caressing one ceramic boot.

"Not now," I said, swirling the remainder of tea in my little cup. "Grady's next door with Denver. They're at story time with Mr. Butters, and I don't want to interrupt their nice moment to deliver bad news." I stretched for the carafe and helped myself to a refill, then warmed Aunt Clara's drink up as well. "This can wait. No one's been hurt, and I'm not in immediate danger." My tummy heated with the weight of the liquid, and my muscles sagged in gentle relief. "This is really soothing," I said, running a fingertip around the cup's edge. "You did something different, and I love it. Do I get to know the secret ingredient?"

"Sure." Aunt Clara peered at me over the top of her rimless half-glasses. "It's schnapps."

A ragged laugh burst from my lips. "What?"

She shrugged. "Mr. Waters had some peppermint schnapps on the shelf the last time I was in Molly's Market, so I picked up a bottle. I'd originally planned to cook with it, maybe bake it into cookies or boil it into icing. Then, this week started down the toilet, and I just decided to drink it."

I had another sip and giggle before setting the antique cup aside. I still had to drive home. "Do I even want to know the tea-to-alcohol ratio?"

"Probably not." Aunt Clara smiled. She finished the gnome's boots and moved him down the line, positioning the next figure before her. "I could use some crushed peppermint for my new Christmas gifts. Since no one will want these guys, I've decided to make hot cocoa jars. The kind you layer ingredients in, then attach a recipe card and the recipient can make it at their convenience."

"You're in luck," I said. "I happen to know where you can find about ten pounds of peppermint in the form of a bat."

She smiled. "May I? I can promise to put it to good use if you can't."

"I definitely can't," I said. "I'm done with all my peppermint recipes for the season." I made a mental note to bring the Waterses' gift with me for Aunt Clara the next time I visited. They'd like to know their gift to me went on to reach so many others.

I lifted one of the finished gnomes and turned it over in my fingertips, careful not to smudge any spots that might still be wet. "Why are you painting all these?" I asked. "You should definitely stop since they're being used in all sorts of crimes, but I don't think you ever told me why you started."

When she didn't answer, I pushed a little more, making a guess. "Are you trying not to think about something?"

Her brush stilled a moment before busying itself once more. "What do you mean?"

I returned the gnome to his ranks and refocused on Aunt Clara. "I mean I think you're upset about something and taking it out on ceramics." I'd never seen Aunt Clara truly angry, but it seemed fitting that she would channel her emotions into a project like this. I baked to take my mind off difficult things. I could do that anytime I needed, but Aunt Clara's favorite pastimes were out of season. Her herbs and flowers, the extensive vegetable garden, even the bees were unavailable for now. "So, what is it?" I asked. "What are you trying not to think about?"

Her head snapped in my direction, lips parted. "How did you know?"

"Because I do this too," I said, waving a hand toward the legion of ceramic men. "Except I bake. And then I eat."

Aunt Clara set the paintbrush aside with a long and labored sigh. "One more way you and I are alike. We avoid unpleasant feelings."

"Who wouldn't?" I asked.

She smiled, but it didn't reach her eyes, and her work on the gnome before her had been all but forgotten.

"You know you can tell me anything, right?" I asked. "It helps to talk about the things that bother us, even if we don't want to. You taught me that."

Aunt Clara finished her tea in one gulp. Then, she finished mine. "Okay." She shook her hands out hard at the wrists. "The truth is I'm feeling a little lost without Fran around all the time. We've practically spent our entire lives attached at the hip and suddenly she's off on a new adventure. Without me. I'm having a hard time processing that, and it's making me feel all sorts of...things."

I folded my arms on the table and rested my chin on them. "It must be a miserable adjustment for you." I glanced away, heat rising to my cheeks. "Jealousy's tough."

Aunt Clara's eyes widened. "I'm not jealous of Fran. I'm thrilled for her."

I nodded, rubbing my chin against my arms. "I meant jealousy toward Janie."

Aunt Clara removed her glasses and covered her mouth in horror. "It shows?"

"A little, but only to me because I've been feeling the same way. I'm not used to sharing either of you with anyone, and I know it's nonsense, and I'm too—"

"Too old to be jealous of someone spending so much time with someone you love?" Clara cut me off. The understanding in her eyes made me smile.

"We're ridiculous," I said, feeling doubly silly as I recalled the way I'd felt about Janie getting to know Grady.

Aunt Clara sighed, resigned. "Yeah."

"And you decided to paint gnomes to stay busy?" I guessed with a laugh. It was definitely an original idea, as unique and slightly eccentric as Aunt Clara herself.

"Originally, I was waiting around to be invited to the party," she said, "figuratively speaking. I thought eventually Fran would need me to step in, help out, or take over some aspect of the planning, but that never happened. So, I started reading more and volunteering a little, then I took one of Mr. Butters's painting classes." She shot me a red-cheeked grin. Aunt Clara had told me what she thought of Amelia's dad more than once, and how she wished she was twenty years younger.

I blushed a little too.

"It was fun and soothing, so I kept going back and I got pretty good. Once the holidays were upon us, I figured I'd paint gifts this year. There was a massive end-of-season sale on garden figures at the nature center gift shop, and I remembered the Christmas lore about *Nisse*, so I bought them out. I thought it would be fun to see a gnome on every porch in town. A little piece of me guarding all my neighbors, family members, and friends."

"You really need to reread that fairy tale," I told her, feeling the effects of the tea take hold.

She wet her lips and frowned, apparently lost in her thoughts. "The worst part is that I'm torn between wanting Fran to get her wish and become the mayor this town needs and wanting her to fail."

I reached for Aunt Clara's hand and covered it with mine. "Don't beat yourself up too much," I said. "You're allowed to miss her. Let's think of the election as a win-win. If things go one way, we'll be thrilled to see her success. If things go the other way, you get your sister back full time."

Aunt Clara squeezed my hand. "I like that."

I sensed there was more. "But?"

"I don't know who I am without her, or where I fit in if she's the mayor. It's sad and scary to think about. One day next fall it might just be me and the gnomes." She offered a mischievous grin and wiped a tear discreetly from the corner of her eye.

"Well, for what it's worth, you'll always have me," I said, sliding out of my seat to wrap her in a hug. "I'm not the same as a sister, but I love you just as much."

Aunt Clara sank into my embrace, hugging me back with all her might. "Thank you." When she pulled away, her usual easy smile had returned. "I guess talking about the hard stuff does help."

"You've never led me astray," I said, dropping back into my seat.

She gathered the excess of a long, shapeless white dress in one fist and crossed her legs beneath the billowy material. She was always wafer thin, but she seemed especially so tonight.

"You should stop by and let me feed you again soon," I said. "A one-on-one ladies' night dinner."

"That sounds lovely." Her newfound smile

suddenly doubled in size. "I noticed you haven't selected your menu for the Holiday Shuffle yet."

I marveled at the strange twinkle in her eye. "Not yet. Why?"

"Is it because you're planning a big surprise?"

I laughed. "I wish I had a surprise. What I have is severe procrastination and no idea what to serve that night. Did you see that Grady's mother-in-law is getting in on the action? Her menu is perfection with generous sides of pizzazz and wow. Anything I make will look amateur in comparison."

"No way," Aunt Clara cooed. "You don't need fancy food to impress anyone in Charm. We're already impressed. And no one visits a seaside iced tea shop for snooty food anyway. People come to see you. They want that special home cooking with a twist that only you can provide. It makes them feel good. *You* make them feel good."

I laughed. "I had no idea a glass of iced tea and some finger foods could do that."

Clara narrowed her eyes. "I think you do." She selected a clean, dry paintbrush and passed it to me. "Since you're here, you might as well make yourself useful," she teased. "I'm going to run these to the kiln tomorrow, then ship them to places that can use them in their gardens like hospitals, libraries, and retirement communities. No need for them to go to waste."

I accepted the brush and she tapped hers against mine in a toast.

Thirty minutes later, we decided the folks at those

hospitals, libraries, and retirement communities might enjoy painting the figures themselves. Aunt Clara boxed up the leftover gnomes, and I loaded the finished ones into Blue's backseat. I'd take them to the kiln for her on my way to visit Mary Grace and the stand-in mayor tomorrow.

"Drive safely," Aunt Clara called from the sidewalk outside her shop door. "Thank you, Everly," she added with such sincerity, my heart soared.

I honked as I pulled away. I wished I could stay and talk with her until Aunt Fran returned to the shop as promised, but I needed to get home and bake cookies for my morning inquisitions. Painting the one and only gnome I'd managed to finish had my mind wandering back to the biggest of our problems: how to keep Aunt Fran from winding up in police custody the week before Christmas.

Grady's truck was parked outside my carriage house when I arrived home. I kept one eye on the darkened vehicle as I reached for the box of gnomes on Blue's backseat. There wasn't any movement in the cab, and Grady wasn't on my porch, so where was he?

Someone stepped out of the shadows in my garden, and I screamed.

Grady's lopsided smile set my heart to skitter. "Sorry. I didn't mean to startle you. I did a perimeter sweep while I waited."

"You're living on the edge," I said breathlessly, "sneaking up on a jumpy lady with a box full of weapons."

"Let me." Grady easily arranged the burden under one arm. He waved me into the moonlight with the other. "Do I want to know why you have a box full of gnomes?"

"Aunt Clara overbought," I said. "These are the last of the finished products. She never dreamed one would be implicated in a murder before she gave them all away." I hooked my hand in the crook of his arm and led him to my front door.

"You still haven't told me why you have them," he said.

I pressed the numbers on my new keypad. A few local historians had made it known that they didn't approve of the keyless entry option on a nearly two-hundred-year-old home, but I'd made an executive decision, and I stuck by it. Keys were too easily lost, stolen, or duplicated. My luck was bad enough without pressing it. The way things were going for me, my next investment should probably be a full house alarm system with motion detectors.

"I'm taking these to the kiln for her tomorrow morning," I said. "Once they're finished, Aunt Clara's going to donate them to charities since she can't give them to locals as gifts anymore."

Grady followed me inside without comment.

I flipped the dead bolt back into place before unlocking the door to my private quarters and heading up the steps. "Right this way."

Once we'd made it to my living room, I flipped all the light switches and plugged my tree back in. The space illuminated in a zing of holiday cheer. I pulled the curtains across the rear wall of windows to add the rolling sea and starry night to our view.

Grady set the box on the counter and watched silently as I headed back to the kitchen.

"Don't get me wrong," I said, "It's nice to see you, but I'm not sure why you're here." I considered telling him that Janie had appointed herself his new contact, but knew that was just me being snarky and a little jealous. I blamed Aunt Clara's tea.

He gave a disbelieving look. "Any chance you've looked at your website lately?"

"Oh." My stomach dropped. "That." Severe unease returned in a crashing wave. Somehow, I'd managed to push the website issue out of my mind while I'd been with Aunt Clara.

"Yeah. That," he grouched, pulling his phone from his coat pocket and turning it toward me. "Why didn't you call when you saw this?"

I couldn't bring myself to look directly at the phone, though I'd likely see the message in my sleep for weeks to come. "I didn't want to interrupt story time." A new thought drew my brows together. "How did you know about it?" I'd only told Aunt Clara.

Grady tucked the phone away when I didn't take it. "I'm registered for your updates." He took a slow step in my direction. "Hundreds of people got the same notification."

"What?" My thundering heart seized. "Who?"

"Your followers," he said slowly, as if I might be suffering from an exceptionally low IQ.

I had hundreds of followers? And they'd been alerted about the threat? *And my uploaded how-to video.* "Oh my goodness," I whispered. "This is bad." Suffering in silence while a lunatic taunted me was one thing. Having half the island know it was happening was another.

"You should have called me," Grady said. "This is a big deal. I know you've received a lot of threats in the past few months, and maybe it's getting hard for you to discern between them, but this was very bad. It's not like dropping a broken statue outside your car or even throwing an armload of them at your house. This was personal *and* invasive. Whoever did this worked at it, so you'd know you can be reached on all fronts. Not even your café's website is outside the limits."

The whooshing sound returned to my ears, and a few spots floated in my vision. I folded myself onto the floor and dropped my head into waiting palms. I focused on breathing.

Grady sat beside me, my laptop on his crossed legs. "This was on the counter. May I?"

I nodded, still working to slow and deepen my quick, shallow breaths.

"What's the username and password for your site?" he asked.

I closed my eyes while I told him, "Username and Password."

"You almost deserve to be hacked for that," he said.

I couldn't argue. Instead, I listened to the steady tapping of Grady's fingertips against my keys, the rhythmic clicking of my touch pad, and finally the satisfied grunt of work completed. "There. I reset it. The site should look exactly like it did before the latest change, and I fixed your log-in situation."

I raised my head slowly. "You did?"

He passed me the laptop. "I did."

I scrolled through the site, noting all the familiar materials I'd painstakingly chosen, written, and uploaded. Including the video I itched to take down.

Grady nudged me with his elbow. "Your new username is BakingGoddess, and the password is GradyLovesLemonCake."

I tipped over against him, resting my head on his shoulder. "Thank you."

A long moment later, his cheek pressed against the top of my head. "What are friends for, Swan?"

"How about sharing some lemon cake?" I asked, forcing myself away from him and onto my feet.

Grady joined me in one lithe movement. "I thought you'd never ask."

We shared half a lemon cake and two glasses each of Grandma's Old-Fashioned Sweet Tea before I remembered I still had cookies to make. There were orders from locals to fill, plus I needed a few delicious props to justify my unexpected appearance at Mary Grace's house and the standing mayor's office tomorrow morning.

I arranged the ingredients for my family's amazing sugar cookies on the counter and smiled. When I cut them out and iced them, people lost their mind in need of more. It seemed like the right recipe for loosening some lips. "Have you learned anything new about the night the mayor died?" I asked Grady. "Found his cell phone? Got any leads on a new suspect?"

"No one with means and motive," Grady said, but something flashed in his eyes.

I froze, hoping it was good news. "What?"

Grady pursed his lips. "It's probably nothing, but Dunfree's wife called in a complaint today, and when I looked into it further, I found a few other complaints from her this year."

I gaped at him. "Complaints about her husband?" There were only a few reasons a woman would call the police about her husband, and none of those were good.

"No. Nothing like that. There's an ongoing spat with a neighbor. The guy put up a new fence at the end of summer and it blocks Mrs. Dunfree's view of the ocean. She doesn't like it, and he won't take it down, so they argue and drag the local PD into it. There are multiple reports from the past few months, but police action has never been taken."

"And she called for the same reason again today," I clarified.

Grady gave a stiff nod. "Twice. The fence is obviously a sore spot. Add the stress and grief of losing her husband, and she's mad as a rattlesnake. This morning, she told the responding officer that the neighbor's taking advantage because her husband isn't here to enforce the rules anymore. I'm thinking that if the fence had actually been against the rules, it would have already come down."

I felt my mouth form a little *o* as I took the new information in. "What does the standing mayor say?"

"Not much," Grady said. "He's promised Mrs. Dunfree he'll look into the bylaws of their neighborhood to see if there was any infringement, but I figure Mr. Dunfree would've already done that. If he can't find a reason to force the guy to take the fence down, she'll either have to learn to live with the fence or move."

I returned my attention to the giant ball of sugar cookie dough on the counter and gave it a few whacks with my great-great-grandmother's rolling pin. *Mrs. Dunfree has a nemesis.* Could he have figured into her husband's death somehow? I used the ancient rolling pin to press the dough ball into a massive quarter-inch-thick spread, sprinkling a fistful of flour over the sticky mix as needed. "What's the neighbor's name?" I asked, trying to look as innocent and disinterested as possible. "Maybe I know him."

Grady chuckled. "Don't even try it."

I got the first round of cutouts into the over, then grabbed the stack of unopened cards from my bag and a wheel of tape to hang them. Better to keep my hands busy if I was going to be alone with Grady much longer, I mused. "Want to help?" I handed him half the stack without waiting for a reply.

He went to work sliding one finger under each flap and freeing the cards. He stood them like teepees over the envelopes in an arc across the counter. "You get a lot of cards. You're running out of windows."

"I'll stick them on the cupboards next," I said, opening a pretty red envelope with a butter knife. No return address, so the sender would be a surprise, but definitely a local. It had been stamped at the Charm post office.

A barrel of red glitter spilled over my hands, counter, and floor. "Goodness!" I jumped back, unsure who thought that was a good idea. "Glitter bomb," I said, dusting my hands and clothes with a dish towel.

Grady was on his feet and at my side. "Did you cut yourself?"

"No." I raised my open hands to him. "Some nut sent me a pound of glitter."

Grady checked the envelope, then gave a soft cuss. The only thing inside the envelope, aside from glitter was a piece of paper with my name on it. Each letter had been x-ed out in heavy black strokes.

"Uh-oh," I said. My stomach ached and twisted. "Another threat." In a holiday card. What kind of sicko did that?

Grady pulled his phone from his pocket again. This time he frowned at the screen. "Denver had a nightmare." He ran a hand through his hair, then looked at the glitter.

"It's okay," I said. "Go." I stripped the apron from

around my waist. "Take the card. I'll gather up as much of the glitter as I can."

He nodded, distracted.

I found a dustpan and whisk broom, and Grady joined me in the cleanup, but his distraction was palpable. Something was wrong with his son, and that came first. Always. And as it should.

"Go." I pressed the sealed bag against Grady's chest. "I'm fine, and I'll lock up behind you. I'm not going anywhere else tonight, and I'm not in any danger. It was just glitter."

Grady gave one stiff nod. "I'll stop at the post office in the morning. Find out who mailed this."

I wasn't sure it was that simple, even in Charm, but I forced a tight smile of acceptance. "Thanks."

I followed him to the door, feeling a small tremor work its way through me. I wanted to make a joke to lighten the mood and erase the worry etched across his brow. Maybe something about an angry crafter on the hunt, or that Mr. Butters should rethink his story choices about child-eating giants. But I knew Denver had much worse things haunting him. Losing his mother to a lengthy cancer battle, for starters. The pain in Grady's eyes said it all. It wasn't a monster that had woken his son. It was remembered heartbreak.

Grady turned to me beneath the mistletoe at my front door and ran a palm down the length of my arm, shoulder to elbow. "Lock up behind me, Swan. Stay safe."

CHAPTER TWELVE

Clara arrived shortly after breakfast the next morning. She stomped snow from her boots and dusted flakes from her hat and coat before hanging both with a shiver. "The weather is atrocious. I've never seen the likes of this in all my days."

"Did you have any trouble getting here?" I asked. I couldn't imagine my great-aunt walking or riding her bicycle in the snow, and she rarely drove her aged golf cart.

"Not at all," she said. "I called the Waterses' niece for a Pick-Me-Up."

I laughed. Lanita had chosen a great place to spend her holiday break. Thanks to the crazy weather, she'd be going back to school a lot richer. "You got all this snow on you walking from the driveway?"

"More," she said. "I stomped off as much as I could on your porch. It's unbelievable out there. You should've seen the meteorologist's face on the news this morning. The precipitation doesn't even show up on his little weather map. He seemed as dumbstruck as the rest of us."

I smiled. "Well, I don't mind. I've always wanted a white Christmas in Charm. Grandma and I sat up late every Christmas Eve talking about what it would be like to sled over the beachy grasses and build snowmen near the surf." My heart warmed with instant memories and nostalgia. "Now it's happening. And she's not here to see it," I added in a whisper.

This wasn't just my first Christmas back in Charm, it was my first Christmas without the woman who'd raised me. "She always called," I said, fighting the instant sting of emotion against the backs of my eyes. "Even when I was too busy to make the time for her, she called."

Aunt Clara's unusually cranky expression turned curious, then softened into something resembling wonder. "Maybe she's calling you now."

I followed her gaze through the window at her side, and a rush of love swept over me. Fat white flakes whirled and cartwheeled through the air.

"It would be just like her," Clara croaked softly, "to send you one last Christmas gift if she could."

My heart swelled and my eyes blurred. "Thank you for saying that."

Aunt Clara wiped her eyes with the pads of her thumbs. "If you're going out there, I suppose you'd better get to it. It's only going to get worse."

"Right." I ran the cuff of my sleeve under my nose, then turned for the café. "I've got the cookies packed up and ready to go. I left them with the gnomes on the counter."

"Excellent. Skip stopping at the kiln if the roads are bad. There's no rush to get the gnomes back since they aren't going to be Christmas gifts anymore," Aunt Clara said. She fished an envelope from her handbag and passed it to me. "I made this for your collection. A holiday card from our shop to yours."

I opened the cheery yellow-and-white card with a smile. "Thank you!" A small cartoonish honey bee had been fixed to the cardstock by a short accordion-folded strip that made him bounce. He had a small red heart between his thin black arms. She'd drawn a sketch of Blessed Bee on one side of the card and Sun, Sand, and Tea on the other. Both shops were decorated for the holidays and dusted in silver glitter snow. A dotted black line curled between them, as if the bee might've flown the loopy path, and *May your days* bee *merry and bright* was scripted above the scene in Aunt Clara's careful hand.

I cradled the card to my chest and gave her another hug. "It's perfect. I love it."

Aunt Clara patted my cheek, then backed away with a smile. She snagged a roll of tape from my office supplies and added her card to the collection circling my nearest café window.

I poured her a large glass of blackberry iced tea while she worked. "You're the best. I don't tell you often enough."

"Maybe," she said, returning the tape and then

accepting the tea, "but you show Fran and me every day, and that's even better." Aunt Clara savored the tea, her gaze drifting through the festive café around us. "Have you decided on a menu for the progressive dinner?"

"I have. Thanks to you." She'd inspired me with her speech last night, and I'd stayed up looking through old family cookbooks for the perfect recipes. "I stopped worrying about showing off and focused on what the holidays meant to me. Then I thought about how I could share that with everyone else."

Aunt Clara beamed. "And?"

I moved closer, biting my bottom lip to quell the thrill I got at the thought of it. "I'm making great-grandma's chicken and waffles with warm maple syrup, served appetizer-style, plus mini baked macaroni and cheese, the shrimp and grits Aunt Fran loves, and maybe some crab and corn chowder cups. Nothing fancy, just good, old-fashioned southern comforts. I'm still working on the cocktails, but I'm leaning toward a few of my favorite teas instead. A hot selection. Two cold, and maybe one spiked."

Aunt Clara set a palm on her middle. "If you need someone to check your work before the event, you'll let me know?"

"Absolutely." I laughed. "Hopefully everyone who stops by will enjoy the recipes as much as I do. I emailed my menu to the *Town Charmer* this morning."

She winked. "Good girl."

I threaded my arms into my favorite down coat

and tied the wide belt in a knot. "I guess I'd better get moving. If there's time, I'd like to stop at the Giving Tree while I'm out. Do you want me to grab a name for you?"

"I've already stopped. I've got two names at home, but thank you for the offer." She paused, her already empty glass positioned beneath the blackberry tea dispenser for a refill. "I guess I should've asked you before I went. I could've saved you a trip."

"It's no trouble," I assured her. "I like going, and it's a tradition, right?"

"It is." She smiled. "Meanwhile, I'll hold down the fort."

I doubted anyone would venture as far out as my place until the snow stopped, but if someone did, I was glad they would find the café open. "I appreciate it," I said, planting a kiss on her cheek. "I won't be long."

"No rush. Be safe," she called after me.

I headed for Blue with a box of gnomes in my arms and a giant delivery bag stuffed with cookie boxes in the opposite grip. It was doubtful that Mary Grace would let me through her front door, let alone entertain my questions, with or without a cookie bribe, but I had to try. I needed to know what she knew about Mayor Dunfree's death, and I was positive she knew something. Anyone who'd planned to be the mayor's running partner in the upcoming election had to know if he had any enemies or current feuds going. Additionally, I wanted to see her face when she answered in case she lied. As far as I was concerned, Mary Grace was still a suspect.

Once she inevitably tossed me out, I planned to meet with the stand-in mayor, previously known as Chairman Vanders. I'd called his office at eight sharp to make an appointment. His receptionist had initially thought his schedule was full, but after discovering there was a dozen assorted cookies from the Swan family cookbooks at stake, she assured me she'd been mistaken.

Blue and I motored slowly through town. Dozens of brave Charmers moseyed in and out of shops along Main Street and Vine. They were bundled to their noses against the cold and snow, eyes down as they moved in case of a slip, I supposed. Cars and trucks had replaced golf carts, and most of the drivers looked half-terrified by the accumulating slush on the roads. A pickup slid past a stop sign by half a foot, and a line of pedestrians scattered for their lives.

I stopped at the traffic light on Middletown Road and glanced at the bag on the seat beside me. I'd brought enough cookies to tempt Mary Grace, schmooze Chairman Vanders, bribe his secretary, and possibly ply Mrs. Dunfree and her fence-erecting neighbor if the opportunity arose. I'd call the outing a success if even one of those people were willing to talk to me about Mayor Dunfree.

I pulled into Mary Grace's driveway several minutes later, preferring to get the worst out of the way. The lights of a Christmas tree were visible through her drawn curtains, and two lopsided snowmen graced the lawn, but no one had shoveled the walkway or steps.

I grabbed a box of cookies and made my way carefully onto the porch. I forced a tight smile and pushed the doorbell. The commotion that followed was enough to drown out a three-ring circus. Children yelled. Dogs barked. Something crashed.

"Quiet!" Mary Grace screamed. She appeared at the front window a moment later, peeling the curtain back carefully, then frowning when she saw me.

The door sucked open, and I leaned back, putting distance between myself and the frightening version of Mary Grace that answered.

"What do you want?" she asked, makeup-less eyes squinting, unkempt hair pointing in every direction. Two pocket-sized Chihuahuas and a trio of kids mashed into the space around her feet and legs.

For a moment, I had no idea what I wanted. The shock of seeing Miss Perfect in a house coat and ratty slippers, surrounded by a gang of wailing dogs and children struck me silent. I'd known she was a mother, but I had assumed she was raising a gaggle of militants trained to obey her every command. Had I known she owned dogs, I would've imagined a pair of Dobermans to reflect her personality. "Cookies?" I finally offered, pushing the bakery box in her direction.

The kids nearly lost their minds jumping for it.

One of the dogs tried to bite me, but he got one of the scrambling kids instead, and the child screamed.

Mary Grace swept the injured one onto her hip and took the cookies. "You've got five minutes."

I followed her through a house covered in toys and plastic sippy cups to the equally messy kitchen. She deposited the box onto her table, and the ensemble of small jumping bodies surrounded it. "Settle down or you won't get any," she ordered.

The child on her hip shimmied onto a chair someone hadn't pushed in when they last left the table. His wiggling bottom lip was pushed out and tears rolled down his cheeks, but his attention was fixed on the box instead of the small red mark on his calf.

Mary Grace untied the crimson ribbon and raised the box's lid. "I'm going into my office," she said sharply. "You each get two cookies only and there had better not be any fighting or you won't play in the snow after lunch."

She shooed the Chihuahuas into a kennel large enough to hold all three kids, and I wondered if she'd ever been tempted to use it on them. "Let Bacon and Elephant out when you finish your cookies. Do not share with them."

She turned a pointed look on me, then marched down a short hallway to an office that looked as if someone had turned it upside down a few times and motioned me inside. "Five minutes," she repeated, securing the door behind us.

I decided to skip the small talk and get out of there in four. "Why did you agree to run with Dunfree as deputy mayor? A few months ago you wanted to be mayor, then something happened, and you agreed to run with him instead of against him. I want to know what changed."

Mary Grace rubbed her forehead. "He was sick."

The rumor was true, but what did it mean? "Who knew?"

She leaned her backside against a cluttered desk. "Very few people. He wanted to keep it that way. It's the reason he changed his mind about stepping down and retiring. He said he didn't have long to live and he didn't want to die a forgotten old has-been. He wanted a big funeral and gravestone where he would be memorialized as Charm's mayor."

I cringed. I wasn't sure if planning the inscription for your own tombstone was good or bad or sad or what, but I was thankful no one I loved had to think about that right now. "I had no idea," I said.

She shrugged. "I agreed to run with him when he told me about his failing health. It seemed like the nice thing to do, and I'd gain priceless hands-on experience before stepping seamlessly into his place."

That sounded more like the woman I knew. She didn't care if it was the nice thing to do. She'd agreed because there was plenty in it for her. "Who would want him dead?" I asked. Not her, I supposed, at least not yet. Not until she was secured as the deputy and poised to take over upon his absence.

"Oh, I don't know," she said, raising her eyebrows in challenge. "Your great-aunt Fran?"

"Be serious," I said. "I don't have any time to waste explaining the obvious to you."

"What's obvious," Mary Grace said, pushing off of her desk and crossing her arms, "is that your aunt was his competition, not me."

I sighed, forced to explain things after all. "Your goal was to take his place one day, just like Aunt Fran's. That doesn't make her a killer. I want to know who might've been angry enough to lash out at him."

"Maybe no one," she said, lips curling into a taunting grin. "Maybe you should take a closer look at your weirdo family."

I balked. Mary Grace knew how much I hated jokes about my family's unusual beliefs and the rumors that occasionally sprouted from them. She'd known when we were children, and she'd used that knowledge to ruin my elementary school life. Twenty years later, she was resorting to the same ammunition, and I refused to let her see how much it still bothered me.

"He'd just come from your creepy haunted house," she sneered. "Maybe one of your family curses killed him."

My chest puffed with rage, and I bit the insides of my cheeks until I thought I might taste blood.

"Mommy!" a set of angry voices called through the door. The voices screamed heated accusations of cookie theft, and the third child began to cry.

Mary Grace slid her eyes shut a moment, then pinched the bridge of her nose, all pretense of superiority gone. The dogs began to howl in the background, and I smiled.

I took a minute to center myself and absorb the fact that the mean little girl who'd once bullied me was now living with three small versions of herself. "Sounds like my time's up," I said brightly, letting myself out of the office and heading back to the front door the way I'd come.

Mary Grace followed on my heels. "So, you admit your family is cursed," she called after me, her voice barely registering above the cacophony of small cries, dogs' howls and general complaints.

"Merry Christmas," I told the child in diapers seated on the kitchen table, covered in icing and polishing off the last of the cookies.

So much for only having two apiece, I thought, bouncing happily down the walk to Blue. Hopefully, her children wouldn't be sick from eating all those sweets in under five minutes.

But if they did get sick, a little part of me hoped it would be on their mother.

CHAPTER THIRTEEN

The Giving Tree was as beautiful as ever. The stately evergreen towered over all the other trees at the nature center. It had likely been growing there since my ancestors arrived to settle the town, and if it wasn't for Charm's lighthouses, the tree might've been the tallest thing on our island. Each year, volunteers draped the pine in white lights and topped her with a star that had the word *HOPE* written across it. The message was powerful in a number of ways. Literally, folks who hung their names on the tree hoped to have a need fulfilled, graciously and without judgment. Figuratively, those four letters, *HOPE*, challenged the members of our community to be better than we were, kinder, more compassionate, and unified. With an election coming next fall and the murder looming over us now, I hoped the tree would remind Charmers that regardless of politics, grief, or strife, Charm was and always would be family first.

I took my time approaching the tree, wanting to

admire its beauty and sorry I hadn't come sooner. The small white cards attached to the branches looked a lot like snow. The sheer volume was both heartbreaking and remarkable. It was a massive visual reminder that everyone needed something, and it was an encouragement to know my neighbors trusted one another to help.

The nature center kept sponsored supplies in a receptacle beside the tree: stacks of carefully cut cardstock squares from the stationery store, small plastic sleeves and precut string from Crafty Corner, and a mound of little pencils from the miniature golf course. It was everything we needed to attach a request to the tree.

I surveyed the branches. Some folks used the opportunity to ask for warm thoughts or a prayer over something that couldn't be fixed with a purchase. Others wanted something for a friend or neighbor who'd been too timid to ask, but most of the cards asked for tangible things the author needed to fill immediate personal needs. Meals. Warm coats for their kids or gas money for a spouse traveling to the mainland for work. Winters were tough in fishing and tourist communities like ours, and everyone understood the fear of running out of supplies or savings before spring. I wanted all the people whose names hung from the tree to get a happy holiday ending, just like the characters in the novels from Amelia's book club. But there were so many names, and Christmas was almost here.

How could I select one need over the others?

How could I leave so many behind?

I closed my eyes and focused on the reason for the tree, *the reason for the season*, as so many liked to say, and I lifted my hands to the branches. I closed each mitten around a card before reopening my eyes. I rubbed my thumbs across the familiar names as a lump of emotion wedged in my throat. There were so many more. So many unchosen. And only a week until Christmas.

I closed my eyes again, remembering a lesson Grandma had taught me. *When you feel lost or like giving up, it's time to stop and give thanks.* This time I sent thoughts of gratitude into the ether. I was thankful my grandma had brought me to this tree every Christmas. I was thankful she'd used the experiences to teach me that everyone could make a difference to someone. That even the smallest of children had power. We could all give joy. Grandma took me to read to folks whose sight had faded. She made meals with me for local shut-ins and stayed with me while we visited them. She'd invited children to play at our house when their parents both had to work, and she'd helped me collect mail or pull weeds for neighbors who were sick or in the hospital. I was thankful for a town that cared for its own, and I was elated that I had the means to help.

Hot tears of gratitude rolled over my cheeks as I opened my eyes. I gathered supplies from the receptacle at my side, and I wrote my name on the outside in large block letters. Inside, I made a request of my own.

I left the tree with my eyes turned skyward, my smile bright, and a fantastic plan brewing.

❧

The sun had burned its way through the clouds by the time I reached the town hall, making the world brighter and the air warmer. I squinted against the blinding gleam of sunlight on snow as I slid Blue into an excellent parking space.

The mammoth mud-soaked Jeep Wrangler to my right cast a comfortable shadow over Blue, allowing my eyes a moment to readjust. I ogled the vehicle before I got out. It wasn't uncommon to see off-roading vehicles outside of town, near the maritime forest and unsettled portions of the island where hikers escaped for solitude. Parked outside the town hall, however, snow or no snow, the Jeep seemed like overkill. I grabbed my bag of cookies and hurried onto the sidewalk, heavily sprinkled with sand to help with the ice and reduce slipping. I gave the Jeep another look as I passed before the massive, filthy grille. Seven letters on the personalized license plate spelled *VANDERS.*

I let myself into the front office at the town hall, triggering the manufactured *ding-dong* of an electronic bell. A blast of hot air tossed my hair into my eyes, and I danced away from the assault with a shocked squeak.

I peered up at a blower positioned above the door and smiled, laughing silently at myself for being startled.

"May I help you?" a woman's voice asked.

I swept hair off my face and turned to locate the speaker.

A narrow woman in a long-sleeved blouse and a pleated, ankle-length wool skirt stood beside the reception desk, a load of files in her arms. Her silver hair had been twisted into a painful-looking bun at the top of her head and serious soda-bottle glasses emphasized her wide green eyes.

"Hello," I said, still working to smooth my hair as I approached.

The woman's mouth fell open. The folders slid and shifted in her grip.

I slowed my pace, unsure what had caused the strange reaction. The room was empty aside from us, and I didn't see any cause for alarm. The nameplate on her desk identified her as Maven Winkles. "Ms. Winkles," I began again, letting my local drawl drip over the words, hoping to put her at ease. "I'm Everly Swan," I continued. "I believe we spoke this morning." I set a logoed bakery box on her desk in reminder.

"Of course." She dragged her gaze from me to the box. "Everly Swan," she said, carefully emphasizing my first name.

"That's me." I worked up a confident smile. "I can't thank you enough for your generosity. I realize my request to see Chairman Vanders was very last minute, and I truly appreciate the favor."

"You look so much like your mother," she said, ignoring my thanks. She stared openly now. "For a moment I thought..." She set the stack of files on her desk and offered me her hand. "I don't believe we've ever met, officially. Not since you were in diapers anyway. Please, call me Maven."

I chewed my bottom lip, never sure what to say when anyone told me they knew my mother. It meant she knew how my mother had died as well, of a broken heart, as my grandma and great-aunts liked to say, or maybe as part of the ridiculous Swan curse, like Mary Grace would claim. Either way, I squirmed, partly worried about what this woman thought of my family and partly elated to hear that I looked like the woman I loved so much but couldn't remember.

"I'm sorry. I'm being rude," Maven said, finally taking a seat at the desk between us. "I'm glad to help," she said. "Did you know your mother was an art student of mine? Four years in high school. I've been retired nearly twenty now, but she will always hold a special place in my heart. Talent like hers doesn't come along very often."

"My mother was an artist?" I asked, instantly rapt and a little ashamed that this stranger knew more about her than I did. "Was she good?" Grandma and my aunts had mentioned how much my mother loved to draw, but they'd never elaborated. I liked to draw, but I wasn't an artist. *Artist* made her seem professional. Incredible. More real and full of potential. My heart sank a bit at that.

"Oh, yes," Maven said. "I still have one of her pieces at home. It hangs in my sunroom. I hear you're quite an artist as well. You just use a different medium."

I tried to smile, but my mouth only wiggled, not quite finding the right position. "I bake. It's not the same thing, but thank you."

Maven untied the bow on my cookie box and opened the lid. She tilted the box until the contents were visible to me. A rainbow of sugar sprinkles shimmered under the fluorescent lights. The soft scents of vanilla and cinnamon wafted up to greet me from cutouts and gingerbreads, snowballs and shortcakes. "This is art," she said. "Trust me. I know."

I inclined my head slightly in agreement. I supposed the finished products were quite beautiful, and they were absolutely delicious. I smiled. "Thank you."

A door opened nearby and two men exited in our direction. I recognized one as a local reporter, his identification lanyard bouncing against the curve of his protruding belly. "Merry Christmas," he called on his way out.

Maven and I responded in kind.

The remaining man was new to me, overdressed in a full suit and tie, shiny black shoes, and a smug grin. "Well, hello there," he said, heading quickly in my direction.

"Chairman Vanders," Maven said, "this is Everly Swan. She owns the iced tea shop on the beach."

He nodded in recognition. "Of course. You caused quite a stir with that one. The council hated the notion of adding a business to a home, but you found the loophole." He rocked back on his feet with a broad smile.

I tried not to scowl. Until three days ago, he had been on that council, and the loophole he mentioned was actually straight fact. My home had been registered as a commercial property since the Great Depression when it changed hands many times, trying to stay afloat. Before my iced tea shop, the property had been a number of things from a boardinghouse to a prep school. I'd done nothing besides point that out. He was right, though. The town council hadn't liked it.

"What can I do for you today, Miss Swan?" he asked, rubbing his big hands together and slinking to my side.

I stepped back to look up at him and smiled, realizing his commanding presence was a perfect match for his attention-grabbing Jeep. "Do you have a minute to talk?" I asked sweetly, hoping his ego might work in my favor. Suspicious people always saw me coming at times like these, but I had a feeling Chairman Vanders was the kind of man who'd assume I came to admire him.

He snaked a long arm in my direction and set a palm against the small of my back. The heat from his hand seeped through my coat as he steered me toward his office.

I cast a backward glance at Maven, who frowned as she selected a cookie.

Chairman Vanders open the door still marked *Mayor Dunfree*. Piles of clutter lined the wall outside the door. Boxes and books were stacked waist high on, under, and all around a traditional metal desk with a faux-wood top. Inside, the office was stunning, hyper-organized and possibly decorated by a professional. The only thing that seemed out of place was an eight-foot painting of Charm, complete with street signs and local landmarks.

Vanders closed the door softly behind us.

I considered cracking it open so I could call for help if I'd accidentally scheduled a private meeting with a killer, but I decided to play it cool. Vanders couldn't kill me in his office. Maven had seen him walk me in.

He directed me to a short leather chair opposite a massive mahogany desk and motioned for me to sit. "Water?"

Before I could answer, he poured a glass from the fancy fruit infusion pitcher on a little silver cart near the window.

"Thank you," I said accepting the glass gingerly.

Vanders unbuttoned his suit jacket, then took a seat in the impressive leather executive chair on the other side of his desk. "What brings you in to see me this morning, Everly?"

"I just wanted to welcome you to your new position and bring you some cookies," I said, producing another box from my bag and setting it on the desk between us. "I only make these at Christmas, so I wanted to be sure you got some before they were gone."

He smiled wolfishly in response. "You know that old saying about the way to a man's heart being through his stomach is true, and I can't wait to dig in."

I leaned back in my seat, slightly concerned with the way his voice had grown deeper as he spoke. "Great!" I cleared my throat. "Your office is so lovely," I said, casting my gaze around the room. The furnishings were far too modern and minimalist to have been Mayor Dunfree's. When I'd been to the office before, making arrangements for the tea shop at my home, the room had been strikingly opposite, stuffed with enough dusty books and memorabilia to rival my great-aunts' attic. Now, things were streamlined. Black leather on brushed metals and glass-topped tables. I turned to stare at the closed door. "What's all that stuff piled outside your office?"

He grimaced. "Donations. I've arranged a pickup as soon as the charity can get out here."

"Cleaning house?" I guessed.

"You could say that. None of it is mine. Those things belonged to my predecessor. Let's talk more about the gifts you're offering," he said, pinching one end of the crimson ribbon from my bakery box between his thumb and first finger. He flashed the wolfish grin again and began to pull painfully slowly on the soft satin material.

I ran a mental calculation. Mayor Dunfree had only been dead for three days, which meant Vanders couldn't have been in the office more than two, assuming he'd come right in the morning after Dunfree's death. Icky, pretentious, and slightly morbid, *but possible*, I thought, watching in horror as he continued the weird cookie box striptease. Vanders had wasted no time moving into Dunfree's office or shoving the former mayor's things out of his way. Not exactly signs of mourning for someone who'd served on the council for Mayor Dunfree several years.

"It must be different without him around," I said, trying to sound solemn instead of accusatory.

The bow finally gave way under Chairman Vanders's slow pull, and his grin widened. "The unwrapping has always been my favorite part," he said, curling the satin around his finger and coaxing it free from beneath the box.

Alarm must've shown on my features because Vanders huffed a sigh and flipped open the box with zero ado. "Everything's fine without him. Like I told the reporter, Charm is a tight ship. Anyone with a little backbone can step in and hold down the fort."

"Really?" I asked, taken slightly aback. "He'd been mayor for so long, I'd assumed filling his shoes would be a challenge."

Chairman Vanders' eyes went cold. "It's not a challenge," he corrected, bristling, as if the mere suggestion had offended his manhood. "I've only been here two days, and I've already got this job locked down. In fact, I like it here so much I plan to run for the position permanently next fall. Meanwhile, I'll be here upholding the rules, regulations, and bylaws that this town is based on with zero tolerance for dissent. That's what keeps Charm chugging along like it always has, after all. People like to complain and say otherwise from time to time, but they know the truth, and I'll make certain folks keep toeing the line."

"Maybe that can be your campaign slogan," I said smartly.

I snapped my mouth shut when I realized I'd said the words aloud.

The chairman frowned. "What?"

"It's a great platform to run on," I said brightly. "Personally, I love it, and I think most people like Charm just the way it is." I pushed a smile back in place.

"Yeah." He relaxed his shoulders a bit and eyed me skeptically.

"I can hardly believe we've never met before," I said, selecting a powdered wedding cookie from inside the open box. "I must've missed you at my Christmas party the other night. Most of the town was there."

He narrowed his eyes. "I was camping with friends."

"In the snow?" I asked incredulously, a cookie poised before my lips.

"Polar Bear Club," he said. "We swim, then we camp."

I tried to imagine Chairman Vanders in board shorts, racing through the snow and into the ocean with a group of equally crazy friends and failed. "I didn't realize we had a Polar Bear Club in Charm." I smiled. "What time would you say you made it home?"

He crossed his arms. "You came here to see if I killed Dunfree."

"What?" I feigned indignation, eyes wide, mouth agape. "I was thinking of joining the Polar Bear Club."

"Cut the act," he said. "I'd hoped I was wrong when I found you out front, looking cute in your little coat and come-hither smile, but I wasn't. You aren't here to congratulate me on my new position or pedal your goods to the new man in power."

"Gross," I said, abhorring both his accusations equally. He wanted to be congratulated for a position he'd gained through another man's murder? And he thought that news of that new position was enough to bring me running?

"If you really want to get someone arrested for Dunfree's death," he said, "talk to your great-aunt Fran. She hated him, argued with him, and opposed everything he stood for. She did all those things openly and regularly at council meetings. She even started that Charmers for Change group to make it seem like she had a backing, but she never fooled me. I saw through her act too. The only Charmer for Change was her." His cell phone lit on the desk beside his arm, and he yanked it up before I could read the screen. "Excuse me."

He rose from his chair and strode past me to the door. "I'm just finishing with a guest," he told the caller, then stared pointedly at me until I stood.

I opened my mouth to proclaim Aunt Fran's

innocence but thought better of it. Arguing with Mary Grace hadn't changed her opinion, and it would take more than my word to set Chairman Vanders straight. Somehow I doubted he ever admitted to being wrong on any topic.

I marched out, chin high, and stopped when the door closed behind me. I ducked out of Vanders's view through the little window on his office door and took a minute to pick through the piles of Mayor Dunfree's things before I left.

I thumbed stacks of old festival posters and cutout newspaper articles on local events. Rolled fishing maps were propped in the corner beside giant wooden lures and bobbers meant to be hung on the walls as art. Encyclopedias. Old storefront signs from businesses long gone. Nothing too personal, but the items were all clearly special to Dunfree or he wouldn't have kept them all these years. I snapped a few pictures for Grady, then texted him the suggestion of letting Mrs. Dunfree know about the office castoffs before the charity arrived to pick them up.

Grady responded to my text before I could get the phone back into my pocket.

What are you doing in Dunfree's office?

I wrinkled my nose at the message. I should have anticipated the response, but Vanders had thrown me off my game.

I peeped through the window on Vanders's door to see if he was looking, or if I'd have to duck-walk past. Vanders wasn't in there. I moved closer and gave the room a thorough exam from my side of the glass. No one.

Apparently the coast was clear.

I waved to Maven on my way out. "Thanks again," I said, approaching her desk with a smile.

"I hope he behaved himself," she said. "I hate to send anyone in there alone with him. He's such a scoundrel."

"I'm tougher than I look," I assured her, "but I think he might be a magician. I looked back into the office a few minutes after he sent me out, and he was gone."

"He does that," she said. "There's a second door. Mayor Dunfree covered it with the painting of Charm, but it leads to a hallway with a private access bathroom and an exit."

Interesting.

I thanked her again and headed for the door before responding to Grady's text.

I'm not there, I replied. I was on the sidewalk.

Vanders's Jeep was still at the curb, so he hadn't made a great escape.

Several hurried steps later, the toe of my boot caught on something hard in the snow and tossed it down the sidewalk ahead of me.

I froze and stared, unbelieving, as a busted gnome's head rolled awkwardly off the curb and into a slush puddle.

I pulled my gaze across the sidewalk to find other gnomes waiting for me, all arranged in the snow outside my ride. I recognized them from the box I'd left on Blue's backseat. These figures weren't broken like the others, but they'd each been vandalized with heavy black marker strokes in the shape of an exaggerated *V* between their eyes. Below the angry eyebrows, someone had drawn jagged, zigzag lines over their former rosebud mouths. All the figures had been splashed with red paint.

~

Grady arrived three minutes later. He'd already been on his way after my text, making sure I'd left as promised and that I hadn't caused a stir while I'd visited.

It was as if he didn't trust me at all.

"Talk me through this again," he said, dropping the last of the angry gnomes into an evidence bag.

I repeated my lame story about cookie deliveries in the name of holiday cheer and tried not to choke on the lie.

He stuffed the final evidence bag into his duffel with a sigh. "It's getting weird in the evidence locker at the station. All those gnome parts on shelves, and now these." The corners of his mouth pulled down. "It's enough to give a guy nightmares."

"Tell me about it," I agreed. "Will you have these checked for prints?" I asked. "Aunt Clara and I painted them last night, so you should find both of our prints on them."

He nodded. "I'll have them sent to the lab after I return to the station."

I crossed my arms over my middle, stomach churning with the overdose of adrenaline my body had produced at first sight of the evil gnome army. "Did you let the Dunfrees know about the mayor's keepsakes?" I asked, hoping for a change of subject and dying to blurt out the real reason I was there. *To snoop.* Exactly the thing Grady had asked me not to do, and look at what had happened.

"I'll share the news when I see Mrs. Dunfree this afternoon." He gripped the back of his neck in one hand and dropped his chin to his chest.

"You okay?" I asked, inching closer. Adrenaline pumped through my veins like a gallon of black coffee. Seeing Grady, the most calm and steadfast man I knew, looking so miserable twisted and pulled at my insides. "Did something happen?"

Grady raised his head and locked his gaze to mine, the tight expression in his jaw slowly lost its edge. "What were you really doing here?"

I wet my lips, mortified by my initial fib. It was time to come clean. "I was delivering cookies." That part was true. "But I only brought them so I could find out what Chairman Vanders thought of Mayor Dunfree. When I learned Vanders was handed the position in Dunfree's absence, I couldn't help wondering if Vanders might have opted to skip the campaigning and just take what he wanted."

"And?" Grady asked.

"Inconclusive," I said. "I don't particularly like him as a person. He's a womanizer and probably a liar, but

I can't say for sure about him being a murderer." I shook my head at the memory of our chat. "He said he missed my Christmas party because he was camping with his Polar Bear Club. I'm not convinced Charm has one of those."

Grady raised his eyes to the building behind me, then leveled me with his gaze once more. "Did he say or do something to you?" he asked, his voice low and tight.

I frowned. "Yeah, he said he was camping with his Polar Bear Club."

Grady groaned. "Not what I meant, Swan."

I took a minute to retrace my words. "Oh. No. He did a weird thing with the ribbon from my cookie box, but other than that, he was just vaguely chauvinistic."

Grady's brows tented. "You've got to stop doing this or I'm going to get an ulcer."

"Hey," I caught his gloved hand in mine. "I wasn't hurt, and I wasn't trying to cause trouble. I had no idea I'd upset the gnome bandit by coming here." I waved a hand toward the black duffel full of angry figurines. "I'd just wanted to see if Vanders and Dunfree had gotten along, and ask Vanders who he thought might have had motivation to hurt his predecessor."

Grady rocked his head to one side, allowing me to keep hold of his hand. "What'd he say?"

My face puckered on instinct. "He said Fran probably did it."

Grady rubbed a hand against his mouth to cover a smile. "Care to tell me more about why you believe he's a womanizer and what exactly he did with that cookie box?"

I laughed. "Maybe, some time."

"How's now?" he asked, tugging playfully on my hand. "May I buy you a hot chocolate, Everly?"

CHAPTER FOURTEEN

The local ice cream shop was quiet when Grady and I arrived. It was barely past breakfast and too early for shoppers in search of lunch. Sandy's Seaside Sweet Shack had become a staple in the community, but the busiest time of day was after dinner in any season. At barely ten in the morning, we had the place to ourselves.

Grady had insisted I grab a seat while he order and pay for the hot chocolates, so I'd selected a tall round table with long silver legs and two matching chairs. The interior decor was quirky, vintage beach-chic. Fifty percent sock hop, fifty percent seaside, and one hundred percent fun. The furniture was straight out of a diner in *Grease*, but the napkins on the tables were stored in small, brightly colored sand pails instead of the classic metal boxes. Long boards and boat oars hung on the walls beside framed vinyl records. Peppy holiday music rocked through cleverly hidden speakers and sand clung to the large black-and-white tile flooring most months of the year, thanks to the close beach proximity.

Grady approached the table with two steaming mugs and a smile. "Sorry that took forever. The cashier asked about Denver. She's missed seeing him, and he's normally a regular in here."

"Too cold for ice cream?" I guessed, unsure what could keep Denver away from his favorite shop.

He passed me a mug without answering and took the seat across from me.

"You really didn't have to pay," I said. "Thank you, though, and cheers." I lifted my mug and waited for him to tap his drink to mine.

"Cheers," he agreed. "I think I'm behind on owing you drinks. I don't think you've let me pay for anything at your café. Ever."

I grinned. "I just like to feed people," I said. "It makes me happy. Especially when I can tell they're enjoying every bite. I wouldn't charge anyone if I didn't have a mortgage to pay."

"I don't doubt it," he said.

His warm smile set off a swarm of butterflies in my core, and I set a hand on my middle to stop them. My attraction to Grady had been difficult enough to deal with when we'd first met and I didn't know him. Now that I could see beyond the unreasonably handsome face and general hubba-hubba exterior, my reactions had gotten significantly worse. "What's Denver been up to?" I asked, circling back to the reason my favorite Charmer child hadn't been out for ice cream in a while and hoping to redirect my thoughts from Grady's stunning smile. Plus, Denver was always a source of interest for me. He was a huge personality in a pint-sized package, complete with his daddy's clear gray eyes and adorable dimple. "Was he okay when you got home last night?"

Grady twisted his mug on the table between his palms. "He was fine. He's a tough little guy. Denise had him baking when I left this morning." He lifted his gaze to mine. An odd expression was on his unreadable face. "His grades were down at school, and Denise thought he might be losing interest. So she did some troubleshooting and found a way to engage him. They practice reading and math skills in the kitchen. When he reads the recipes without help and completes the measurements as required, she lets him take the finished products to school and share with his class. Needless to say, his grades are soaring and so is his popularity among Charm children." Pride emanated from his words and seemed to reach across the table to fill my chest as well. "They made your seven-layer bars from the video you posted."

"What?" I set my mug down with an awkward clatter. Heat rushed over my face. *Denise and Denver watched my cookie-making video.* "Did you watch it?" I asked cautiously, feeling like a complete moron for posting it to begin with. I wasn't a cute, co-ed culinary school student anymore. I was...well, different.

I let the question rattle around in my mind. So much had changed in a single year, and most of me was still reeling from the force of it all. I'd accepted Wyatt's rejection, then he'd moved home and pledged to make up for having hurt me. I'd sworn off love, then Grady had arrived and confused me. Add in the number of times I'd been stalked, attacked, or nearly killed this year, and I had to wonder: Was I still the kind of woman who made how-to-bake videos? I wasn't sure, but I wanted to be, and I hoped that was enough.

Grady watched me silently with that look that always made me wonder if he could somehow read my mind. "I was the one who told Denise about the video," he said. "It was good. Are you planning to do more?"

I blinked. Grady had already told me that he subscribed to my website's updates. It shouldn't have surprised me that he'd watched the video, but it did. And he thought it was good. I struggled not to smile as the feeling of pride returned. "I've always wanted to create a video library," I said, pulling my attention away from his smart gray eyes so I could think more clearly. "As a teen I'd wanted to be one of those celebrity chefs who hates everything she tastes until she suddenly finds the most amazing dessert under heaven and makes that baker a star." I waved a dismissive hand and laughed. "All that changed after I started culinary school and had the opportunity to be the one called out for her terrible work. I knew then, what I'd probably always known. I never want to be the kind of person who makes someone else feel bad."

Grady's lips tipped into a barely there smile.

I unbuttoned my coat, suddenly overheated by the hot chocolate. "How's it going with Senator Denver?" I asked, directing the focus off me before I rambled on about some other personal and irrelevant thing.

The mention of his mother-in-law did the trick. "She's stifling," he said. "She's unimpressed with Denver's rearing for starters." He made finger quotes around the word *rearing*. "And she hates the idea of him living on an island. There aren't enough choices. No private schools. No Trader Joe's."

"We don't need a Whole Foods Market because everyone gardens," I said.

He looked at me as if I'd sprouted a new head. "Can you imagine Olivia Denver in a sun hat and filthy gloves?"

"No," I admitted.

"Neither can she." He laughed. "She's insistent that it's my fault she's forced to stay here, but I didn't invite her."

"She's unhappy, but she plans to stay and run for mayor?" I asked, puzzled.

"Politics is in her blood," he said, "and she's an equal opportunity complainer."

I laughed.

Grady stiffened. His expression went flat. "Sorry. I didn't mean to rant. A simple, 'she's fine' would've been the sane answer."

"I wasn't looking for sane," I said as kindly as I could, knowing he must feel exposed right now, exactly the way I had after going on about being a celebrity chef. "I was looking for honest." I offered him a warm smile.

Grady released a labored breath. "I've got to tell you something."

The timbre of his voice stood the fine hairs along my neck and arms at attention. I couldn't find the words to ask what it was, so I sat frozen in wait.

He leaned forward over the table between us. "Olivia wants me to move back to Virginia and reopen her husband's case."

I felt my eyes widen in shock. *Her husband's case.* What did that mean? Could he still be alive? Did she know he was alive? Is that why she hadn't had a funeral for him? If so, where was he? "What?"

"I said I wouldn't move. Denver and I like it here, and I won't uproot him again. And I said no to rejoining the Marshals. I didn't like who I was then. Denver deserves better than some strung-out, workaholic father more focused on an elusive fugitive than the son right in front of him. I won't ruin this life for us. Not even for Mr. Denver."

My chest warmed, and I realized some part of me had always assumed Grady would leave one day. He'd told me once that he'd come to Charm to heal, and it was obvious he and Denver were doing great. But he wasn't leaving. He didn't want to. "You're staying?" I asked, needing to hear him say the words again.

"I'm staying." Grady slid his hand across to table in my direction, then stopped, seeming to think better of it. He curled his fingers, then dropped the fist onto his lap.

The almost touch left my heart in a sputter and my mind on something else his mother-in-law had said. "When your mother-in-law was in for tea the other night, she mentioned something that's stuck with me."

He narrowed his eyes. "Go on."

"About Denise," I began timidly, realizing that I had no right to ask about his personal relationships no matter how badly I wanted to. "She said Denise was handpicked for you."

Grady gave a stiff nod. "That's right. Olivia assured me that Denise was the best. I wasn't in any kind of shape to make decisions after Amy died, and I was too mired in grief to care. I wasn't the father I should have been. I've told you that, but Olivia never judged. She did a good job assigning Denise."

I lifted a finger. "See, that's the thing. You and Senator Denver both say Denise is on assignment. It's a weird way to talk about an au pair." I shifted in my seat, not wanting to continue, but I'd said too much to stop now. He'd know I had more to ask, and the whole thing would become more awkward. "Also, the senator said Denise was chosen for you *both*."

He nodded, eyebrows knitted. "She was assigned to care for us," he said. "She does everything for the both of us."

Heat flamed in my cheeks. I bit into the thick of my lower lip and cringed. "Does she?"

Grady squinted. Slowly, his expression morphed

into a mask of shock and understanding. "No." He leaned low over the table, voice firm. "No. No. Not like that."

"Okay," I said with a shrug that was intended to look casual but felt more like rusty gears working up and down. "I'm just repeating what was said to me."

Grady was still for a long beat, then his jaw flung open and his eyes went slightly unfocused. He laughed, deep and genuine. When he looked at me again, his face was as red as mine felt. "There were times early on," he began, then stopped. "She acted strangely when I came in from a run or out from a shower, anytime I didn't have a shirt on. Mowing grass. Cleaning stables. I was never sure what to make of it, so I learned to keep my distance and wear all my clothes. All the time." He groaned. "Olivia must've scared her half to death. I spent months trying to figure out how to make her comfortable, worried she might leave. She was the glue keeping things together while I got my life back on track." He pressed his lips tight. "She must've thought Olivia and I had some kind of *agreement*." He hung his head. "I owe her so many apologies."

I laughed. "I'm sure she'll understand. I think after three years of living with you, she's figured things out."

Grady leaned back, relenting his intense position and stretching his long legs beneath the table. "I'm sure Olivia meant well, but she can't replace Amy."

"No one can," I said. "No one should want to."

He drew in a breath and his eyes softened at the corners.

It might've been all the time I'd spent at the Giving Tree earlier, but there seemed to be a measure of hope in the expression.

He shifted a moment later, pulling his phone from his coat pocket and scowling at it. "It's the mayor's office. I've got to get back there and talk to Vanders and the receptionist. See if they know anything about who might've set up the angry gnomes." His lids slid shut. "I can't believe I just said that."

I stood and pulled the strap of my purse over my head. "Have fun. You should ask Chairman Vanders if trying to fill Mayor Dunfree's shoes has been a challenge."

"All right," Grady agreed slowly. "When I finish there, I'm headed to the post office to ask about the glitter bomb. Any other advice before I talk to Vanders?"

"Yeah. Don't watch him unwrap anything."

CHAPTER FIFTEEN

I checked my watch as I pulled up to the Dunfrees' house. The morning had taken some unanticipated turns, and Aunt Clara was going to have to open Sun, Sand, and Tea without me. I wasn't ready to tell her about what had happened to the final round of gnomes we'd finished together last night. And I couldn't bring myself to head home until I'd at least tried to talk with Mrs. Dunfree about her feud with the neighbor. I'd even packed an extra box of cookies to soften the blow of my appearance on her doorstep. I made her box with extra peppermint fudge since she thought my aunt had recently killed her husband.

I slowed at the end of her packed driveway and gawked as a small crowd of huggers said hellos on the porch. Mrs. Dunfree's face was red and streaked with tears as she accepted a covered dish and welcomed the group into her home. I gave my cookies a sideways glance. It was probably not the best time to visit, even with the gift. She was clearly in the middle of a wake or memorial of some kind, and I didn't want to make a difficult day worse. Not to mention, she'd likely call the cops, and I didn't want to push Grady. He was still dealing with the last Everly-related mess.

I moved on, crunching over tightly packed snow a plow had flattened to the road and eyeballing the houses on either side of the Dunfrees. Both were still and silent, but one belonged to an offending neighbor. I circled the block to determine which. A narrow, pitted alley provided the perfect venue for scoping the backyards. A particularly tall strip of fencing came immediately into view, sticking out like a sore thumb among the shorter rows of white-picket planks along the alley.

A string bean of a man, out walking a little dog, watched me as I turned Blue around. I had no idea what I'd say when I knocked on the front door.

The man paused at the rear gate of the home in question. He had a dog leash in one hand and a little baggie, presumably for his pet's business, in the other. The dog was small and white with puffy ears and a dinky pom-pom-topped tail that resembled a lollipop. She wore a pale pink quilted coat and matching collar with rhinestone accents connected to the long retractable leash. Without the coat and leash, the poor little dog would blend into the piles of snow lining the alley. And without a lift from the man guiding her, she probably couldn't have gotten through her unplowed yard on her own. The man tossed the little baggie into a trash bin at the curb. *His* bin, I realized as he lifted the little poodle into his arms.

"Hello!" I chirped, parking Blue and hopping out before the pair could get away. "Merry Christmas! Good morning," I greeted. "I'm Everly Swan. I own and operate Sun, Sand, and Tea, the iced tea shop on the beach."

He smiled. "Gene Birkhouse." He offered me a hand, and I accepted with a shake. "Out enjoying the scenery? We don't see snow like this often."

"True, and it's beautiful, but I'm actually making my rounds. I wanted to say happy holidays to everyone I missed at my party a few nights ago. I don't think I saw you there."

He chuckled and reached for the knitted hat on his head, shifting it around before leaving it where it had started. "Meg and I weren't prepared for the weather, and most of the shops in town had been wiped out of their snow gear, so we were homebound until our online deliveries came in."

I brightened up my smile. "Well, I'm glad to see you got your deliveries." I lifted the white bakery box with the pretty gold-and-scarlet bow. "Would you and your wife like some cookies? They're made fresh daily at my shop."

He accepted the box with a quizzical look. "I'm not married."

My gaze flicked to the dog. A little silver charm dangled from her collar. A three-letter inscription explained the mix-up. *Meg.*

"Oh, sorry. My mistake," I apologized and leaped for another subject. "I wish I had a good pet-friendly recipe for times like these. Even the drive-through attendants at the bank have treats on hand for island fur babies."

The man's smile warmed. "I think I can help you. I have a growing collection of canine biscuit recipes for Meg. I've been making her birthday cakes for a decade." He gave the dog's small head a loving pat. "Would you like to come inside? I'd love to share one with you. If you like it, maybe you can offer it at your café. A little something to-go for guests to take home to their pups. I've been thinking of selling my biscuits on consignment through a few of the shops on Main Street to see what folks think."

"Smart," I said, appraising his size before accepting the offer. I wanted to continue the conversation until I found an opportunity to ask the questions I'd come to get answers for, but I wasn't in a hurry to go inside alone. It was hard to judge what kind of physique might be hidden under the ski coat, but his legs were long and narrow like a stork and his face was gaunt. I suspected that without the winter coat, hat, and gloves, Gene Birkhouse probably looked a lot like Ichabod Crane. I was guessing I could get away from him in a hurry if needed. "Thank you," I said confidently. "I'd love to."

I followed him along a narrow path that had been shoveled through the backyard snow, surrounded by a too-tall and partially unfinished fence. Most of the completed sections had been painted barn red, and I imagined the weather was the only reason the last few sections hadn't been set into place and painted to match the rest.

I stomped snow off my boots before stepping into his small, warm home. A collection of paint cans and supplies lined the wall inside the door. "Painting?" I asked, curious about the unfinished work outside.

"I was," he said. "The weather ruined that."

He crossed into a small kitchen and motioned for me to join him. A round oak table with two chairs and a simple white cloth anchored the room. Similarly basic curtains hung in the windows. The appliances were new, but the cabinets were old. A typical work in progress. I could relate.

He gave Meg a treat from an antique container with a small bone painted on the front, then opened the bakery box and arranged my cookies on a small glass serving tray. "Would you like a hot cup of tea while I dig up those recipes?"

"Oh, no," I said as sweetly as I could, in case he didn't take kindly to rejection. "I don't want to impose, and I have to keep an eye on the time. I've got to open my tea shop soon, but I would love to know your secret to delicious doggy-safe treats." I smiled. "You bake and you paint. Sounds like you have a creative streak. Maybe even an artist's heart?"

I cast my gaze around his shabby-chic decor. Neat as a pin, with an eclectic mix of old and new. I could appreciate his style, though unlike my place, where twinkly lights and holiday decor engulfed everything, Gene had opted for a lone, sensibly decorated tree in the front window.

He set the cookies on his kitchen table. "I try," he said, stripping off his coat and scarf to reveal exactly what I'd expected. A long-limbed, slow-moving man who had a foot on me in height, and nothing on me in weight. A center of gravity like that had to be a curse. I could definitely knock him down if he tried anything funny. Moreover, any man with a ten-year-old female purse poodle who served cookies on glass trays probably didn't have a murderous bone in his body.

I blew out a sigh of relief and refocused on my fact-gathering mission. "I noticed you started to paint your fence out back before you finished putting it all up. That was an unusual choice."

His lips turned down in distaste. "That's a long story," he said.

I smiled. "I'll bet it's an interesting one."

Gene's eyes narrowed, and for a moment I wondered if I was wrong about his potentially murderous bones. "My neighbor had a problem with the tall fencing. He said it was against regulation and I couldn't enclose my yard with it, so I only used the six-foot pieces along the alley. Those were the most important. They block Meg's view of the people and traffic that bothers her when she goes out to tinkle. I'd put up shorter fencing along the sides of the yard where she was only visible to the neighbors."

That explained the partial paint job. The pieces

that were already in place along the alley had been painted when they went in. The newer pieces, still being erected along each side of Gene's yard, would need the paint when he finished. "You're changing out the short pieces for tall ones now?" I asked.

"Yeah, and I'm getting it finished before anyone can stop me."

"Why would anyone stop you?" I asked, attempting to look mystified.

His eyes lit. "The mayor lives next door, or he did."

I let my jaw drop.

He grimaced. "I've wanted a proper fence out back for years. I wanted Meg to be able to run free on our property, but Mayor Dunfree nixed my permit request every time. He made Charmers get permits before doing anything because he wanted to control us. He wouldn't sign off on my request unless I adhered to some outdated mandates on height and style. Apparently, every fence on the island has to be wrought iron or white picket and stumpy. Nothing over thirty-four inches tall. It's ridiculous."

I thought of the low scalloped fence surrounding the elaborate gardens on my property and the very similar one serving the same purpose at Aunt Clara and Aunt Fran's house. Both white. Both picket. "I didn't realize," I said, stepping close and selecting a cookie. "How frustrating."

"You have no idea," he said, looking suddenly livid. It seemed that just talking about the situation was enough to get him riled up, even if the mayor was dead and the wife, who Grady said he had the beef with, was nowhere to be seen.

"At least you were able to put up some tall pieces in the back," I offered.

He hacked out a throaty derisive sound. "Dunfree left a loophole in the wording on the permits. No fence taller than thirty-four inches shall be installed around a yard or property perimeter," he quoted in a scathing tone. "I didn't install tall sections around the entire yard. I only used those pieces where they mattered most. I adhered to the rules for the rest."

"How did that go over?" I asked, certain I already knew.

He turned his attention to the window facing the Dunfrees' home. "He lost his mind, and his wife went nuts, but I hadn't done anything wrong and he knew it." His mouth curled into a wicked grin. "They came over here screaming about how my fence blocked their view of the coast, but I didn't care. Then, he claimed there was a rule against it. *Shocker.* I demanded to see this magical book of rules he always used to get his way, but he couldn't produce it. Probably because it doesn't exist. So they went home, and the cold war began."

"Why was it so important to have a six-foot fence?" I asked. I raised my palms in surrender when he spun on me, eyes flashing hot. "I'm just curious. I don't think I've ever seen such a tall backyard fence before, and it eliminates your view of the coast too. Don't you miss it?"

"No, because I can walk outside and see the coast anytime I want, as long as I'm not in my backyard. I live on an island for criminy sakes. And so did he."

He must've seen the alarm or confusion on my brow because he went on. "Meg needs a fence tall enough to protect her from a dognapper. She could be seen over a thirty-four-inch fence and through the bars of an iron one. Besides, if people could see in, then she could see out, and she'd bark at everything. Then the Dunfrees would've been back to fine me for some made-up noise ordinance violation."

Meg was asleep on a plaid pillow bed near the fireplace in the next room. Photos of her life lined the mantel. Clearly this poodle was important to Gene, but would he kill for a private place for her to run?

"He was such a pretentious bully," Gene boomed. "He made Meg spend the best years of her life on a leash because he was too power hungry to give in on one little thing, or too lazy to stand up and see the coast on the rare occasion he even went into his backyard." His face turned deep red and he slammed his palms against the table. "Dunfree's wife and that spineless council are going to have to live with what they stole from Meg, but I'm done letting local politicians run over me. I'm building that fence and I'm giving Meg the life she deserves, even if she has fewer years ahead of her than behind. I'd like to see someone try to stop me."

I pulled my phone from my pocket and pretended to check an incoming message "Oh, look.

My great-aunt is looking for me," I said, tapping the screen of my phone in an equally fake response. I'd been wrong to assume the lanky man before me couldn't be dangerous. I hadn't considered he might be hiding a wild temper. "There." I smiled up at him. "I let her know I'm with you now, but I'll be there to open the café in ten minutes." I hoped if Gene was a killer, he could read between the lines. *Someone knows I'm with you, so don't try anything stupid.*

"I'd better grab that recipe," he said, collecting himself.

"No worries," I said. "Email me." I rushed back outside and nearly dove into Blue, my heart hammering wildly. Could Gene have killed Mayor Dunfree? If so, I hated to think of what his real intentions had been for inviting me inside.

I pressed my foot to the floor and raced back around the block. The number of vehicles parked at the mayor's house had grown, and I didn't dare slow down. I was too shaken to ask another question. Instead, I pointed Blue down Middletown Road, toward the boardwalk and my home.

Grady's truck came into view as I approached the mayor's office. For a moment, I considered stopping to tell him about Gene Birkhouse's temper, but I wasn't in the mood to be scolded for having questioned the Dunfrees' neighbor. I'd had a massive fright for my effort and that was punishment enough.

I tried to keep my eyes on the road, begging them not to linger on Grady's truck or search for the detective, but my will was weak when it came to warm pastries and Grady Hays.

His gaze flicked to mine as I drew near, as if he'd somehow sensed my approach. The fierce expression on his face sent a quiver of fear down my spine.

Beside him, the words *Charmers for Change* had been graffitied over Vanders's Jeep in sloppy red paint—the same red paint that had been splattered on the gnomes.

The same shade I'd seen in Gene's mudroom.

CHAPTER SIXTEEN

I swung Blue around and parked beside Grady and the Jeep.

"What happened?" I asked, vaulting into the slushy lot. Was this why the mayor's office had called while Grady and I were having hot chocolates? "Who did this?"

"No witnesses," Grady said, "but I'm going to take a guess on the guilty party." He pointed a ballpoint pen at the messy red words.

Charmers for Change.

"Okay," I agreed slowly, "but who is that?"

Grady tucked the pen and a small notebook into his inside jacket pocket, then lifted the free hand toward his truck. "Got a minute?"

I followed him to the passenger side where he opened the door for me. I climbed inside with the weight of unanswered questions flattening my lungs. The truck was running and warm. Delicious scents of cologne, vanilla, and spice circled my head as I waited impatiently for him to join me.

Grady folded himself behind the wheel a moment later and rubbed his hands briskly in the stream of air spilling from the vents. "Any idea where your Aunt Fran is right now?" He worked the cell phone from his pocket and cast me a tentative look.

"Considering it's nearly eleven on a workday, she's probably at Blessed Bee," I said, letting a little venom drip over the words in fair warning.

"You sure about that?" He fastened his seat belt, then turned his cell phone to face me. The speaker function was on, and the device began to ring. The recorded message for my aunts' store played. He disconnected.

"She's probably with a customer," I said. "Aunt Clara is watching Sun, Sand, and Tea for me, which means Aunt Fran is handling everything, from stocking shelves to ringing up sales, by herself on the busiest week of the year. She can't answer every call. It would be impossible."

Grady sucked his teeth and shifted into gear. "That wasn't my first call."

I fastened my seat belt. "Where are we going?"

"I'm going to start with Blessed Bee, then head over to her home. If I can find her, I'd like to know if she has any insight into who might've painted Chairman Vanders's Jeep and what it could mean."

I narrowed my eyes. "You think Aunt Fran did this."

"If the paint matches," he said, setting a hand on

the black duffel bag between us. The bag he'd filled with red-paint-splattered gnomes just an hour earlier.

"Unfair," I protested, but my heart wasn't in it. This was just one more link in someone's chain of false evidence meant to redirect attention from themselves. Surely Grady knew that. I settled against the seat and rested my head on the soft leather back. Grady was following evidence. *He has to*, I reminded myself. *He won't allow the gossips any room to say I'm impacting his investigation.*

Grady took it slow through snow-lined streets teeming with golf carts in various winter enclosures and frequently with reindeer antlers fixed to the doors and red pom-pom noses attached to the fronts. His black pickup looked big beside normal vehicles. Compared to the golf carts, it was a four-wheeled King Kong.

I waved at shop owners on the sidewalks dousing the cement with ice melt and shoveling away excess snow. Twinkle lights danced in the windows, and town banners waved from lampposts, encouraging all to *Have a Happy Holiday*.

Grady slid into the last open space outside Blessed Bee. The shop was dark, and the *Closed* sign was still in the window. "Should I knock?" he asked. "Any chance she's in there setting up for the day and just hasn't opened yet?"

"Why don't I call her?" I asked.

He twisted to watch me. "Find out where she is and ask her to stay put. Let her know I want to talk to her."

I pursed my lips and dialed Aunt Fran's cell phone number. Several moments later, the call went to voicemail. "No answer," I whispered. My heart rate kicked up a notch. What if something had happened to her? "I have a key," I said, digging into my purse. "I'm going to call Aunt Clara before we go storming inside. If she says Aunt Fran's supposed to be in there, we're going."

"Hello, sweetie," Aunt Clara cooed. "How's the cookie delivery going?"

"Hi," I said. "Everything's good."

"Excellent. Take as long as you like," she said. "I have everything under control here."

"Okay, but I'm looking for Aunt Fran and Blessed Bee is closed. Do you know what's going on or where she might be?"

"Of course," she said. "Just a minute, dear."

I covered the phone with my palm and turned to Grady. "Aunt Clara knows where Aunt Fran is," I said. "She told me to wait. She might be helping one of my customers." I held the phone between us and engaged the speaker function.

Grady leaned closer, listening intently to the shuffling sounds on Aunt Clara's end of the line.

"Hello?" Aunt Fran's voice sounded through my cell phone. "Everly?"

"Hey!" I perked. "You're at Sun, Sand, and Tea?"

"Yes." The answered sounded tentative, but I beamed at Grady anyway.

He shifted into gear once more and headed toward my home.

"Great. Don't go anywhere. I'm on my way back, and Grady's with me. He has a few questions for you."

"Super," she said flatly. "Can't wait."

Ten minutes later, I'd convinced Grady there was no hurry and he'd taken me to get Blue before following me home.

The café was busy without being full. Several customers were scattered throughout the space, chatting merrily and enjoying plates of mixed cookies and cups of iced tea.

Aunt Clara and Aunt Fran had taken over the sitting area near my bookcase. Poster boards and paints covered the low table near my rear deck.

Aunt Clara hugged me first. "We're making campaign signs together. Isn't that great?" she asked. The joy in her tone and on her face was almost enough to make me smile.

The frown on Aunt Fran's face was more than enough to keep my enthusiasm in check.

"What's this about?" Aunt Fran asked, arms crossed and eyes on Grady.

He forced a tight smile and shoved his hands into his back pockets. "The signs are looking good," he said. His gaze lingered on the little jars of red paint. "How long have you two been at it this morning?"

"Not long," Aunt Clara said.

Aunt Fran's thin arm snaked out. She caught her

sister's elbow in a purposeful grip, effectively shutting her up. "You haven't told me why you're asking," she said, shifting her gaze from Grady to me.

"Someone painted 'Charmers for Change' on Chairman Vanders's Jeep," I whispered, checking over both shoulders for eavesdroppers and lookie-loos.

Grady stepped closer, filling in the small space between Aunt Fran and me. He scanned the room. "Is there somewhere a little more private where we can talk?" he asked. "Maybe there?" He pointed to the archway connecting my café to the empty former ballroom.

"Of course." I hurried in that direction, double checking the tea levels in customers' jars on my way past. Everyone seemed to have enough cookies and drinks to keep them busy a few minutes while my aunts and I set Grady straight.

Grady hung back until we'd all passed into the room, then he blocked the archway behind him, keeping watch on everything from his position. "What brought you here to make posters?" he asked Fran without wasting any time. "Why not work at Blessed Bee where you can keep your store open and bring in Christmas sales while you work?"

I frowned. He was supposed to be on our side, but his questions sounded a little too pointed for that.

Fran squared her shoulders and tipped her chin high. "I came here after I heard about what happened with the gnomes this morning. I didn't want Clara to be alone, and I wanted to be with her when

Everly returned so I could see for myself that she was okay."

I swung my head in her direction, shocked. "You know about the gnomes?"

"What gnomes?" Aunt Clara wondered.

"Someone broke into Blue and took the box of gnomes we finished last night," I explained, trying to sound as easy-breezy as possible about a horrible experience. "Whoever did it drew angry faces on the gnomes, then lined them in the snow around Blue."

Aunt Clara made a strangled sound.

"Maven called to let me know," Aunt Fran explained. "She didn't want me to worry if I heard the story from someone else. So, I called Clara to see if she could use some company. I figured we could kill two birds if I brought the campaign materials with me, and as a bonus, I'd get to tell Clara in person."

Aunt Clara spun on her sister, tears swimming in her wide, sincere eyes. "You didn't tell me."

"You were busy," Aunt Fran said. "We've barely traded ten words, and I didn't want to upset you in front of everyone."

Aunt Clara stepped away from her, the tears beginning to fall. "I don't need you to protect me. I need you to be my sister."

I reached for her. "Aunt Clara, I'm sure she didn't mean to..."

"You!" Aunt Clara dodged my hand. "You should have called me. As soon as it happened. You never call and I worry and it's not fair. It's selfish."

Grady waved his hands like an umpire across his middle. Frustration mixed with curiosity on his brow. "The mayor's secretary called you?"

Fran nodded. "Maven and I have been friends for decades. Her husband was on the council for twenty-five years before his passing. She understands how this island works, and she's keeping an eye on Vanders for us. Us being the council," she clarified. "He's not qualified for the position, and no one elected him, so we have to make sure he doesn't go rogue."

"No chance of that," I said. "When I talked with Vanders, he assured me he's just the man to keep everyone in line. He plans to make certain nothing changes on his watch." I thought of him on the phone and something else flashed into mind. I looked at Grady. "Did you ever find Mayor Dunfree's cell phone?"

"No. We've searched the area numerous times. It didn't walk away on its own after the murder, so we think someone took it and powered it off. Probably the killer. Anyone else would've powered it up or turned it in by now. The minute it comes on, we'll be able to track it. Tech services is keeping watch."

A set of heavy footfalls moved across the café floor in our direction. Wyatt appeared behind Grady, smiling, hat in hands. "Hey, y'all. Am I interrupting anything?"

I huffed. I wasn't sure when he'd moved from brooding cowboy to genial boy next door, but it bugged me. Everything about him bugged me.

Especially the history we shared, and the handsome all over his face.

"Nothing at all," Aunt Fran said. "I was just explaining to Detective Hays that I've been here with Clara for nearly an hour, chatting and visiting with her and several of the lovely café customers, so he's barking up the wrong tree."

Aunt Clara nodded eagerly. "We have several finished signs to show for it."

Wyatt shot me a perplexed look. "Has something else happened?"

I couldn't answer, or even hold his gaze.

Grady's suddenly pursed lips might as well have been screaming that an hour wasn't long enough to clear Aunt Fran of the vandalism completely. I tried to do the math in my head.

Grady and I had parted ways when the mayor's office called him. I checked my watch. That had been nearly two hours ago. I'd been with Grady for the last forty minutes. So, where was Aunt Fran before that?

"Where were you before you came here?" Grady asked, speaking my thoughts.

Aunt Fran straightened further. "Home."

Wyatt whistled long and low, reminding me of a falling missile. He shouldered his way past Grady to face my aunts directly. "This seems like a bad time, but is there any chance you're opening your shop soon? I've been tracking the wild mustangs before and after work all week and my lips are chapped. I could really use some more of your bee balm."

I gave his big bicep a push. "Wyatt. We're in the middle of something."

He made big innocent eyes. "I'm just asking."

Grady shifted his annoyed expression to Wyatt. "You're out and about every day. Talking with folks at the nature center. Tracking the horses. Have you heard of Charmers for Change? Know anything about them?"

Wyatt looked stumped, something I was beginning to think came naturally. "They're a group of Charmers who want change?" he asked Aunt Fran.

"Don't look at me," Aunt Fran said. "I don't know anything about them. I don't know who they are, where they meet, or even what kind of change they want."

Wyatt puckered his brow. "I thought you were their leader or founder or something."

I turned Wyatt around by force and shoved him back through the archway. "That's a rumor and it's wrong."

He stopped letting me move him when we reached the service counter. "How about you and the good detective? Still claiming that rumor's false too?"

"That's none of your business." I hugged myself to keep from pushing him some more. "I'll ask my aunts to call you when they get back to Blessed Bee, and I'll personally buy you a lifetime of bee balm if you never ask about my love life again."

"No deal," he said smoothly. "As much as I like to keep these lips in good working order, I'll foot my own bill on the bee balm." He reached for my cheek and brushed a strand of hair away from my mouth. "Who you're involved with matters to me, so I'm going to keep asking."

"Why?" The word was barely a whisper on my tongue, and I hated how easily Wyatt could still pull me into his orbit.

His mouth hitched into a cocky half smile, and his thumb grazed my cheek. "Because you matter to me."

The words *old habits are hard to break* came to mind, and they'd never felt so personal or so true.

Grady cleared his throat, and I jumped back from Wyatt's touch.

Wyatt grinned as his hand fell away. "Nope. Nothing to that rumor at all," he murmured.

I wasn't sure if it was sarcasm or belligerence in his tone, but I disapproved of both.

The heat from Grady's body warmed me as he angled himself at my side. "I'm going to have a talk with Maven. Are you okay here?" He lifted his gaze to Wyatt, who was smiling smugly back at us.

"I'm good." My cracking voice probably cast a little doubt, but Grady had the decency to pretend he hadn't noticed.

He looked into my eyes for long beat without speaking.

"Really," I assured. "I'm fine."

He relented, reluctantly, with a tip of his hat, and walked out.

Wyatt watched from his perch on the barstool he'd

retreated to when Grady had appeared. He'd propped an elbow on the counter and rested his stubble-covered cheek in one open palm. "If you want, I can go up to your place and check all the rooms for trouble." He wagged his brows, then flexed his opposite arm beneath a heavy wool-lined coat.

A sudden and unexpected belly laugh broke the tension in my mood. Much as I wanted to toss him into the snow, Wyatt had always made me laugh, and currently, I needed it. "I can take care of myself these days," I said with a wide grin. "I've got a peppermint stick."

CHAPTER SEVENTEEN

I shuffled into the café at insane o'clock the next morning and stripped the next tea bag off my advent calendar. Just six short days until Christmas, and I was no closer to clearing Aunt Fran's name than I had been the day Mayor Dunfree died.

Wind howled around the deck doors and window panes, rattling the aged glass and echoing my dreary mood. Thanks to the glorious southern sun, we'd had a beautiful winter day after my aunts had gone to open Blessed Bee. Folks had been thrilled to be out without fear of slipping on icy sidewalks or sliding into a snowbank on Main Street, so Sun, Sand, and Tea had stayed busy until close. I'd been exhausted from the emotional morning and all-day rush, then stayed up late preparing for tonight's Holiday Shuffle.

I'd had high hopes for the dinner. Warmer temperatures meant folks would walk stop to stop instead of drive, which meant I'd be able to blend into the masses on the sidewalks and eavesdrop. Surely there would be plenty to overhear with the entire town out and about. I'd mentally selected my walking routes between stops, not by scenery or ease of commute, but according to which paths I expected to be heaviest with foot traffic.

Sadly, a wicked cold front had moved in while the town had slept and transformed the newly melted snow to ice. Now, the world beyond my windows was encased in crystal. Unprecedented. Beautiful. And a traveler's nightmare.

I was doubly thankful for yesterday's busyness because today was sure to drag. *Another blessing*, I reasoned, seeking a positive spin. I'd been up late creating enough drinks and hors d'oeuvres to feed an army. I could use today's downtime to prepare the café. I sipped coffee and examined my night's work. The refrigerator was stuffed with appetizers ready for the oven and gallon dispensers of tea ready for consumption. The volume of product was probably overkill, the result of extreme wishful thinking, but any leftovers could be used as tomorrow's Sun, Sand, and Tea menu. A win-win in my book.

I stretched and wandered around the first floor for several minutes, collecting steps for my fitness bracelet before slogging back upstairs to dress for the day. I moved in slow, steady strides, groggy from the late night and discouraged from my lack of progress in Aunt Fran's case. I wrapped my hair around two sets of giant rollers as I wracked my brain thinking of possible ways to point the proverbial finger away from

Aunt Fran. Yes, it looked bad, her standing over the body of her enemy with the murder weapon in hand, but obviously she hadn't killed him. It was obvious to me, anyway. I just needed to imagine a scenario where evidence appeared to the contrary. What could it be? What was I looking for? And where could I find it? Mayor Dunfree's cell phone would help, but that was likely with the killer who'd been smart enough to take it.

I applied a few strokes of mascara, taking in the fact the killer had thought ahead, or at least fast enough to know the victim's cell phone might reveal their identity. So, it was safe to assume the mayor had spoken with his killer by phone at some point, even if it wasn't that night. I drove a lip gloss wand around my lips and pressed them tight before blowing a kiss to my reflection. I hadn't bothered with so much makeup in months. Now I knew I was procrastinating. I chose a festive holiday sweater to go with my comfiest jeans and fur-lined boots, pulled the curlers from my hair, and gave my head a generous shake.

It was time to start my day.

I still had no idea how to help Aunt Fran, but I looked good, and that made me feel a little peppier. I bounced back to the café and opened my laptop to bring up the *Town Charmer*. I hadn't gotten far with my interviews yesterday. I'd learned the Dunfrees' fence-building neighbor needed anger management and the stand-in mayor needed a cold shower, but neither had copped to murder.

Movement caught my eye in the foyer, and I grabbed the hefty peppermint stick from beneath the counter. "Who's there?" I demanded, my voice shockingly confident.

Maggie meowed. She slunk into the café, bright green eyes flashing.

I released the candy in favor of digging my fingers into her soft fur as she came near. "Where have you been?" I asked. "And why can't you talk?"

She rubbed her cheek against my palm and purred. It wasn't an answer, but I softened at the sound of her contentment.

"Fine, you win," I said, heading for the fridge. "I boiled some chicken last night in case you came to see me while I was making all those hors d'oeuvres. I'll reheat it for you."

She waited patiently on my vacated chair while I prepared her meal, then horked it down as if she hadn't eaten in days, which I knew was untrue. I felt guilty anyway. What kind of cat mother was I when I didn't know where she was ninety percent of the time? I cleaned the counter and dropped the empty container into the dishwasher. When I turned back, Maggie was gone.

I sighed onto my chair and dragged the laptop close again.

There wasn't any new gossip about Mayor Dunfree's death on the *Town Charmer*, but the list of progressive dinner stops was up with finalized menus and printable maps for anyone unfamiliar with the best routes from place to place. I reviewed the web page, but my night's itinerary hadn't changed. I'd hit the busiest stops by way of the busiest sidewalks... assuming the ice had melted by then.

First stop was my place. Sun, Sand, and Tea for hors d'oeuvres and predinner cocktails. The cocktails were mostly composed of my favorite and most popular iced teas, but I'd allowed for one hot option: an apple cinnamon tea I'd blended with nutmeg and pumpkin pie spice. From here, I'd head over to Blessed Bee for soups and salads with my aunts. Theirs was always a popular spot. People loved their store and their stories. Aunt Clara couldn't host a crowd without regaling everyone with tales of unwritten history that could raise doubts about the afterlife in even the most cynical Charmer: me.

Much as I wanted to protest Senator Denver's attempt to lure the town into her good graces, I'd be there for the main course. Along with the rest of the island, no doubt. If I wanted to hear what folks were saying, I was guaranteed to hear the most people at her place. So, I couldn't miss it. From there, I'd head back to Main Street for desserts and nightcaps with Amelia at Charming Reads. By then, I imagined, I might be ready for a cocktail.

The day had dragged by as expected, long and lonely inside the café. I'd mentally rehashed my chats with Mayor Dunfree's neighbor and Chairman Vanders, plus Maven and relative discussions with my aunts, Amelia, and Grady. I'd replayed the moments after finding Aunt Fran with Dunfree's body, and I'd relived each gnome threat to no avail. I was practically dizzy from running in mental circles by the time my first guests of the evening arrived.

I was fizzing with excitement at the sight of other humans and had to restrain myself from hugging them and dragging them inside. Lou had shown up at lunchtime with something red on his wings, gobbled up his crustaceans, then puffed up and flew away before I could ask him what he'd gotten into, and I hadn't seen Maggie since breakfast. After eight hours alone with my thoughts, I was desperate to get out of my head.

Folks piled inside as if they'd been waiting on the porch for five o'clock to roll around. I took their coats and shook their hands greedily. "Merry Christmas! Welcome to Sun, Sand, and Tea," I sang. "Come inside. Make yourselves at home. Plates are on the counter and everything's waiting for you to dig in."

A long buffet stretched across the service counter, now lined in greenery to hide the bases of the warming dishes and add a festive effect. The soft sounds of holiday classics played through the speakers of my old boom box on the bookshelf, and everything smelled like homespun magic.

Amelia arrived with her dad after the initial crowd had swept in. I gave both Butters a hearty squeeze. "Thank you so much for coming. I know you have a million things to do by the end of the night."

Mr. Butters chuckled. "Please. We wouldn't miss

your piece of the spotlight. Besides, we have the easy part, desserts and cocktails. Everyone loves desserts, plus they'll all be stuffed by the time they get to us, and it's hard to make a bad cocktail."

I wanted to argue with that, but it was Christmas, so I smiled.

"Amelia made all the sweets last night," he continued. "They're waiting in the fridge. All that's left to do is open the doors and dish out the goods."

"And bartend," I said.

Mr. Butters beamed. "I was a bartender in Kokomo one summer." He waggled his eyebrows. "Quite an experience."

I laughed. "Prove it. Impress me with your skills tonight."

He kneaded his hands in anticipation. "Challenge accepted."

Amelia shook her head. "Don't get him started. I beg you." She wrapped one arm around her dad's back and shoved a book in my direction with the opposite hand. "I found *The Greatest Gift* in the return bin at Charming Reads and figured you must be ready for another holiday classic."

I turned the new offering over in my hands. "*A Christmas Carol*?"

Her smile widened. "It's my favorite Christmas read."

I laughed. "They're all your favorite Christmas reads," I said. "Thanks."

"You'll read it?" she asked.

I sighed. "Why not?"

Amelia bounced and clapped silently.

Her dad crept out of her reach, then turned for the buffet with a grin.

Amelia fell into line behind him.

I'd arranged the tea dispensers at the end of the food line. The silver thermal unit kept my hot apple cinnamon warm while three glass dispensers showcased my favorite sweet teas of the season: Iced Blackberry Vanilla and Iced Cranberry Mint. The adult selection was a combination of sweet wines from the cellar, plus brandy, lemonade, sugar, and a healthy amount of orange juice, which seemed counterintuitive to all the other not-so-healthy ingredients, but made for a killer sangria. I'd mixed in several chopped apples and sliced oranges for good measure. Considering the amount of ice still on the ground, anyone having a refill from the adult dispenser might want to call Lanita for a ride to their next stop.

Amelia returned with a small sampler plate of everything and an extra-large smile. "I almost forgot to say how much I enjoyed your how-to video. It was delightful. When will the next one go up?"

My stomach knotted and my smile fell. Grady had seen the video. Denise and Denver too. "You watched it?"

"Yes," she said slowly, dragging the little word into several syllables. "I was watching for it. Remember? And I loved it, like I knew I would. Everyone's talking about it."

Everyone.

My mouth went dry. "People are talking about it?" I struggled to repeat her words with my sticky tongue. "Who?" And what were they saying? I scanned the cheerful faces throughout my café. Had any of them seen my video? Was it too late to take it down? "Define everyone."

My fingers itched to grab the laptop and remove the link. I curled my hands into fists at my sides and reminded myself to be still and look calm. For the next thirty-five minutes, I was a happy hostess who wanted all her current guests to return again as customers, hopefully with friends.

Amelia pulled her lips to one side in a smug expression. "As if you haven't been checking hourly to see how many times the tutorial was viewed and read every comment."

"There are comments?" I ducked behind the counter and nabbed the laptop.

Amelia followed, peeking over my shoulder as I brought up my website. "See," she said. "More than one hundred views and over half as many comments."

Breath caught in my throat. My eyes stung with emotion and my fingertips froze on the keyboard before I could scroll down to see what people were saying. What if they all hated it? What if the commenters were cruel?

Amelia reached around me and hit the down arrow on my keyboard until the comments came into view.

I smashed my eyes shut for a long beat. I gave myself the world's lamest pep talk, then pulled one lid open.

> *What a fun video! Will there be more?*
>
> —Shelia in Charlotte

That wasn't bad at all. I opened the other eye.

> *So glad I found this site! The cookies were a hit at my office party! When will the next video go up?*
>
> —Manny in San Diego

> *Fantastic tutorial. I'm a mess in the kitchen, but this helped me get it right. I even impressed my mother-in-law!*
>
> —Anita in Los Alamos

I speed-read through the comments with plans to return to them later and savor the kind words. Everyone was gracious and happy, and they weren't only from Charm. Folks all over the country had watched and tried the recipe. *And they'd liked it.*

My heart soared.

"So?" Amelia asked. "When are you posting the next video? You only have six days until Christmas. You'd better get moving. With a response like this, you should make videos a weekly thing after the holidays. Give it a snazzy name like Tutorial Tuesdays to draw attention. Then, your subscribers can anticipate their next lesson and plan accordingly. Oh!" She rocked onto her toes. "You should make a newsletter. Provide baking tips or kitchen hacks and a recipe of the month. I can help with the setup. I took an entire course on newsletter writing in business school, and I have a great one I use for Charming Reads that we can modify for Sun, Sand, and Tea."

My head lightened. Words piled on my tongue with a hundred offerings of gratitude and appreciation my brain couldn't sort into sounds. So, I hugged her instead.

Thirty minutes later, my time was up, and the crowd moved on. I rushed through the café, cleaning up and putting away the leftovers before locking up on my way out.

It was officially my great-aunts' turn to steal the show. Aunt Clara and Aunt Fran had chosen to hostess the soups and salads portion of the evening, and they were guaranteed to wow the crowd with dishes made wholly from the produce and herbs grown in their gardens. They'd toiled over the cinnamon and butternut squash soup all afternoon. Aunt Clara had called twice to ask me for advice while Aunt Fran had cussed the concoction in the background. Ultimately, they'd been satisfied with their results and texted to wish me luck just before the dinner started. Now, it was my turn to support them and make sure they knew they'd outdone themselves.

I hurried onto the boardwalk, careful to make each

step count and planting my boots in the snow as often as possible. Snow offered a little grip on an otherwise iced-over world. I slipped and skidded several times before reaching the section of frozen planks that drew nearest to Ocean Drive, then I crunched across a narrow patch of icy grass to the street.

The streets were gritty beneath my boots, heavy with sand and road salt to melt the ice. I caught up to a slow-moving clutch of people on the corner of Main and Middletown, then adjusted my pace to theirs and listened. Mostly, they were discussing their strategies to stay upright and the likelihood of getting a cab home if they had a couple of nightcaps later.

I excused myself from behind them and hurried to catch the next group. They were discussing the hors d'oeuvres at their previous stop. I tried not to take offense that they'd chosen another location over mine.

We passed a man leaning against a pillar at the edge of the walk. He turned as we passed, and I smiled, ready to welcome him into our fold.

His face was grim, eyes hard on me, and my breaths faltered. The man was Gene Birkhouse, and he made no move to join us. He just watched as I hurried along.

"Whoop!" someone called several yards ahead. Her arms pinwheeled and one leg shot forward.

I sucked in a breath, hoping she wouldn't fall. The man at her side caught her under the arms with a chuckle and set her upright before she hit the ground. He held her closer as they began to move again.

Something tugged in my heart as I slowed to take the couple in. My gaze travelled to the other folks out for a walk in my hometown. Braving the ice to participate in a Charm tradition. Choosing to be part of something greater and sweeter than just one family could ever be. Everywhere I looked, folks were laughing, smiling, and holding onto one another a little tighter thanks to the unfavorable weather conditions. The ice hadn't stopped them, it had only added to the memories being made before my eyes.

Behind me, Gene Birkhouse was gone.

I breathed easier, concentrating on the muffled sound of distant rolling waves despite the snow-globe-worthy scene around me. Overhead, stars twinkled in an inky, moonless sky while the entire earth seemed to be encased in crystal. Each tree branch and power line, street sign and roof glistened with the reflection of holiday lights. The view was beautiful in the extreme, surreal and almost otherworldly. In reality, however, people were struggling to stay upright, and they were cracking up about it. Joyful tingles worked their way across my skin, engulfing me in the sensation of a warm hug, despite the freezing temperatures. Suddenly it seemed as if anything was possible.

I blended in with the next group that passed, then proceeded in the direction of Blessed Bee feeling light enough to float away. My portion of the dinner had been well attended and the selections well received. My video had been a hit, and the viewers wanted more. My smile grew impossibly wide as I stepped across the threshold to my aunts' shop.

Merry chattering and lively music filled the space, punctuated regularly with an abrupt round of laughter. I followed a line of new arrivals toward Aunt Clara at the buffet, cheeks rosy and expressions giddy with delight.

Blessed Bee's interior smelled like warm vanilla and honey. Happiness seemed to drape over each guest and fill the room from floor to rafters. I helped myself to a cup of cinnamon squash soup and an arugula salad Aunt Fran had tossed with candied pecans, feta cheese, and a homemade honey dressing.

Aunt Clara was dazzling in head-to-toe white, an extreme version of her usual angelic attire. Tonight's flowing dress was fancy with gold accents, bell sleeves, and a scoop neck lined in rhinestones. The look coordinated seamlessly with her blond and silver hair. "Everything we're serving tonight came from our gardens," she explained. "We harvest fruits, produce, herbs, and honey, then can, freeze, and preserve them to make condiments, dressings, and products for Blessed Bee all year long."

"It's all marvelous," an older woman replied. Her comment was supported with multiple other accolades rising up from the crowd.

My heart warmed further still at the group's kindness. People could've chosen to be mean or even boycott this stop on the dinner tour if they truly believed Aunt Fran was a killer. The significant turnout and positive enthusiasm proved that most Charmers were smart and loyal, or at least still ran on an innocent until proven guilty mentality, and I appreciated that.

I turned in a small circle, seeking Aunt Fran in the crowd.

She sat in the back of the store with a mug in her hands. Her gaze was distant, her smile weak and manufactured. Janie sat at her side, gently stroking her arm.

I made my way through the crowd with my food and took a seat on the opposite side of Aunt Fran. "What's up?" I asked, casting my gaze from my aunt to Janie.

Janie's eyes met mine first. "Fran's thinking of dropping out of the mayoral race," she said. "I've been trying to talk her out of it, but she won't listen to me."

"Aunt Fran?" I asked, shocked at the suddenness of the announcement and a little offended it hadn't come from her.

She nodded slowly, absently. "Everything's just gotten out of hand," she said softly. "Maybe it's time to face the fact that a stint as mayor was never in the cards for me." The quiet despair in her eyes was enough to break my heart. Fran wanted to be mayor. She had for years, and it was beyond unfair that a murderer had dragged her into his crime spree and taken the hope from her.

"Hey," I said softly, lifting her hand in mine. "I know it's been a tough few days, but don't forget how long you've wanted to do this. You can't let one horrible person's actions steer you off the path. Stay the course," I told her. "Isn't that what you always told me?"

Aunt Fran raised weary brown eyes to mine. "You can't fight fate, chickadee."

I grimaced at the word. *Fate.* The nonsensical idea of family curses flashed into my mind. Though that wasn't what Aunt Fran had been referring to, it was the question of fate I struggled with almost daily, and everything inside me rejected it. All of it. "Fight," I said. The strength of the word reverberated through me like a gong had been struck. "I believe in fate," I assured her, "but I also believe in free will. The will to challenge things we don't agree with and fight for things we do. Nothing can be set in stone so long as we have the will to change it. So, if you truly want to leave the race, I'll help with your withdrawal any way I can. But, if you want to stay and fight…" I let the sentence hang as I squeezed her hand.

Janie pumped her fists in silent approval of my awesome speech.

Aunt Fran's lips curled slowly at the sides. She reached for my cheek and gave it a gentle pat. "You've always been the fighter in this family."

"And who do you think I learned it from?" I asked, pressing my hand against hers on my cheek.

"Everly?" Grady's voice cut through the white noise around us. He closed the remaining distance in three long strides. Deep lines had gathered across his forehead, and a mix of fear and concern battled in his eyes. "Are you okay?"

"Sure." I glanced at Aunt Fran and Janie. We'd been having a moment before he'd interrupted, but we weren't in any danger, if that was what he'd meant. I gave his grim expression another moment of consideration, then checked behind him for Denise and Denver. Wasn't he supposed to be enjoying the progressive dinner with them tonight? And why hadn't they stopped at my place?

Suddenly his expression and his son's absence sent a jolt of alarm up my spine. "What's wrong? Is it Denver?"

Grady's expression softened slightly. "No. He and Denise are at Olivia's." He glanced at the women beside me before fixing his gaze back on me. "I was worried about you."

"Me?" Shock set me on my feet. I moved in close to his side. "Something else happened?" I guessed.

He gave a stiff nod in affirmation. "Mayor Dunfree's phone came online about thirty minutes ago. The lab called and I've been tracking it."

I set my plate of untouched food on the empty seat beside Fran. Victory crackled over my skin. Dunfree's cell phone was the key to everything. I could feel it in my bones, and now we had it in our reach. "Let's go," I said, "Where is it?"

Grady's hard gray gaze slid from my face to Aunt Fran's. "Here."

CHAPTER EIGHTEEN

I tensed as the weight of his statement settled over me.

Mayor Dunfree's formerly missing phone had come online, and it was here. Which could only mean one thing: the killer was here also. *With us.* Enjoying my aunts' tasty soups and salads as if he or she hadn't brutally murdered a man only a few days ago.

"How do we know who has it?" I whispered to Grady, craning my neck for a better look at his phone screen. There were at least fifty people filling the quaint little shop. "Can you tell which direction the signal is coming from?" I lifted onto my tiptoes and scanned the room for signs of Mary Grace, Chairman Vanders, or Gene Birkhouse.

Grady drew his brows together and shook his head. "It's not a metal detector. The tracking service uses GPS coordinates. The phone is in this building. That's all I know."

"So, how do we find it?" I asked. "We can't exactly

pat everyone down." Personal space violations aside, mandatory police pat downs had to be an invasion of rights.

Grady scanned the smattering of jolly faces. Some guests browsed the displays. Others stood around rented tables. All had food in hand and appeared perfectly at ease. He checked his watch. "I don't have time to pat them all down."

I narrowed my eyes, wondering if he'd truly considered that an option. "Maybe we can disguise the search as a game," I suggested. "We can ask them to unload their pockets for some reason. Pretend we snuck something into one guest's possession and the one who has it wins a prize."

Grady continued to watch the group, likely seeing more than I could, despite our identical views. "Whoever has Mayor Dunfree's phone won't reveal it willingly."

"So, we're back to the pat downs?" I asked.

Grady gave a soft laugh. "No."

"Why do you think the killer powered the phone on now?" I asked. "After three days and during a party?"

Grady walked away, shoulders square. He had a plan.

Thank goodness. Only eight minutes before folks would leave for their next destination.

Grady climbed onto an empty chair beside the buffet station arranged across the room. He swiped a fork and glass from the buffet on his way up, then tapped them together. "Can I have your attention?"

Authority boomed from the words, sharpening the request to a demand.

The room quieted.

Grady tapped his phone's screen and waited. *Calling the mayor's phone*, I realized, *waiting for it to ring*. But there was only the tense silence of a group wondering what the good detective wanted.

"For any of you who don't know me, I'm Detective Grady Hays," he said finally. "It has come to my attention that someone here has something I'm looking for. Something that will help me with the investigation of your mayor's recent murder."

Whispers rolled through the crowd. Faces pinched in distaste. I didn't blame them for the sour response. They'd managed to put the ugliest part of the week aside and focus on the Holiday Shuffle, a treasured annual tradition. Now, less than two hours in, the local fuzz was disrupting their night with talk of a murder. It was an understandably unwelcomed return to reality.

Grady raised his palms apologetically, though I suspected it was also to regain their silence and attention. "I know I'm wrecking your night, and I'm sorry for that, but there's a family in this town that is grieving, and they want the truth. They want justice and closure. I think you can all support that."

"What do you want us to do?" A man's unfamiliar voice rose from the crowd and was quickly accompanied by others offering words of support and compliance.

Grady motioned me forward. "I'd like you all to show Everly or me your cell phone before you leave tonight. We have about five minutes until everyone heads off to enjoy the main course, so we'll make this quick. We don't need to touch the phones or see anything personal. We just want to see you unlock the phone and open a personalized app of your choice. Email. Photos. Social media. Anything that says, this is your phone."

The crowd murmured and shifted. Those on the fringes moved closer to Grady as I reached his side. Guests dug into their pockets and handbags, willingly producing cell phones, e-readers, and tablets.

"Just cell phones," Grady said. "If you have more than one on you, I'd like to see them both."

A man I recognized as a local construction company owner inched toward the door.

I nudged Grady with my elbow, but he was already trailing the man with his eyes.

My heart rate doubled. Was he the killer? Why? Had the former mayor done something to make him snap? Was it building code related? Something else?

Grady stepped off his chair and moved toward the door. "Excuse me," he said softly, setting a hand on my shoulder as he passed.

I stayed on task, watching as my neighbors and friends unlocked their phones and showed me photos of their families and pets. "Thank you. I appreciate your help. Merry Christmas," I told folks one by one.

The man opened the shop door to escape, and Grady followed.

Aunt Clara took up position at my side, packing to-go containers of soup and salad from the buffet, then offering them to every person I cleared to leave.

My gaze traveled to the door on repeat. Had Grady followed a killer into the night?

Aunt Clara caught my eye with a curious stare. She had no idea what was happening, I realized. She'd simply found a use for herself and jumped in to help.

Across the room, the chairs where Aunt Fran and Janie had been were empty, and I didn't see either of them in the thinning crowd. A bead of panic lifted in my tightening chest. Were Aunt Fran and Janie okay?

"Is that it?" The elderly woman before me asked. The tiny screen of her ancient flip phone glowed up at me. "I don't know what you mean about unlocking it. I just pull it apart and it opens like this." She flipped the device open the shut a few times in demonstration. "I've never bought a lock for it."

"Yes, thank you," I said. "Merry Christmas."

She tucked the phone in her bag and moved on to collect her to-go box from Aunt Clara.

Grady returned several minutes later and joined me in assessing the final few phones.

Aunt Fran flipped the dead bolt and lodged her fists in the curves of her narrow waist as the last guest moved into the night. "Well, what now?"

Grady tented his brows. "Now it's your turn."

Aunt Clara, Janie, and I showed our phones to Grady. Aunt Fran did the same.

"What happened with the man who took off?" I asked. Clearly Grady hadn't made an arrest or he wouldn't need to see our phones. "Did you lose him?"

"No." Grady returned our phones with an audible exhale. "I caught him before he reached his truck. He ran because he had two phones on him and only knew the password to one of them. He said he took his kid's phone earlier this week for breaking curfew. The kid's a senior in high school, and he didn't know the password."

I wrinkled my nose. "That was it? Why'd he run? Why not just tell us that story when it was his turn in line?"

Grady raised a weary gaze to Aunt Fran. "He said if people are willing to believe Fran Swan is a killer, then they wouldn't hesitate to see his second cell phone as evidence he was involved too. An accusation like that would ruin his business, so he tried to slip out unnoticed."

"Okay," I said slowly, "but if you couldn't unlock the phone, then how can you be sure it wasn't Mayor Dunfree's?"

Grady smiled. "The lock screen's background is a photo of the man and his son on a fishing boat this summer."

"Aww," I said.

Grady nodded. "Yeah. I think seeing the picture made the guy rethink his kid's punishment. He was choked up when he got into his truck, saying what a good kid he has, and how much he's going to miss him when he graduates in May. He was already accepted to a school in Miami." Grady's prideful expression suggested he'd put himself in that man's shoes. One day too soon, little Denver would grow up and leave too.

"The guests have all left and no one had the phone," I said, a new problem registering. "How's that possible?" Did somebody lie to us? "Could one of the guests have shown us their personal cell phone, then walked back out the door with Mayor Dunfree's device?"

My question fostered the return of Grady's unreadable cop face. "According to GPS tracking, Mayor Dunfree's phone is still here."

I gave a long, slow blink as he turned his phone to face me. The little red blip on his screen hadn't moved. "It's somewhere in the store? Hidden?"

Grady slid the phone into his pocket. "That, or someone got spooked and left it behind. We can dust it for prints when we find it. I'll need a list of everyone who was here tonight in case the phone's been wiped clean."

"So, this is good," I said. The plan had worked! Grady asked to see everyone's cell phones, and they'd complied. No pat downs required. Unfortunately, I realized, having the phone turn up in Aunt Fran's store didn't exactly help her case.

"Let's split up," I said. "We've got to find this thing."

My aunts, Janie, and I headed in four different directions.

"Remember," Grady called after us. "If you find it, don't touch it."

A sharp whistle stopped me short several minutes later. Grady appeared at the stockroom door. "Fran?" he said. "Can I see you for a moment?"

Aunt Fran cast her gaze to her sister, then me and Janie. "Sure."

The four of us converged on him, moving in from our separate directions. We formed a line, shoulder to shoulder, before Grady.

I wet my lips, terrified of what he'd found. "Is it the cell phone?" I asked, hoping it was nothing more gruesome. *No more gnomes*, I begged the universe.

"Come with me," he said, moving back through the stockroom door.

We followed.

He stopped before a set of cabinets along the far wall. The two nearest him had been personalized. Each with one of my aunts' names on it. Beside them, a pint-sized version of the cabinets sat on a cubby. The small one had my name on it. The cabinet on the other side of mine was Grandma's.

Grady snapped a blue latex glove over one hand and reached into the already open cabinet marked *FRAN*. He pulled a cell phone from the pocket of a smock inside her locker.

My eyes widened, and the trio beside me gasped.

I turned to see color drain from Aunt Fran's face.

"That's not Mayor Dunfree's phone," she said. "I found that in the store earlier today and set it aside. I assumed whoever had forgotten it would be back. I was so busy after that, preparing for the party and then having it, I forgot the phone was here."

Grady pressed the speaker button on his cell phone and made a call.

The four of us were silent with anticipation.

The phone from Aunt Fran's locker began to ring.

"You have reached Dudley Dunfree," the voice recording stated. "Please leave a brief message and I'll return your call."

My stomach sank and my head lightened. There must've been too much noise for it to be heard from the party before. Standing in the quiet stockroom, my ears began to ring.

Grady turned regretful eyes on Aunt Fran. "You found it, so I'm guessing your prints are on it?"

She covered her mouth with both hands and nodded.

He shot me a pointed look, then turned his full attention back to Aunt Fran. "I'm afraid I'm going to have to ask you to come with me to the station."

"No!" I yelled, throwing my arms wide and jumping between them. "That phone was obviously planted here by someone who knew Blessed Bee was hosting part of the Holiday Shuffle. They wanted it to be found in her possession."

"Everly," Grady warned. "Don't."

"How can I not?" I pleaded. "She didn't hurt Mayor Dunfree, and you know it."

Pain flickered in his eyes. “Fran? Shall we.”

My vision blurred with unshed tears. “Don’t go,” I told her. “Please.”

Aunt Fran kissed my cheek, then stepped around me. “It’s fine. I’ll go.”

“No!” I tried again, but she moved to Grady’s side. “He would take anyone else in at this point, and I can’t be given special treatment or the town will get the wrong idea. They’re still giving me the benefit of the doubt, and I don’t want to take advantage of that.”

My head swam. I chased them through the store and clutched Grady’s arm. “The phone is going to help her, right?” I asked. “Tech services will find something on it to clear her name so you can release her.”

Grady didn’t answer.

“You’ll know who Mayor Dunfree was heard arguing with that night,” I said. “You’ll know who’d been calling him. Everyone he’d been in contact with. You can listen to the messages and see if there are any angry ones. Maybe someone was harassing him. Maybe that crazy neighbor, or Mary Grace, or Chairman Vanders had been giving him trouble.” I sucked in a ragged desperate breath and tightened my grip on Grady’s arm. “What about the widow? Why’s she in such a rush to arrest Aunt Fran? There could be a big insurance policy, or maybe they had a nasty lover’s quarrel.”

Grady stopped moving. “Give us a minute?” he asked Aunt Fran.

She stepped away to hug her sister and Janie.

Grady turned to me, a storm of emotion in his eyes.

"Please don't do this," I begged. "I can't lose her. It's Christmas!"

Grady's heartbroken expression sent shocks of pain through my chest. He rested his palms on my shoulders and bowed his head to mine, creating a little space just for us. "The red paint in the back matches the paint used at multiple recent crime scenes," he said quietly. "I can't ignore what's right in front of me, Everly. Not anymore. Not if I want to be respected in this town."

"Something else is going on," I said, emotion erasing the last of my composure. "I saw that same color paint inside the Dunfrees' neighbor's house too. It's just paint. Not a smoking gun. At least talk to Gene Birkhouse before you arrest Aunt Fran. *Please.*"

Grady's jaw locked and his spine stiffened. He dropped his hands from my shoulders. "Why were you inside Gene Birkhouse's place?"

I pursed my lips and squared my shoulders. "You know why."

Color spread slowly over his face, changing his expression from compassionate to a little angry. "Leave this alone. Understand? Do not test me."

I released his sleeve and crossed my arms, defiance lifting my chin.

"This thing is escalating, and I can't have you in the middle of it," he said softly. "I can't see you hurt again."

Electricity zipped and zinged through the air between us. Heat spread through my chest, crawled up my neck, and flooded my cheeks. My arms fell limply to my sides.

"Do you understand what I'm saying?" he asked softly. The protective edge in his voice was new and intense, and it softened my heart.

I nodded dumbly. The familiar tug of instinct in my gut said there was a deeper meaning to his words. It said that Grady couldn't see me hurt again because he cared about me. Not because I was a citizen he'd sworn to protect or because I was a friend he'd grown to trust. But because *he cared.* The proof was right there in the cutting edge of his voice, the rigidity of his stance, and the fire in his steely eyes. Grady cared for me.

And it knocked the breath from my lungs.

"Don't worry, Fran," Janie said as Aunt Fran moved back in our direction. "I'll get you a lawyer. You'll be out before breakfast. This is all circumstantial."

I worked to swallow the lump in my throat and regain my wits. Not easy given the circumstances. I wanted to know if I was right about Grady and his feelings for me, though it wouldn't matter if he arrested my aunt for murder. Especially given the fact he knew she was innocent.

Grady dragged his gaze from mine, then turned to escort Aunt Fran out the door.

I wished more than anything that Janie was right, but the evidence against Aunt Fran was stacking up fast. She was going to need a Christmas miracle to escape the web being woven around her. I just hoped I could summon one of those before it was too late.

CHAPTER NINETEEN

Aunt Clara, Janie, and I were left alone to process what had happened. Aunt Clara wiped her eyes with a handkerchief and sniffled. "I suppose it's time to clean this up."

I recognized the simple eyelet hankie from my childhood. Aunt Clara's initials were embroidered in one corner, a gift from her one true love. She didn't speak of him often, and I couldn't recall his name, but he'd been drafted into the Vietnam War immediately following their engagement. He hadn't returned. Another alleged casualty of the Swan curse.

"Let me help," I said, moving to her side and beginning the teardown process.

Janie swept into view, coat on and cell phone in hand. Her eyes glistened with unshed tears. "I'm going to find a lawyer."

We wished her luck, considering the hour, and I locked up behind her.

Aunt Clara and I worked in steady, companionable

silence until the shop was righted and all evidence of the soup and salad portion of the evening had been erased.

"I suppose that's that," she said threading thin arms into a long wool coat. "We've missed the main course, and I'm ready for a nice toddy and bed. Not that I'll be able to sleep."

I hugged her. "The toddy will help."

She nodded. "I'm going to call Lanita for a Pick-Me-Up. I want to go home."

I waited to see Aunt Clara off and wished Lanita a Merry Christmas, then I headed next door to Charming Reads. I needed a nightcap, and I wanted to vent my complaints to a rational listening ear. Amelia was exactly the woman for that job.

Lively holiday tunes flooded from hidden speakers inside Charming Reads. A tree dressed in tiny hardcover books and typewriter ornaments stood at the window. Amelia had arranged tables where chairs normally stood for guest speakers and the book club, then covered them with white linens, a plethora of chocolate desserts, and an army of filled champagne flutes. Mr. Butters was in a Santa costume, minus the beard, working a cocktail shaker Tom Cruise–style at a small rolling bar near the register.

I smiled, despite my horrendous evening.

Amelia spotted me from her position at the dessert buffet and hurried in my direction. The bell of her vintage red swing dress was puffed with white crinolines that swished against her knees as she walked. Her heart-shaped neckline showcased a string of perfect antique pearls, and the black patent leather pumps she was working would make a diva from any decade jealous. “I heard what happened,” she whispered, grabbing my arms and pulling me away from the crowd. “I’m so sorry I wasn’t there. This night has been crazy, and it took a lot longer than Dad and I expected to set up the buffet tables and arrange the seating.” She stroked long, side-swept blond bangs off her forehead and pierced me with sympathetic blue eyes. “What can I do?”

I gave a limp shrug. “We’ll know more in the morning.”

Amelia pursed her lips and scanned my face carefully. “I have alcohol,” she said. “Come on. This kind of stress calls for a cocktail, and Dad’s mixing peppermint martinis.”

She released me and turned for her dad. I waited, thankful to be standing on the fringe, mostly unnoticed, instead of in the midst of a crowd that was probably discussing the reason Aunt Fran was seen in the local detective’s truck after dark.

Amelia swiped a pair of completed martinis from the table where her dad worked and ferried one back to me. She sipped the other. “What do you think is going on?” she asked, tapping the little candy cane from her drink against the side of the glass. “Why does all the evidence keep pointing to your aunt?”

I sampled the drink to keep myself from shouting or crying. The martini was delicious and went down too easily. Not good, especially after the night I was having. I lowered the drink away from my mouth before I finished it and wanted more. "Aunt Fran's being framed. I don't know why."

"Finding Mayor Dunfree's body and picking up the murder weapon was probably the springboard," Amelia said. "It makes sense for the real killer to keep pushing Fran as the guilty one since there's already evidence against her."

"That's possible," I said. Why reinvent the wheel when there's a perfectly acceptable one already in motion? "I need to narrow my suspects. I've talked to everyone on my list except Mrs. Dunfree, and in my opinion they all have motive. And since the murder weapon was on my porch, they all had means. I'm just not sure if one of them is a killer. Though, the Dunfrees' neighbor had a fast temper, and the paint he's using on his fence has been at nearly every crime scene."

"You mean him?" Amelia asked, her wide eyes staring over my shoulder.

Behind me, not three feet away, Gene Birkhouse sipped a flute of champagne and glared back.

ᘐ

If there was an upside to being too upset to sleep, it was the resulting massive productivity. Thanks to my racing thoughts and anxiety-knotted stomach, I'd cut myself off after one peppermint martini and gone home to catch up on my cookie orders. From there, I'd worked on a second how-to video for my website, Classic Coconut Macaroons, and by 8:00 a.m., I was ready to call it a night.

I brought the final trays out of the oven, settled them on the stove top, then collapsed into the nearest chair. I folded my arms on the table, forming a pillow to rest my head. My eyelids drooped, and the nerve-induced nausea I'd battled all night began to fade. For the first time since Grady pulled Mayor Dunfree's cell phone from Aunt Fran's apron pocket, my mind and body were in harmony, and they were ready for sleep.

Something beeped, and I nearly swallowed my tongue leaping from the chair. "What!" I yelled into the quiet room, looking from the foyer to the stove, struggling to place the familiar sound through the haze of fatigue.

The beeping came again, and my gaze fell to my wrist. *Be more active.*

I blinked fast and hard at the little screen, trying to make sense of what was happening.

Be more active, the screen flashed.

My mental capacities returned like a slap in the face, along with all the terrible memories of my week. I groaned at the little rubber bracelet, then crammed my finger against its button until I thought one of the two might break.

Be more active.

"Come on," I whined, lifting my heavy legs in a

half-hearted attempt to march in place when pushing the button didn't help.

The demand vanished, apparently satisfied I was moving, and I considered throwing the bracelet into the ocean.

My laptop dinged, and I groaned. "Now what?" I asked the computer, marching behind the counter to check the screen.

There was a comment on the new video. I hesitated a moment before scrolling to read the words. Uploading the file seemed more like something that had happened in a dream than reality.

> *These look delicious! Keep the cookies coming!*
>
> —Anna Marie in Peoria, IL

Relief washed through me, releasing the tension in my shoulders, and lifting the corners of my tired mouth into a smile. I marched a little more proudly as I shut the numerous open tabs. I'd spent the time between cookie batches looking into Mayor Dunfree, hoping to uncover some useful thread of information I could pull until the case against Aunt Fran unraveled.

Unfortunately, I hadn't found any angry articles about him or evidence of current legal issues. The only new information I'd found was about a lawsuit filed against the town nearly twenty years ago. Someone had fallen from a cliff near the maritime forest and the results had been fatal. The lawsuit claimed the accident could have been avoided if proper signage had been posted. Mayor Dunfree was named in the case, and the issue had been settled out of court for an undisclosed amount of money. It didn't seem like much of a lead, especially since so much time had passed and the one filing suit had been paid off, but someone had died, so I made a mental note to ask my aunts if they remembered the case. I was in elementary school then, and had no recollection of the incident.

I grabbed a stack of flat, white rectangles and worked a dozen bakery boxes into existence. They submitted easily under my practiced hand, and I filled them with the bounty of last night's bake fest. I tied them with ribbon and scribbled a holiday message across the box tops along with the recipients' names.

I arranged the leftovers from each batch on a large glass pedestal display then covered them with a matching dome. Sugar cookies, snickerdoodles, and shortbreads were plated beside thumbprints, peanut butter cups, and pizzelles. Seashell-shaped cutouts lined the pedestal's perimeter, shimmering in pale blue and white sugar crystals.

I sent a text message to Grady asking when I could see Aunt Fran, then went out to feed Lou. I'd barely opened the deck doors when I spotted him soaring in my direction like a kite on the ocean breeze. He landed on the railing with impressive grace, wings outstretched and obviously showing off.

I smiled, a little jealous of his utter freedom and

apparent imperviousness to the cold, until a patch of red along the tip of one wing caught my eye. I moved toward him slowly, teeth chattering from the frigid air and quick shot of adrenaline. I knew that shade of red. I'd seen it on a dozen threat gnomes and scrawled in big messy letters across Chairman Vanders's Jeep.

"Lou?" I asked, setting the tray of shrimp and fish on the snow-covered rail at his side. "You've got a little something on your wing."

He hopped closer, keeping one beady black eye on me as I angled for a better look at the bright red smudges.

"May I have a look?" I asked, wrapping one arm around my middle for warmth and gesturing at the wing in question with the opposite hand.

Lou cocked his head and outstretched the wing without missing a beat on the shrimp. It was as if he'd understood, but that was impossible. Anthropomorphic and silly. Wasn't it?

I pushed the thoughts aside and refocused on the red marks. *How had they gotten there? And how long ago? Was the paint dry?* I suppressed the urge to reach out and check. Lou was a meticulous feather cleaner. I couldn't imagine him allowing the mess to stay. *Unless he'd wanted me to see.* I shook my head hard, trying to dislodge the nutty notion. "What have you been up to?" I whispered.

Lou craned his head, gave me a pointed birdy stare, then flung himself into the sky.

I collected the empty tray and scurried back inside.

My phone buzzed with a response from Grady, and my heart grew light. I could visit Aunt Fran anytime.

Immediately seemed perfect.

I called Aunt Clara to let her know I'd be there to pick her up soon, then I marched upstairs to get ready for my day. I called Lanita for a Pick-Me-Up and decided to reserve her services for the entire morning. There was no reason to brave the cold in Blue when I could ride in a new model SUV with a proper heater and radio. I'd deliver the cookie orders after seeing Aunt Fran.

I'd bundled up for the day in soft jeans, Sherpa-lined ankle boots, and a cable-knit sweater I'd owned for years. The sweater used to be bigger, but it still worked for warmth. I made a harrowing trip down the icy front steps to visit the mailbox, then tossed half a bag of ice melt on my porch and walkway while I waited for my ride.

Lanita hugged me when she arrived. "I heard about what happened to your great-aunt," she said. "My aunt and uncle are a mess over it, and all their friends are arguing over whether or not your Aunt Fran could really have done it. Her ride to the police station was a hot topic during all eleven of my Pick-Me-Ups last night."

She loaded my bags of delivery boxes into her front seat while I struggled to process what she'd said and formulate a response. I'd hoped that the progressive dinner and general merriment of the evening had distracted folks from Aunt Fran's predicament, at least a little.

Lanita opened the back door of her SUV for me. "Ready?"

I climbed numbly inside. "Yeah, thanks."

Lanita pointed us in the direction of my aunts' home and we trundled down Ocean Drive.

"What were people saying about Aunt Fran last night?" I asked.

"Different things," Lanita said. "I heard she confessed, but most people think it was under duress."

"She didn't confess," I said. "There's nothing to confess."

Lanita cast a remorseful smile over her shoulder as she settled the silver SUV into my aunts' driveway. "Sorry. That's just what folks were saying."

"It's okay," I said. "I asked."

I opened my door and climbed out. "I'll get Aunt Clara."

Lanita joined me. "I always greet my clients at the door," she said. "I'm more personal than a taxi. Cheaper than a town car. More practical than a limo."

The scarlet red door sucked open, and the wreath of greenery and holly berries rocked wildly on its hook.

"Ready!" Aunt Clara called. She buzzed past us to the car. "Let's go. I don't want to waste a single minute of whatever amount of time Fran's allowed." A massive overnight bag bounced against her backside, and she gripped a set of pot holders to a steaming slow cooker in her hands.

Lanita scrambled after her, and I took up the rear,

engulfed in a salty ham and cheddar scented cloud. Lanita opened the SUV's back door and waited while Aunt Clara set the slow cooker on the floor. She tossed her bag inside and climbed in after it. Lanita shut the door.

I climbed in on the other side of Aunt Clara and buckled up. "What's in the cooker?"

Lanita made notations of our pickups in the notebook she kept in her console, checked her mirrors, then backed out of the drive. "Smells delicious."

"It is," Aunt Clara assured her. "This is Fran's favorite breakfast casserole. I made it for her to share with the officers and any cell mates she might have. I brought plates, forks, and napkins in the bag, along with her necessities. Pajamas, a few changes of clothes, books, toiletries, cards for solitaire, and a portable DVD player."

It took a minute for me to decide where to start. "You still have a portable DVD player?" I asked. "I didn't know they made those anymore."

Aunt Clara made a sour face. "You know Fran loves her movies, so I packed all of those too."

"I don't think she can have any of that stuff in jail," I said. "Have you talked to Grady?"

"Was she arrested?" Lanita asked.

I jumped, having nearly forgotten she was there. "No. I think she's being held for questioning." At least I hoped that was the plan. "The police can keep her for up to seventy-two hours before making an arrest. The idea is to build a case while they have a suspect in custody, but I plan to have enough evidence to prove her innocence before then."

Aunt Clara gripped my hand on the seat between us. "Thank you."

I squeezed back.

"I heard you're pretty good at stuff like that," Lanita said, navigating the island with proficiency. "My aunt and uncle think it's amazing."

A fist pushed into my core as vivid memories of being abducted and nearly killed came rushing to the surface. "I think it's pretty amazing how well you get around Charm for someone who just got here," I said, truly impressed and hoping to change the subject.

Lanita smiled. "I've been doing a lot of Pick-Me-Ups this week, plus it's not my first trip to the island. I came here a bunch of times with my folks as a kid."

"You did?" I supposed that made sense. Her aunt and uncle lived here. I struggled to remember seeing her before, but didn't think I had. Lanita was younger enough than me that I wouldn't have paid any attention to her if I'd seen her when I lived here before, and she wouldn't look the same after all these years.

"Every other year for a week," she said. "Until middle school when my parents got divorced. I've only been here twice since then, but my aunt taught me to drive here. My mom was so mad when she found out. I was only fifteen."

I laughed. "It's a great place to learn. Low traffic. Safe roads."

"Do you have any suspects?" Lanita asked, switching the subject back to me.

"A few, but none are really panning out," I admitted. It would've thrilled my inner child to see Mary Grace behind bars, but she was being groomed for Dunfree's job. She didn't make sense as the killer. And Vanders wasn't even in the running for mayor before Dunfree died. He hadn't seemed to know he wanted the position until he'd gotten it. I wasn't sure what other motive Vanders could've had for killing his predecessor, but becoming mayor didn't seem like it. Which left me with Gene Birkhouse, the fence-obsessed neighbor who'd turned up twice last night, just before and just after Aunt Fran being taken into custody. Gene's quick temper and long-standing grudge against Dunfree made me suspicious and queasy in familiar and frightening ways. He believed the mayor had shorted his beloved poodle on her chance at a full and vibrant life. Mrs. Dunfree might've been the one making reports with the police, but it was the former mayor that Gene had called out in our talk. "I need some real evidence to back my gut."

Lanita pulled into the lot outside the police department. "If I hear anything, I'll let you know. People sit back there and seem to forget they aren't alone."

I'd experienced that myself.

"Thanks," I said. "I'd appreciate it."

Aunt Clara handed Lanita some cash between the seats. "Thank you, dear. You did a lovely job."

"My pleasure," Lanita said, accepting the money with a smile, then making a notation in her book.

"Help yourself to the cookies in the box with the teal ribbon," I told her. "I made those for you, and I'm not sure how long Aunt Fran can have visitors. I'm guessing not long. If you get bored or cold, the nature center is fun."

Lanita smiled at the nature center through her windshield. "You're not joking," she said. "There's a cowboy in there who could change a girl's life."

I cast a wayward look at Wyatt's shiny blue pickup in the lot. "Don't I know it," I mumbled, then opened my door and climbed out.

CHAPTER TWENTY

"You know," Aunt Clara said, nearly running to the station door. "During my meeting with the local historians last month, I learned that Mayor Dunfree had an appointment scheduled with the people who grant historic town status. He's been looking into it for ages, but there are so many details and specifics involved that it always wound up on the back burner. The historians were thrilled. It's the first time Charm has gotten far enough along in the process to have a committee come out for evaluation. It's a very big deal. I hope Chairman Vanders will keep the appointment. Historic status comes with financial perks. Grants to restore and upkeep qualifying properties, plaques to identify them, and Charm's name will go on the national register."

"That's interesting," I said, rushing around her to haul open the door. "I wonder if that meeting was the reason he'd been so adamant about his neighbor's fence size and construction?"

"Probably," Aunt Clara said. "The application and acceptance process can take quite a while, and keeping a whole town of citizens, residents, and businesses in line with historic expectations is a full-time endeavor. Plus, he still had his responsibilities as mayor to keep up with."

A uniformed officer met us in the lobby. "Come on in, Ms. Swan." He greeted Aunt Clara with a smile, then nodded at me. "Everly."

I squinted at the guy for a long moment before I placed him as Brayden Castle, a kid I went to high school with. Brayden had been an upperclassman who didn't know I was alive back then. Now, he was a cop, and I was frequently entangled in murder investigations, so he recognized me on sight and not the other way around. Guess I showed him.

I lifted my fingers in a hip-high wave.

"They're waiting for you in the back," he said. "Here. Let me help." He lifted Aunt Clara's big bag off my shoulder and hooked it on his, then took the slow cooker from her hands and strode away.

We hurried along in his wake.

"Who is 'they'?" I whispered to Aunt Clara as we scuttled down the hall.

"Everyone," Brayden answered from several yards ahead.

"Nothing wrong with his hearing," I muttered, earning a smile from Aunt Clara.

"Nothing at all," he agreed, then shot a wide smile over his shoulder.

Good thing I hadn't commented on the fit of his pants.

Brayden turned through an open doorway with lots of jovial conversations flowing out.

I stopped to gawk upon arrival. Four officers sat around a table with Aunt Fran and a deck of cards. Grady leaned against the wall behind them, sipping a cup of what I assumed was coffee and smiling at his view of Fran's hand.

Aunt Clara ran for her sister.

The cards went facedown when the officers got a whiff of the cheddar, eggs, and ham. Brayden set the slow cooker on the break room countertop and plugged it in. Chairs scraped over the linoleum floor as the other lawmen jumped to their feet.

I hugged Aunt Fran when Aunt Clara finally released her. "How are you? Why aren't you in a cell?" I checked her over head to toe. "What are you wearing?"

She looked down at her baggy black sweatpants and hooded sweatshirt with *CHARM PD* in a large, white font. "Grady brought them to me before bed. I didn't have any pajamas, and it's not as if I could sleep in my holiday dress."

I raised my eyes to Grady and mouthed the words *thank you*.

He lifted his cup slightly in return.

"I'm fine," Aunt Fran continued. "I wasn't arrested, and Detective Hays let me sleep on a cot in the empty office beside his. We played cards and listened to oldies music until I was sleepy enough to doze off. Then, I slept until almost eight!" Her eyes were wide with amusement. "I haven't slept past five-thirty since the Kennedy administration. I might have to come here more often."

"Don't say that," I said. "I didn't sleep at all I was so worried about you."

She patted my cheek. "Your Detective Hays took good care of me."

I swung my gaze back to Grady, suddenly overwhelmed with appreciation.

He shrugged.

"There's an attorney coming over from the mainland," Aunt Fran said. "Janie called a firm with more names than I can remember, and they're sending an associate. She told me not to talk to these guys until the attorney gets here, but I like to play cards."

Brayden laughed. "She's crushing them," he said. "It's not much of a game."

Grady peeled himself off the wall. "I'll assure Janie they only talked cards," he said.

I bristled nonsensically. "You're planning to talk to Janie?"

He dipped his chin and eyed me carefully. "She's called a couple of times to ask me about Fran, and she'll be here with the attorney later."

"Oh." I forced a tight smile. "That's nice." I briefly considered staying to see the attorney too, but there were other things I needed to get done today, and I was down to half a lemon cake in my private sweets stash. That wasn't nearly enough sugar to get me through the trauma of watching Janie flirt with Grady in person.

Grady patted Fran's shoulder as he passed. "She's not talking about the case, but she's definitely having a good luck streak. I hung around to see if she was cheating," he teased.

Aunt Fran did an exaggerated eye roll. "I beat you last night because you weren't paying attention. I beat them because they aren't any good."

The officers returned to the table, their plates and mouths full of melted cheddar, ham, and eggs. They didn't seem to mind the insult.

Grady moved closer to my side. "How long can you stay?"

I gave my giddy aunts a look. They held hands on the table as if they'd been parted for years instead of overnight. "I'd planned to stay an hour, or as long as you'd let me, but it doesn't look like Aunt Fran needs me, and her attorney is coming, so I should probably get going. I've got some cookie deliveries to make. Lanita's waiting outside."

"I'll walk you out," he said.

I hugged my aunts goodbye. Aunt Fran assured me that Janie would drop Aunt Clara off at Blessed Bee after the attorney left. Aunt Clara promised to call me with details from the meeting. Grady set a palm on the small of my back and escorted me to my ride.

Lanita dropped me off at Sun, Sand, and Tea an hour later. With her help, I'd made all the deliveries in half the time it would've taken me in Blue, plus there were no icicles hanging from my nose and my fingers weren't blue.

I flipped the window sign to *C'mon in Y'all!* and went to await the customers.

I started when I heard Aunt Clara call my name. My eyes blinked rapidly as I peeled my cheek off the table where I'd accidently fallen asleep in the silence. I wiped drool from the corners of my mouth and waited while the world came into focus. "Hello?"

Aunt Clara peeked her head around the corner. "I have a surprise for you," she sang.

"Is it a pony?" I croaked.

"Better." She stepped into the café and flung her arms out. "Ta-da!"

Aunt Fran danced into sight, smile wide and arms swinging overhead. "I'm free. I'm free. I'm free-free-free!"

Joy shot me onto my feet, and I ran to scoop her into a hug. "Oh my goodness! How are you here?" Had Grady found evidence to prove her innocence while I'd been out delivering cookies and napping in my café?

Janie slipped into view from behind them. She did a shy wave. "The attorney was as good as he claimed," she said. "It took him less than ten minutes to set this PD straight."

Aunt Fran ran a palm up and down Janie's back.

"The next time they haul me in, they'll have to arrest me," she said, "but the attorney seemed confident that wouldn't happen. Not without more to go on."

My stomach dropped. That was the problem, wasn't it? Someone was throwing chum into the waters, and the police were eagerly taking the bait. Who knew how soon the next falsified or planted evidence would show up?

Janie tipped her head against Aunt Fran's shoulder. "In other good news, I think your aunt has come to her senses and decided to stay in the running for mayor," she said. "It's wonderful. Charm wants a new, fresh approach to island politics, and Fran Swan is the woman for the job." She pulled Aunt Fran tight against her side and laughed. "She can hardly say no now. Look at what happened the last time she thought of dropping out."

Aunt Fran rolled her eyes. "I hardly think the two are related, but I did have time to contemplate things while I was in jail, and I believe I could do nice things for this town if it let me."

Janie smiled. "Tell us about it."

Fran nodded and began to pace. "I could be the voice of the people during council meetings, shutting down otherwise unanimous votes to keep things as they are for no other reason than continuity. Sometimes change is good, and we need to start thinking about how a few targeted changes would help our town."

Aunt Clara watched her sister with clear admiration. "What sort of changes?"

Aunt Fran stopped to face her. "Specifically, our perception and response to tourism, local arts, and the wildlife population. Money from summer tourism feeds many of our local families for the entire year. We treat the summer influx as a hassle, but it helps our citizens live better lives. Not to mention, it could lead to new residents. Adding fresh Charmers to the population would mean gaining new and diversified talents for our community. Also, I want to see our summer arts festival marketed widely and aggressively. It's the coolest thing that happens in any Outer Banks town, and we hold onto it like it's a secret. Plus, we treat our artists as if there's only one week a year when they can be bold about their art. That's bubkes! We're an artistic community. There should be art everywhere. Murals on municipal buildings, sculptures on the square. We should be proud. We need to showcase our talents and develop a fund to encourage the arts in our education system. Don't even get me started on our beautiful maritime forest and abundant wildlife populations. We're so busy keeping everyone away from our wild mustangs, we're missing major opportunities to nurture their community and grow their numbers. Wyatt's got a great plan for both, and I think he can do it with some support, but that would mean changing the way we perceive and respond to the horses too. Right now, no one in the position to permit change will." She saddened at that.

I beamed. "You're going to be an amazing mayor."

No one cared more about our island and every member of its communities—human, animal, or otherwise.

Janie climbed onto a high chair at a tall bistro table near the deck and crossed long, thin legs at the knee. "I agree. I think we should find a way to reach out to the CFC and organize a rally or something. Get people excited about your campaign again."

Aunt Clara made a *T* with her hands, like a referee at a sports game. "The CFC vandalized Chairman Vanders's Jeep. Fran should distance her name from a renegade group like that."

Fran joined Janie at the table. "Clara's right. I plan to base my campaign on change, but that group seems like a set of loose cannons."

Janie nodded. "I can see that. I guess we don't need them for exposure." A coy smile budded on her lips. "At least my BMW's still dressed for the job."

The chimes and jingle bells over my door rang, and I headed back across the room to welcome my guest. "Merry Christmas," I called, "Welcome to Sun, Sand, and—" I stopped short.

Wyatt sauntered into view, cowboy hat in hands, broad smile on his lips. "Don't stop on my account," he said. "I enjoy a formal greeting."

I smiled. "I know you do." I filled a jar with ice and Old-Fashioned Sweet Tea, then handed it to him.

He put his hat on the counter between us, winked at me, then tucked a stool beneath him. "You remembered."

I shook my head, hoping to look annoyed, despite

the blooming smile. "You were just here this week," I said. "Don't read too much into it."

A trio of men entered behind him. They scanned the area, then joined Wyatt at the counter, exchanging nods and words of greeting. The men ranged in age from early twenties to retirement, and they wore matching nature center polos.

Wyatt grinned. "I told the guys this was the place to go for homemade lunches, so they agreed to give it a try."

I set straws and napkins in front of each man. "Merry Christmas and welcome to Sun, Sand, and Tea." I smiled at their genuine expressions as they took in the café décor and giant chalkboard menu mounted on the wall behind me. "I'm Everly Swan. I keep twenty flavors of iced tea on tap, and you're welcome to sample anything you'd like."

The oldest man settled a pair of glasses on the end of his nose and peered at the chalkboard. "That's amazing. I didn't know there were twenty flavors of iced tea."

"There are more." I grabbed a stack of juice glasses and began tapping the containers one by one. "I can only manage twenty at a time. How about a few samples?" I lined the filled glasses before them and refreshed my smile. "You can do the same with the menu, if you'd rather try a little of everything than a full serving of just one thing. Or I'd be happy to fix you up a full serving of everything." I raised my palms in surrender. "No judgment here. It's all delicious."

Wyatt leaned on his forearms, hands clasped. "Got any more of that homemade chicken noodle soup back there? We've been tracking wild mustangs all morning and could use a little something to warm us up."

"You and your chicken noodle obsession," I teased. I turned to Wyatt's cohorts. "Does that sound good to everyone?"

The men nodded. No bells and whistles for them.

"Homemade soup, bread, and cookies. Coming up." I took orders for their choice of iced tea when the samples were gone, then grabbed a container of soup from the freezer and a pot to heat it in. I sliced a few fresh loaves of bread while the men chatted.

I set a warm, yeasty loaf in front of them, then took a second loaf to my aunts and Janie.

"Everything okay?" I asked, delivering a tray with glasses and a pitcher of tea onto the table's center. I set the tray of fresh bread beside the first.

The women dug in.

"I'll be back with soup in a few minutes," I said. "Wyatt and his crew over there just made the request, and I have enough on the stove to feed ten."

Aunt Fran smiled around a mouthful of bread.

I laughed. "Be right back."

Wyatt watched me return. His gaze drifted over my shoulder from time to time.

"What?" I asked, checking behind me as I arrived at the counter.

My aunts and Janie were leaning toward one

another, filling up on bread and tea. Janie glanced our way, then pulled her eyes and smile back to my aunts.

Wyatt tugged his bottom lip. "I swear I know her from somewhere."

"Here we go again," I said. "You know her from here. She's lived in Charm a few months now."

He scratched the back of his head and frowned. "Nah. That's not it."

I left him to ponder while I ladled hot soup into bowls. By the time I'd served everyone and pulled a chair up to my aunts' table for a little lunch of my own, the wind chimes sounded.

I hung my head in defeat. I could always reheat it.

"Welcome to Sun, Sand, and Tea," I said, turning to face the door.

Mary Grace glared at me from the threshold. "I need more cookies."

"Super." I made my way to the counter and grabbed an order form. "What would you like and when would you like it?"

"I want an impressive spread of your best sweets delivered to the mayor's office first thing tomorrow. There's a committee coming in to discuss the possibility of Charm as an historic community."

I dared a glance at Aunt Clara who'd told me as much this morning, though she hadn't known when the meeting would happen. I was surprised it was slated to happen so soon following Dunfree's death. Another coincidence? Or was the timing significant?

"I want to impress these people," Mary Grace said.

"If I can get this done for the town, I'm a shoo-in for mayor. I might even be able to force an immediate election given the circumstances."

I poised a pen over the order pad. "How thoughtful and selfless of you."

"Now, just a minute," Aunt Fran said, already headed our way. "What's this about a meeting and why didn't I know?"

Mary Grace scoffed at her. "Gee. Maybe because you were in jail when I spoke with the council this morning. I knew this was on his books, so I reached out and they were willing to come." She shot a smug smile around the room, making sure everyone present had heard the wonderful thing she'd done.

Aunt Fran's olive skin went scarlet, then eggplant.

Aunt Clara hurried over to mediate. "That's lovely," she said. "And now that Fran has been released, she'll be able to attend the meeting. Isn't that nice, Fran?"

Aunt Fran's left eye twitched.

"Whatever," Mary Grace said. "Just make the cookies and charge them to the town. Put them on Vanders's account or whatever you do for things like this."

I stared at her. I had no idea how to charge the town for anything, or if that was even a possibility. "The town doesn't have a tab here," I said. "No one does. If you want to place an order, someone has to pay."

"Then charge them to Vanders," Mary Grace said. "He's the standing mayor. For now."

I shook my head. "I can't charge him without his permission."

Her jaw swung open. "This is ridiculous. What kind of operation are you running here?"

"One where I don't work for free," I said.

Wyatt snorted. The men seated at the counter with him all looked away.

Mary Grace stiffened. "Fine. Charge me." She slapped a Visa on the counter.

"Glad to help out," I said, scribbling the order and presenting it for her to sign.

She gave the bottom line a dirty look but signed. "I'll have Lanita pick them up and deliver them to the meeting in the morning." She returned the Visa to her wallet and gave Aunt Fran a sideways look. "The meeting starts at ten. Try not to get arrested again before then."

"I wasn't arrested," Fran snapped.

It was too late. Mary Grace had already pushed her phone to her ear and started out the door.

My aunts headed back to their table. Aunt Fran grumbled about the meeting to make Charm an historic town. Too many rules and regulations.

I followed on their heels. "Speaking of history," I said, retaking the seat at my bowl of tepid soup. "I saw Mayor Dunfree's name in a lawsuit from about twenty years ago. A teen fell from a cliff at the bluffs. Do you remember that?"

Aunt Clara looked sad. "I do," she said softly. "It was awful."

Aunt Fran nodded, sobered by the memory.

Janie watched them, appearing equally horrified and waiting for details.

Aunt Fran rolled a napkin between her fingertips. "I believe that was actually when the idea of pursuing historic town status first came up."

"Why?" I asked, unable to make the connection.

Aunt Fran shifted on her seat. "The attorney in that case suggested historic status would help justify the absence of signs near the cliffs. Even if Charm was only beginning to pursue the option, it would have explained the lack of warnings. Though, a fence might've been required to make it right. I can't honestly recall."

"There were rumors," Aunt Clara said. "People said Dunfree blamed himself for what happened to that boy."

Aunt Fran shook her head, a look of regret in her dark eyes. "None of us ever gave the cliffs a second thought before that. We'd all been warned away as children. As adults, we cautioned others, but folks rarely venture out that way, and we don't get many tourists," she told Janie.

Everything Aunt Fran said was true. Despite the teen's death, I wasn't sure how I felt about the necessity of signage at the bluffs. Anyone could easily see the drop was deadly.

Janie looked green. "I visited the bluffs this fall. There still aren't any railings or fences to keep people away from the edge."

"True," Aunt Fran said. "Though we added a hand-carved sign at the trailhead and one along the roadside warning folks to explore with caution. We thought that had been enough until last fall."

I covered my mouth as a memory rushed to mind. "The birder," I said. Of course! I turned to Janie, knowing she hadn't been in town for the near-tragedy, and the explanation would help pull a few more pieces of our puzzle together. "Charm gets a lot of birders in the fall when our maritime forest draws various species to the area. Birders follow, hoping to catch a glimpse of a rare species or one that's new to them. A woman was out bird-watching and wanted to get a photo without scaring the bird away. She later admitted that she was paying more attention to the shot than her footing, and she fell. Thankfully, she was several yards away from the peak, putting her only about fifteen feet above the beach at high tide. She survived with minor injuries and a major scare, but it was all people talked about for weeks. If she'd been up a little higher or fallen at low tide, she could have died." I released a huff of air, suddenly understanding why her fall had caused such a commotion in the community. "Most folks probably remembered the death of the teen years before, and the injured birder brought those old feelings back to the surface."

Aunt Fran nodded. "Dunfree never stopped talking about getting historic status for Charm, but I'm sure that fallen birder was the catalyst for his recent renewed interest."

"Guilt is a powerful motivator," Janie agreed.

Aunt Clara looked heartbroken. "Well, he must've finally gotten his act together if the committee was willing to come tomorrow."

"I wonder what changed?" I asked.

Gene Birkhouse's six-foot privacy fence came to mind.

CHAPTER TWENTY-ONE

I rubbed fatigue from my eyes and removed the next quilted tea bag from my advent calendar. Four days until Christmas. I frowned. Aunt Fran was out of police custody, for now, but a killer was still at large.

I sent Grady a text to see if he felt like breakfast, and received an affirmative reply less than a minute later.

I warmed at the instant response, then looked around for some way to stay busy until he arrived. Snow floated outside the windows. Not another near white-out or the wet mush that had been coming lately, but big fluffy flakes that I wanted to twirl in.

I shrugged into a heavy coat, stuffed my feet into boots, and pulled a knitted cap over my hair. I hadn't collected the mail yesterday, and that seemed like a perfectly grown-up reason to head outside. I tugged wool mittens over warm fingers and wrapped a matching scarf around my neck before whisking out into the snow.

The sun was warm and melting the ice from trees and rooftops, but an overnight burst of precipitation had dumped an additional six inches of snow on the town. It was the perfect combination. Warm sun. Lots of snow. The steady rush of the sea. I pulled in a deep breath, savoring the crisp winter scene of a postcard-perfect world. Then, I dragged my shovel off the porch to clear the snow from my walk. Aunt Fran had kicked an early morning path through the worst of it when she'd come to collect the cookies for the council meeting, but there was work yet to do. When I reached the end, I emptied the mailbox.

Grady's truck swung into view as I flipped through the post. Holiday ads, a couple of bills, and two brightly colored envelopes.

I watched as Grady headed my way in long purposeful strides. He moved like the hero in a movie, right before he swept his heroine off her feet and spun her around. I imaged the scenario with Grady and I playing the leads. Me in his arms. His smile burning bright. I'd reach for his sexy black Stetson and put it on my head when he returned me to my feet. White flakes would fall around us like the untouchable contents of a snow globe, but we wouldn't notice. We'd have one another to keep us warm.

"It's freezing," Grady said, shoving both hands into his front pockets. "Why are you just standing out here?"

I blinked. "I was waiting for you," I said, reluctantly returning to reality. "I saw you pull up. I was also getting the mail. And shoveling." I extended both hands, the shovel and envelopes backing up my story. "Coffee?"

"Yes. Thank you." He relieved me of the shovel, smiled, then set his palm against my back as we walked to the door. Tingles danced up and down my spine. When he'd made the same move at the police station, I'd dismissed it as a fluke. Twice in two days, however, was no accident. I hoped he might even make it a habit.

Grady released me to turn the knob and push my front door open. "After you."

He left the shovel on the porch, and I dropped my mail on the counter.

I poured two cups of coffee, then whipped up some pancake batter with a generous amount of blueberries. "How's the investigation going?" I asked. "Any idea who sent me the glitter bomb or vandalized Chairman Vanders's Jeep? Have you gotten any new evidence from Mayor Dunfree's phone?" Surely that had turned up something.

Grady worked his jaw. "It's coming together," he said. "These things always do. One piece at a time."

"What kind of pieces?" I asked, ladling batter onto a skillet. The familiar sizzle and rising scent of melting butter raised the hairs on my arms. Thrilling every time.

Grady sipped his coffee, watching me. Probably choosing his words and preparing to deflect me. "We're going through surveillance footage from the post office on the day the letter was stamped. There were dozens of people in and out that day, but it creates a list I can use to compare and contrast."

"Okay," I said slowly. "Have you seen anyone on the footage who's also on your list of possible suspects?" If so, was that person on my list too?

"I'm working on it," he said.

I huffed, flipped the pancake, then struck a hands-on-hips pose. "Are you being unintentionally coy, or are you refusing to talk to me about this?"

"I'm politely avoiding a conversation we shouldn't be having," he said. "Details of an ongoing investigation are private, and for the record, I'm never coy."

I narrowed my eyes. "It's not as if I'm going to leak the details to the press. We're just having a casual conversation."

He wrapped his long fingers around the mug and laughed. "You might be all T-shirts and ponytails on the surface, but there is nothing casual about you, Everly Swan." His cool gray eyes glimmered, and I lost my train of thought. "Plus, you have a way of getting involved in my work that makes me crazy."

Spell broken.

I plated the first pancake and poured more batter into the skillet. "Here." I set the plate before him and delivered a mini pitcher of homemade syrup to its side. "Did you know Mayor Dunfree was named in a lawsuit against our town when I was a little girl?" I asked. Having toiled over the concept all night, the subject was still on my mind. "No one ever talks about it," which was a statement on its own, "and I still wouldn't know if I hadn't been digging online for something about Dunfree to explain his murder."

Grady had a mouth full of pancake, so I kept going.

"My aunts said the accident gave him the idea to pursue historic status for the town. I'm willing to bet getting Charm into historic-status-worthy condition was the reason he wouldn't budge on Gene Birkhouse's giant fence. A fence he'd been painting with the same shade of red someone splattered on the gnomes and used to vandalize Vanders's Jeep."

Grady forked another bite of pancake into his mouth.

"Well?" I asked, giving the second pancake a flip.

He nodded. "Delicious."

"Thank you, but that's not what I was asking." I waved my spatula at him and tried again. "Did you know about the lawsuit? What do you think about it? Could it be relevant to this case?"

Grady chewed slowly. Intentionally.

I dropped a second pancake on his plate. "A boy died. It could have been the catalyst that led to Dunfree's obsession with keeping everything in this town unchanged, all so he could make Charm an historic community. So he could justify the lack of warning signs on the cliff." I poured another round of batter into the skillet and felt my shoulders droop. "Maybe he wasn't such a horrible person after all. Maybe he was just living under a load of guilt and shame."

Grady ran a napkin over his lips and sighed. "The

boy's name was Tony Boyles. Seventeen. A senior at his local high school in Milwaukee. He was a trumpet player, a swimmer, and an Eagle Scout with a full academic scholarship to the University of Nebraska waiting for him."

I flipped the next pancake, feeling unreasonably slighted. "You knew." I waited a minute for the pancake to brown, then turned off the stove and slid my breakfast onto a plate.

He dipped his chin once in answer.

I took the seat at his side. "I wasn't able to find any of that information about him when I looked."

"It was in the accident reports," Grady said. "Commentary from his parents. Details from the obituary. It probably never made the papers outside of Charm and Milwaukee. The aftermath was rough here. Tony's dad petitioned hard for a year or two, wanting Dunfree thrown out of office. His wife brought friends and members of her church to sit vigil at the cliffs a few times, maybe trying to raise awareness, but none of it amounted to much in the way of publicity. Eventually the case settled upon the condition his parents let it go. They accepted the cash and the terms and never returned to Charm as far as I can see."

"I don't blame them," I said, suddenly losing my appetite. I pulled the mail across the counter in my direction and selected the holiday cards. Both had local return addresses. I ran a fingertip under the first flap.

"Who's that from?" Grady asked.

I unsheathed the card and opened it for a read. "It's from the Realtor who sold me the house." I smiled, then set it up to admire and opened the second envelope.

A photo of my face drifted onto the counter, surrounded in red glitter, both eyes gouged through with something sharp and wide. Festive font on the back stated simply:

I didn't want to have to hurt you,
but you were warned.

~

I climbed gratefully into Grady's truck. I didn't want to be alone, so I packed my big quilted tote with some supplies and the giant peppermint stick. Grady said he'd take me to my aunts' after the police station. Maybe Aunt Clara would be in the mood to make the cocoa jars she'd mentioned.

My teeth chattered from fear and excess adrenaline as we made our way to the police station.

Grady reached across the space between us and ran his palm up and down my arm, then squeezed my elbow before returning his hand to the wheel. Two blocks later, he wheeled into the parking lot outside the police station and settled the engine.

I unbuckled my seat belt, and Grady's gaze shifted past me to my window a second before someone rapped on the glass at my ear.

"Jeez!" I yipped, spinning to find Wyatt. I climbed out, unsure what else to do. "You scared me."

"Sorry." He smiled. "Hope I wasn't interrupting anything."

Grady moved around the front of his truck. "No, you didn't."

Wyatt winked at Grady, then pulled a card from his inside coat pocket and handed it to me. "I know how much you love getting cards. I'd planned to bring it by your place later, but since you showed up at my work, I figured. Fate."

I cast a look at the nature center standing proudly beside the Charm police department.

"Couldn't wait to see me again?" he guessed.

I laughed. If only something as trivial as a crush had brought me back to the police station this week.

Grady extended a hand to Wyatt in greeting.

The men shook while I opened the card.

Wyatt had turned an old photograph of the two of us at a rodeo into a holiday card. A string of sketched colored lights acted as a border. We looked young and happy. I was seated on the top rung of a metal gate inside the arena, and Wyatt's arm hung protectively over my shoulders. I looked as if I'd won the lottery, beaming brightly at the camera. Wyatt looked downright starstruck, but he wasn't looking at the camera. He was looking at me.

Inside, he'd written:

E,

This Christmas, I hope you'll find yourself immersed in the same unspeakable amount of joy that your love once brought me.

Forever your cowboy,
Wyatt

It was senseless, but knowing I really had meant something to him, seeing it in his words, scripted in his hand…broke my heart.

I slid my arms around his waist and hugged him. "Thank you."

He embraced me immediately, as if it was the most natural thing in the world.

I stepped back, emotionally wrecked by the day before lunch. "Merry Christmas, Wyatt," I said, through a tightening throat. "See you later."

CHAPTER TWENTY-TWO

Grady walked silently at my side until we reached the police station. "What's the story with the two of you?" he asked once we were safely inside the station.

"Complicated," I groaned. "Frustrating. Confusing."

Grady led me to his office and shoved the door open. "That's for sure."

I took a seat in the chair opposite his desk, unsure which adjective Grady had agreed with. I decided it didn't matter.

Grady dropped the baggie of glitter and my ruined photo onto his desk and pushed a pad of paper in my direction.

"I know the drill," I said, pulling the items to me. "Write an account of the event in my words. Sign and date it."

"Right." Grady took a seat at his desk and unearthed a bottle of antacids from his drawer. He shook a few into his palm, then tossed them back and chewed.

"How are things with your mother-in-law?" I asked, distracting myself as I explained how a second threat had arrived at my door dressed as a holiday card.

"Great," he said, not sounding as if he thought anything was great at the moment. "Olivia is insistent I help find her husband. I'm guessing that's the real reason she moved here." He rubbed his brow. "If moved is even the right word. I checked online. She hasn't put her old place on the market."

I paused the pen. "So, what's she doing?"

"Manipulating me," he said. "She claims she can't sell the other place in case her husband comes home and she's not there, but she and I both know she'd have to move a lot farther than North Carolina to stop him from finding her."

"How far?" I asked, instantly curious as to the limits of a motivated CIA operative.

"Mars?" he asked with a dry laugh. Emotion blazed in his eyes. "I'm considering her request. My agreement could mean leverage. I could get something in return. Peace, maybe."

"You'd help with conditions," I said.

He nodded. "I could help on the condition she drop the pretense of living here. It's confusing to Denver and upsetting Denise."

I turned my attention back to the paper, processing what his agreement might mean for him specifically. Would he leave Charm? How long would he be gone? I pushed the things I couldn't control from my head and focused on what I could. I scribbled the remaining details of opening a second threat letter, then returned the paper to him.

I tried desperately not to imagine what kind of horror might come next.

"Hays!" A voice called from outside the office door.

A heartbeat later, Brayden arrived. "You've got to go."

The urgency in his voice set us both on our feet.

Grady rounded the desk and reached for me in three fluid strides. "What's wrong?" he asked, moving through the door behind Brayden with me in tow.

"There was an attack on town hall," Brayden explained over his shoulder. "A fire. The council's in a meeting upstairs, and some of them are trapped."

My stomach lurched, and my feet faltered.

Aunt Fran was at that meeting.

~

I held on tight as Grady's truck roared out of the police station lot and tore down Bay View to the town hall. Fire and rescue was already there, and the wail of an ambulance cried out behind us.

My mind screamed with things I didn't dare say.

What if Aunt Fran was hurt? *Or worse.*

And what if it was my fault?

What if I'd pushed Dunfree's killer too far?

"Hey." Grady's voice was low and reassuring inside the warm truck cab, his words unhurried despite our physical speed. He brushed a tear from my cheek and cupped long fingers beneath my chin. "She's going to be okay," he said, glancing briefly to me before applying his attention back to the road. "And no matter what you're thinking, this isn't your fault. The only person responsible for this fire, and any damage or injury it causes, is the person who started it."

I nodded, wishing what he'd said was true but knowing it wasn't. Not completely.

Grady angled his truck into the space beside a cruiser and climbed down from the cab.

Local men and women had formed a loose perimeter several yards from the building, not gawking and staring, but directing traffic around the hall and relaying information between the sparse emergency personnel. Behind us, an army of trained help poured in.

Ambulances. Fire trucks. On-call EMTs in personal vehicles. More cruisers.

Dark smoke billowed from the windows on both floors of the town hall, curling like gnarled fingers into the bright winter sky.

I ran for the door. "Aunt Fran!"

Grady caught me around the waist before I reached the sidewalk. "You can't go in there."

My eyes blurred and stung with smoke and panic. "What if she doesn't get out?" What if she was one of the ones Brayden had said were trapped? The thoughts were knives on my tongue, slicing my throat and my heart.

Grady held tight to me as firefighters in full gear jogged past us. "They've got this, and I've got you."

I turned against him, clutching the fabric of his coat, desperate for some small measure of his strength.

Chaos swirled on the street around us as harried and choking men and women were escorted from the building and EMTs rushed to meet them. I held my breath as I watched the front door, praying selfishly that each new face would be Aunt Fran's, disappointed when it wasn't. My heart seized as a uniformed officer strode from the building, his face marred with soot. Maven was unconscious in his arms.

Grady's hold tightened around my waist until I thought he was the only thing keeping me upright.

I watched in horror as the officer set Maven on a gurney outside an open ambulance bay. He spoke to the EMT, but their words were muffled by the cacophony of sounds on the street and the ringing in my ears.

Grady's mouth brushed my hair. "Here she is."

My body stiffened as I dragged my gaze from Maven to the town hall's front door. Fear and anticipation turned my mushy bones to stone as I strained to see my aunt in the haze of smoke around us.

A fireman walked Aunt Fran from the building. Her face and clothes were dirty. The hems of her long skirt and bell sleeves were singed. But she was upright and moving on her own power. Overwhelming joy launched me forward.

I stopped at the open ambulance bay where the firefighter led her. I waited as the EMT helped her onto a gurney. He snapped an oxygen mask over her face and went to work assessing her condition. I flung myself at her and sobbed.

She patted my back.

The EMT unplugged a stethoscope from his ears. "Minor burns. Smoke inhalation. I'm taking her in for observation, but she's going to be okay."

Grady swung an arm overhead, drawing the attention of the officer who'd carried Maven to another ambulance. "What happened?"

The officer changed trajectory, frustration in his eyes. "Town council was gathered in an upstairs meeting room," he said, eliminating the distance between us. "Looks like someone sprayed an accelerant on the first-floor carpets and curtains, then lit it. The receptionist was locked in the supply room. She inhaled a lot of smoke yelling for help. Smoke carried through the vents. Fire spread quickly."

"Smoke detectors?" Grady asked.

A deep frown settled on the officer's face. "Smashed. There's something else." His gaze drifted over Aunt Fran's face before hardening on Grady. "Carpet burns seem to indicate the accelerant was sprayed in a pattern. Letters."

My stomach gave another hard kick. "CFC."

A stiff dip of the officer's chin confirmed it.

"Anything else?" Grady asked.

The officer lifted his hands. "That's all I know. I was patrolling when the call came in. I heard Maven pounding on the stockroom door when I arrived. I went after her, but she was out cold by the time I got the door open. Firefighters were here before we made it out. You know the rest."

Aunt Fran tugged the mask away from her mouth, thin lips quivering. "Someone blocked the conference room door," she said. Her voice was raw and gravelly. "Smoke kept coming in. Underneath the door. Through the vents. We couldn't stop it. Couldn't get out. We thought we were going to have to jump from the window."

I turned in horror to stare at the burning building. A two-story drop onto concrete sidewalks packed in snow and ice. "The fall could've killed you."

Aunt Fran put the oxygen mask back on, her red-rimmed eyes brimming with tears. And I understood. *The fall* might *have killed her. The smoke and fire absolutely would have.*

A female firefighter headed our way. "Detective Hays?"

The officer excused himself, and the firefighter reached for Grady's hand. After a shake, she handed him a piece of paper. "This was taped to the exterior of the lobby window."

Someone had scrawled *Human Safety over Historic Status* in thick red script.

Recognition dawned, and I grabbed Grady's arm. "This is about the lawsuit." My mind raced over stories of the family's protests. "Could this be Tony Boyles's father?"

Grady stared at the paper for several long beats, then raised his eyes to the burning building. The line of ambulances. Victims being treated for a failed attempt at mass murder. "Stay with Fran," he said, his attention still drifting over the smoky street. "Go to the hospital. I'll be there as soon as I can." With that, he walked away, barking orders at a group of uniformed officers gathered near the building entrance.

"Ready?" the EMT asked.

Tears rolled over Aunt Fran's sunken cheeks.

"Ready," I said.

~

The hospital waiting room was packed with neighbors, family members, and friends of the council and Maven. No one was seriously injured. They were being evaluated, treated, and released one by one.

Janie and Aunt Clara huddled in a pair of chairs near the observation rooms. They'd been at Blessed Bee when they got word of the fire, and they'd headed over when they saw the ambulances leaving the scene.

Amelia sat at my side, clutching my hand. "You can't investigate this anymore," she whispered. "You can't let one dangerous situation become the catalyst for another."

Grady walked in before I could respond. My quilted bag hung over his shoulder. I must've left it in his truck at the fire.

I hurried in his direction, and Amelia followed.

He stopped to crouch before Aunt Clara's chair,

then gripped her hands before rising to wrap her in a hug.

Aunt Clara smiled, and my heart melted a little.

"Everything going okay?" I asked, allowing my gaze to drift from her to Grady.

Janie stood and wrapped thin arms around her middle. "Someone said CFC was burned into the carpet at the town hall. That has to be some kind of silver lining. If it's true, then it should prove Fran's not associated with them. Right? I mean, she can't be the leader of a group who'd attack a building with her inside."

Grady nodded. "It should help sway public opinion."

Amelia and I moved in close, tightening the semicircle in front of Aunt Clara's chair.

"None of that matters now," I told them. "The arsonist left a note that might as well have been a signed confession. This has all been about the boy who died at the cliffs."

Aunt Clara sucked air, her eyes wide with horror. "What?"

Grady turned to face me, jaw tight. "We don't know that. Meanwhile, I want you to go home with your aunts tonight. I made arrangement to add a patrol to the street. I'll add one to the front stoop if necessary." He passed me my bag with a little smile. "You'll need this."

"Swan?" A nurse called.

Aunt Clara pushed onto her feet. "That's me," she said. "Maybe Fran can finally get out of here."

Amelia squeezed my arm, then reached for Aunt Clara. "I'll go with you. I haven't gotten to see her yet."

I waited for them to go. Questions piled in my mind. What did Grady know about the fire and Tony Boyles's dad. He was being careful about what he said in the crowded waiting room, but would he tell me later, if I asked?

Grady's phone screen lit up with a new message. He stared at it a short moment. Whatever was there caused a slight tilt to his mouth. "Gotcha," he whispered.

I leaned closer. Grainy surveillance footage of the town square caught my eye. It was time-stamped before the fire. I recognized one or two pedestrians in the distance and Lanita's silver SUV driving away.

Grady pocketed the phone, eyes dancing. "Surveillance footage from cameras outside the jewelry store show a vehicle leaving the area today that matches one that visited the post office on the day your first threat letter was mailed."

Lanita? It couldn't be. Could it? I swallowed hard, my mouth and throat suddenly parched and pasty. There was no mistaking her vehicle or the Duke University parking pass dangling from the rearview mirror. "And the license plates?" I asked. "Did they match too? Do you know who the car belongs to?"

Grady smiled. "We're running plates now. Go home and grab your things. Head over to Fran and Clara's place. I'll be there as soon as I can."

I covered my mouth, unsure if I wanted to smile or

throw up as he walked away. I wanted to call out. To tell him I knew that vehicle, but I couldn't. So, I stood silently by and watched him go. This was an arrest I didn't want to be a part of.

Janie nudged me with an elbow and a broad smile. "Come on," she said. "We can get your things and come back here to wait for Fran's discharge. Then, we'll all head to their place together. Safety in numbers and all that, right?"

"Right," I agreed half-heartedly. My instincts said I wasn't in any danger. That Lanita wouldn't hurt me. That all the silly little threats I'd received, broken garden gnomes and piles of glitter, weren't that bad. Weren't dangerous. But I followed orders. I'd get my things. Meet Grady at my aunts, then hear the story of why Lanita had done what she'd done.

Janie and I told my aunts the plan, then climbed into her BMW. "You okay?" she asked, pulling out of the busy lot.

"I will be," I said. I chewed the inside of my lip as Janie navigated the increasing traffic and falling snow. "It was Lanita's car on the footage," I said. "That makes me sad."

Janie offered a comforting glance, still being careful to keep her attention on the road. "I'm sorry."

I nodded. I was sorry too.

The late morning sky had turned a dismal gray, saturated with clouds, all dumping their contents on my town. The snow seemed gloomy instead of festive, a reflection of my sinking heart more than the weather.

Lanita knew the town inside and out. She'd been here often before. She had family here. Her mother had grown up here. Had worked for Mayor Dunfree and been treated poorly. Lanita's family despised him. Lanita had told me all those things herself, and I hadn't let them add up.

An old Garth Brooks song began to play on my phone, and I pulled it from my bag with a nostalgic smile. "Hello, Wyatt," I answered. "Aunt Fran's okay, if you're calling about the fire."

"No," he said, a sharp edge of panic in his voice.

My muscles tightened. "What's wrong?" Had something else happened? What could it be? Who had been hurt and where?

"Where are you?" he asked, the words sharp as knives.

"Headed home to grab some things," I said. "What's going on?"

My stomach clenched to the point of pain. I'd seen Wyatt tie himself to an angry bull and smile. I'd seen him wheeled into emergency surgery telling me things were going to be okay, but I'd never known him to be rattled.

"I know why I recognized that lady your aunts are always hanging with," he said. "I remember why, and I was wrong. I didn't know her."

"Okay," I said, dragging out the little word. "And?"

"I couldn't place her at first because she's so much older now," he said. His breathing was heavy through the phone, as if he'd broken into a jog.

I shot a silly look at Janie, hoping to silently communicate I had a story to tell her as soon as I got off the phone. But she didn't look my way.

She passed the turn onto Ocean Drive.

I covered the receiver with one hand. "You missed the turn," I said, thinking of how Lanita never would have. *Lanita the killer.* My brain rejected the words. *Impossible.* "You can catch the next right and backtrack," I suggested.

Janie stepped on the gas, and we fishtailed over the ice in her expensive little car before regaining traction. She blew past the next street with a menacing frown.

"What are you doing?" I yelled, gripping the dashboard to steady myself.

"Everly!" Wyatt's voice boomed through the phone's speaker at my ear. "She's that kid's sister," he said. "The guy who fell from the cliff. He wasn't alone that day. He was with his little sister. Janie Boyles."

CHAPTER TWENTY-THREE

I turned slowly to look at Janie, her thick brown waves spilling over her shoulder. She had the face of a cherub. Could she also have the heart of a killer?

Could she really be Janie *Boyles*?

My heartbeat hitched and ice shimmied down my spine as the truth of it settled in. Janie had means and motive. She had access to Aunt Fran, to the red paint, the gnomes, me. She wanted Aunt Fran in office to make a change. To toss Mayor Dunfree out. To bring justice into town for her brother.

I dragged my attention away from her before she noticed me staring and saw through my barely veiled horror. "I'm with her now," I told Wyatt as calmly as possible. "We're getting some of my things, then heading back to the hospital to pick up my aunts. I'm staying with them tonight, and Grady's going to assign us a protective detail."

Wyatt swore. "That's no good. You've got to get away from her. What if she's the killer?"

"Yes," I said. "Exactly. You should come by and see us. We're on Ocean Drive now, but we missed the turn. We'll be there soon."

Janie's arm flashed out in my direction and pain crashed through my head as it collided with the passenger side window. She tangled her fingers into my hair and gave me another hard shove for good measure. A distinct cracking sound ricocheted around my skull with the second impact.

"Everly!" Wyatt screamed, but my eyes had shut with the pain. Confusion scrambled my thoughts.

I peeled one lid open to gather my wits, and a smear of blood came into view, clinging to the window at my side. Something warm trickled slowly down my face. "Wyatt?" I asked, unclear what was happening or where he'd gone. "I'm bleeding."

I touched a cautious fingertip to the source of the pain and winced. My phone fell onto the floorboards. My finger came away dark with blood.

Janie jammed the brakes, and the car slid sideways on the empty road.

Outside there were only trees and frozen grasses followed by endless beach and sea to the horizon. We were headed for the maritime forest. Heading for the bluffs.

She leaned across my legs and snatched the cell phone away from my feet, then threw it out her window with a grunt. "I hate this unholy town," she said, jamming the shifter back into gear and tearing down the road.

My spinning head collided with the seat back and another flash of pain locked my teeth together.

The world went dark.

❧

The earth bounced and pitched beneath me. I opened my eyelids to half-mast, unsure how much time had passed or where I was. My head and neck ached, blood rushed and whooshed in my ears. My stomach revolted with every tiny movement.

Janie turned to me. Her perfect face pinched in anger. "I came here to get peace about what happened to my brother. Your Aunt Fran was supposed to help me. She was supposed to be the change this town needs!"

I closed my eyes against her scream, trying and failing to thwart the nausea. "I think you gave me a concussion."

"Poor little island princess," she taunted, "you got a headache. So what? My brother is dead!"

I lifted my hands to my ears, protecting them against her suddenly screeching voice. My stomach didn't approve of the movement, but I couldn't bring myself to care if I puked in her car. Janie had already made me bleed on her window, and had clearly lost her mind. "You wanted Aunt Fran to fix the town, but you just tried to kill her in a fire, and you framed her for murder. It doesn't make any sense."

"It wasn't my fault she stormed out of your party

at the worst possible time and found the mayor in the snow. She set herself up for speculation the minute she picked up his murder weapon with her bare hands. I've been trying to redirect suspicions to the CFC ever since, but this town never lets anything go. I made them out to be the bad guys. I made the CFC threaten Fran. What else could I do?"

I rolled my head against the seat back, eyes squinted in pain. "You planted his cell phone in her apron. You set her up."

Janie growled and pounded her palms against the steering wheel. "She was going to drop out of the campaign! I was mad. I had to teach her a lesson after everything I'd done for her. She couldn't just drop out before we got started." Her knuckles turned white as she repositioned her fingers on the wheel. "She needed a night in jail to make her reconsider the decision and choose to stay the course. Don't forget she'd still be in there if it wasn't for me. I'm the one who got her that lawyer."

"After you had her thrown in jail," I yelled. My head and gut retaliated, and I tipped forward to retch.

"My car!" she screamed. "Ugh. I am so tired of cleaning up after you people!"

I rested my forearms on my thighs and dropped my head between my knees. "You tried to burn down the building she was in."

Janie smashed her foot against the brake and the car spun out, tail end overcoming the front again and again before rocking to an abrupt stop.

I cried out in misery.

"Stop doing that!" she said. "Stop twisting things around. I wanted to prove Fran's innocence. To show the authorities that she wasn't the killer. The killer was still on the loose. I needed them to stop investigating her so she could keep working toward our goal. And I wanted the council to know their actions have consequences."

Even with a head injury, I saw the irony.

"Is that why you killed Mayor Dunfree?" I asked. "To punish him for his actions? Or inactions?" I added to cover the bases.

She didn't answer.

I lifted my head slowly until I was upright once more, my back pressed against the warm leather seat. I peered through the windshield at the barren land. We'd passed the maritime forest and stopped at a set of massive cliffs overlooking the sea. I needed to get out of the car before it started moving again. I needed to get help or at least hide until someone found me. Would someone find me?

I racked my addled mind and drudged up a faint memory of Wyatt's voice. *Wyatt called.* He knew I was with Janie, and he knew who she really was. Surely he would contact the police. Surely my aunts would realize we hadn't returned to the hospital as planned.

Janie stared into the distance. "When I confronted Mayor Dunfree about the need for warning signs at the cliffs, he said he knew who I was. He said he was sorry about what had happened to Tony." She released a sad round of laughter.

I squirmed in search of the door handle, trying not to draw her attention.

"He was sorry?" she growled. "Sorry won't bring Tony back. Sorry doesn't un-ruin my life. Sorry doesn't put signs up where they can save others. And Charm is not a historic town!" she screamed. "That's just some lame excuse for your complete lack of concern for public safety! And my true identity wasn't his to tell. I hate him!"

"So you killed him," I said, finally finding and curling my fingers around the narrow handle. "Then, today, you tried to kill twenty more people," I said. "You're mad that there weren't signs to warn your teenage brother away from an obvious cliff, so you're on a murder spree in his name."

"Shut. Up," she warned, her eyes wild with rage.

I clamped my lips together to keep from telling her everything else I wanted to say.

I was mad, my thoughts were fuzzy, and I was in excruciating pain, but Janie Boyles was on the wrong side of cuckoo. And I wanted to make sure I stayed on top of the cliffs.

She released her seat belt and flung it away from her. "I didn't want to burn the people trying to make this a historic town," she said. "I wanted to make them go out the window."

A rock of fear lodged in my throat. She'd tried to make them fall like her brother.

"This town took my brother's life, drove my parents to divorce, gave my dad severe depression, and made my mother an alcoholic. You want to know what that did to me?"

I had a pretty good idea, but I kept it to myself.

My head swam and sickness glued me to the seat. I released the door handle in favor of covering my mouth before I was sick on the floorboards again.

Janie threw her door open. A gust of icy wind whipped inside and stole my breath. When she slammed the door, I whacked the armrest in search of the power locks while I heaved.

"Hey!" she screamed, slamming a palm against my window when the door didn't open.

I pulled myself up again, desperate for my next move. I couldn't call for help. She'd thrown my phone out the window. Could I drive in my condition?

The door locks popped up, and Janie wiggled her car keys outside my window.

I hit the lock button again and swiveled on the seat in search of a weapon. If I couldn't flee, I had to fight. A red-and-white-striped miracle peeked out at me from the bag I'd settled between our seats.

Janie unlocked the door again. This time, she jerked it open before I could stop her.

I swung the giant peppermint stick at her head.

The hard candy connected with her face in a hellacious *thwack*. Shards of candy burst into the air. The formerly tight plastic wrapper ripped around the center and scattered its smashed contents across the snow outside my door.

Janie screamed and doubled over, one hand pressed against her cheek.

My stomach flopped and my vision blurred, but I slid onto my feet beside her, then I ran.

The earth slanted beneath me with every step until I fell onto my hands and knees, sinking elbow-deep in the frigid snow. Drops of crimson dotted the ground before me, dripping from the wound on my forehead.

"Stop!" Janie yelled, storming to my side. She grabbed me under one arm and pulled me onto my feet, then glared at me with one perfectly made-up eye and one horribly swollen one. "That's it. I think it's time you go the way Tony did. Maybe that will get this town's attention."

I scanned the area. To my horror, the cliffs were only a few yards away. She'd driven me to the bluffs, and I'd run straight for the edge. A hard tremor wracked my limbs.

"This is where everything changed," she said, shaking me by my arm.

I jerked free and fumbled away, careful not to get too close to the edge, now masked by tiny hills of snow.

"Tony was seventeen," Janie said. "I was eleven. He was smart and funny, the hero of my little world. We were here for our last family vacation before he started college, and I was soaking up every minute with him before he left. When I wanted to go exploring, he asked Mom and Dad for the car keys and drove me around the island." A wistful expression crept over her pale features and tears glistened in her eyes. "When we got to the cliffs, he asked me to take his picture. He did crazy poses and pretended he was going to fall." She pressed a hand to her mouth and shook her head.

"Janie," I whispered. "I'm so sorry."

"I was eleven!" she screamed. "And I watched it happen. At first, I thought he was faking, but his expression changed, and I knew." She choked back a sob. "I raced after him, but it was too late. I watched him go all the way down."

I stepped toward her, arms extended, unsure what to do or say.

Her knees buckled, and she fell into the snow. "I couldn't drive. I didn't know where we were or how to get back. I didn't want to leave him. I didn't know what to do. Eventually, I just started walking in the direction we'd come. Someone saw me and stopped." She lifted her chin to stare blindly past me, the horrific memories playing clearly over her tear-stained face. "I tried to explain what had happened and where we'd been. They found the car a mile away, and I was able to lead them from there. Tony was still down there. The tide hadn't taken him yet. He was just looking up at me. Wondering why I'd let him fall."

I crawled to her side. "That's not true. You can't think that. He wouldn't blame you. He was your big brother. He'd protect you. He wouldn't want to know you've blamed yourself for his recklessness. It was an accident."

Janie blinked long and slow, her porcelain face

regaining its wrath. "I don't blame myself. I blame this place! It's been almost twenty years, and I still dream about him every night. I see the fear on his face as he loses his balance. I watch in helplessness as he falls. Then that dead-eyed stare when he lands." She forced herself upright and yanked me up with her. "You'll see."

I cringed at the punch of pain and nausea from the sudden movement.

Janie shoved me toward the cliff's edge. "Your mayor should have done the right thing," she snarled. "He didn't and another person fell! That birder you told me about was from Pasadena. I'll bet you didn't know that. Pasadena is just twenty minutes from LA. We're practically neighbors. When I saw what happened to her on the news, I knew it was a sign. I had to come back here and make sure nothing like this ever happened again." Janie's wild eyes went feral. "I won't let you stop me."

"You don't have to do this," I pleaded, struggling to stay away from the jagged, snow-covered edge. "Aunt Fran can still help you. I can help you."

"Oh, you're going to help me," she said, giving me another push. "Maybe after one of Charm's beloved Swan women falls from this place someone will do something about it."

Her gaze suddenly jumped to something over my shoulder. Considering we were at the edge of a giant cliff, there couldn't have been anything but snow, clouds, and ghosts of her past out there. Still, her expression grew fearful and her eyes widened with shock. "No," she whispered. "It can't be. Not again."

Before I could turn to assess the sky behind me, a large shadow darkened the snow. Two wide gray wings sliced through the air only inches above our heads. I jumped away as the wings began to flap and beat at her head.

Janie stumbled, hands in the air, swearing and blocking the bird's attack.

I bumbled further on unsteady legs, begging my vision to clear, willing the unyielding pain in my head to ease so I could find a place to hide.

"Stop!" A deep tenor boomed through the silence. The distant crunch of snow drew our attention toward the place where we'd left the car. Wyatt jogged into view, palms out, arms wide. "Janie Boyles!" he called, as I nearly collapsed in the snow.

The attacking bird lifted into the air. As if responding to Wyatt's voice or accepting his intervention, the gull swept away, sailing gracefully toward the sea.

Janie frowned, fear and frustration swirled in her harried expression. She raked wildly at her hair and patted her face, as if in search of injury. "What are you doing here? Go. Away! You aren't supposed to be here!"

I turned to watch the gull as it circled overhead. It might have been the head injury, but there seemed to be something red on its wing.

Wyatt marched forward. "I had to come. I finally realized where I knew you from."

"Go away," she repeated, but the heat had slipped from her voice.

Wyatt slowed his pace and chuckled. "I'm afraid I can't do that. Everly is important to me, and it looks like you might mean her harm. I swore a long time ago I'd never let anyone hurt her," he said. "A cowboy has to keep his promise."

I lunged forward, throwing myself in Wyatt's direction. Hot tears streamed over my frozen cheeks.

Wyatt reached for me and dragged me against him in one easy motion. He kept his eyes on her as he opened a palm in retreat. "We're going to go now."

A heavy sob racked my chest. Janie was unarmed and no match for Wyatt. I was safe.

"I don't think so," she said, stalking forward, regaining herself. Her shoulders squared and her jaw set.

A large silhouette rose behind her. "Janie Boyles," Grady said, moving into clear view. "You're under arrest for the murder of Dudley Dunfree, one count of arson, the attempted murder of our entire town council, the receptionist, and a few folks from the mainland, multiple counts of vandalism, postal threats, and the abduction of Everly Swan."

Wyatt curled a familiar and protective arm around my back, then swept me off my feet with the other. "I've got you, E," he whispered, turning away from my captor as Grady snapped handcuffs onto her wrists.

I closed my eyes and gave in to the tears.

CHAPTER TWENTY-FOUR

I welcomed Christmas Eve with a mild headache and the blessed ability to move around without wanting to die. As it turned out, concussions were worse than they sounded, and two hearty rams of my head into the passenger-side window had given me a mild one. Aesthetically, things were grim. While the unattractive swelling on my head had gone down, the multi-hued pallet of a healing goose egg was sprawling and evident. My minimal makeup skills were no match for the awful greens, golds, and grays surrounding my right eye and stretching across my forehead. Plus, the skin was still tender to touch. I'd attempted to remedy the situation with bangs which I'd hastily hacked into existence around lunchtime.

The front door chimes and jingles bells had barely stopped ringing since then.

Thanks to the moment of inspiration I'd had at the Giving Tree, a steady stream of locals, neighbors, and friends had made their way to my place all afternoon.

Now, at nearly dinnertime, the countertops and work spaces at Sun, Sand, and Tea overflowed with casseroles, side dishes, and helping hands.

I was up spinning like a top through the remaining space, another Christmas miracle just four days after my abduction.

Outside, golf carts and other personal vehicles were lined up in front of the house, delivering supplies and picking up finished meals for delivery to island nursing homes, shut-ins, and any family suspected to be struggling financially. We were also delivering to anyone who might be alone. Sweetly, many of those people had returned to the café with their delivery driver, eager to help. Wyatt and his band of wild horse trackers from the nature center had taken the first hot, homemade meals of the evening to on-call crews throughout the island. Policemen at the station, firefighters at the firehouse, EMTs waiting for a call. The way I saw it, whether folks needed food, family, a sense of community, or just to be remembered at Christmas, what we were doing tonight covered it all.

The multitude of women helping behind the counter made my work possible. They pulled hot pans out of the oven and slid waiting ones in. They kept the baking dishes clean, greased, and ready to be filled. Their efforts had streamlined mine, and the result was a nearly unbelievable amount of hot homemade meals entering our community.

Aunt Fran and Aunt Clara moved finished products into throwaway containers, then packed the completed meals into boxes. They wrote holiday greetings and the delivery addresses across the tops before tying them with a bow. The boxes weren't nearly as beautiful as the gesture itself, but they would help keep the foods from spilling or losing too much heat while they travelled.

Amelia hummed along with the festive tune on my radio. She hadn't stopped smiling since she'd arrived hours before. She ran a sleeve across her forehead, hands covered in cartoon lobster oven mitts, before pulling the next round of baked hams and scalloped potatoes from the oven. "I love that we're all here doing this together," she said. "It's a perfectly magical show of town spirit and love. I think we all needed this after everything we've been through these last two weeks."

I slowed my wooden spoon, midstir in a massive batch of pasta salad, and smiled. "I was hit with the inspiration bug after visiting your book club."

Her blue eyes widened with a brilliant gleam. "Really?"

I nodded with a joyful smile. "All those amazing holiday reads had a common thread. Hope. Standing in front of the Giving Tree, I thought of those books and how the characters aren't so different from us. They always get a happy ending at Christmas. Why couldn't every name on the tree get one too?" I cast a loving gaze around the bustling room, admiring the unthinkable volume of food and volunteers, all singing, smiling, chatting. All glad to be there, doing their part to make another person's holiday brighter. "I knew *I* couldn't make a difference to everyone, but together *we* can accomplish anything. So I put out a call for help. This is so much more than I'd even dared to hope for."

Amelia batted tear-filled eyes, then threw her arms around me.

I'd written my name on the outside of the envelope before hanging it on the tree. I hoped seeing my name there would get at least a few people's attention, and it had. Inside, I'd explained that though I had so much, there was still something I wanted but couldn't get without help. I wanted to know that no Charmer would go without a warm Christmas dinner and the knowledge that they were loved. I didn't want anyone on my island to think for a second, like the man in the story had, that he or she wasn't seen, had been forgotten, or just didn't matter.

I promised to turn all groceries brought to my place on Christmas Eve into holiday meals for the other names on the Giving Tree. I vowed to cook until the supplies were used up and deliver the results until they were gone. Emotion itched the backs of my eyes and tickled my nose as I released Amelia and gave the overflowing café another prideful look.

Folks had done more than drop off groceries. They'd brought finished dishes and some complete meals. They'd rolled up their sleeves and dug in to help cook, clean, prep, and pack. They'd driven all around the island delivering food, acknowledgment, and love to their neighbors and friends.

I ended my request at the Giving Tree by asking that each reader consider my request, then put the note back on the tree for someone else to see.

And word had spread like wildfire.

Amelia sniffled. "I'm so glad Wyatt and Grady saved you from that lunatic. It was a whole other Christmas miracle that they made it in time."

My gaze jumped to the wall of windows facing the sea. Lou sat on the railing, puffed up to twice his normal size and keeping watch over his portion of the world. I considered telling Amelia the strapping male heroes in her story had a little aviary help on the cliffs that day, but decided to keep it to myself. The incredible generosity and compassion of our community deserved top billing for now.

Across the room, Denise helped Denver wrap cookie platters and dessert trays in brightly colored plastic wrap. Others set the wrapped sweets on top of the packed bags heading out for delivery.

Grady darted in and out through the foyer, loading the waiting cars.

To my surprise, Senator Denver had arrived early and taken up a post near the door. She'd assigned herself the role of forewoman, directing bodies and keeping volunteers on task. She did these things with a smile.

Denise left Denver with the cookie trays and cut through the crowd to the counter. She looked as young and strikingly beautiful as usual. For the first time since I'd met her, I wondered if she was happy here and if she could be long-term. Could she meet someone and fall in love on our little island? Was love something she wanted? I made a mental note to reach out to her more often. She deserved a break sometimes. Some laughs or a drink with friends.

I smiled at her sweater as she approached. An image of Charlie Brown stood proudly beside his pitiful little tree, one red bulb hanging precariously from the bowed limb.

"We're almost out of desserts," she said. "Should Denver and I move to another station, or do you have more cookies back there somewhere?"

I pointed at the stack of bakery boxes near my fridge. "Those are full of cutouts, sugar cookies, and fudge. Believe it or not, I have more of everything else in the freezer." I wiped my hands on my apron, then pulled another mass of sweets out to defrost. "Thank you for being here," I said.

She smiled. "We wouldn't have missed it. Though, maybe you could reward our hard work with a new cookie-making video. Denver's itching to get back in the kitchen. It wasn't easy for him, being the new kid on a small island, but we bring cookies to his class weekly now, and the other kids love him."

I laughed.

She loaded the bakery boxes into her arms. "Your cookies are changing lives."

Grady jogged inside, dusting snow from his hat and shoulders. His eyes sought mine immediately, the way they had continually tonight.

Denise shot me a little cat-that-ate-the-canary smile before sailing back to Denver with the cookies.

Grady made his way in my direction.

And I in his.

"You doing okay?" he asked, pulling the cowboy hat from his head.

"Perfect," I said. "Thank you for helping. For bringing Denise and Denver. And your mother-in-law." I tipped my head in her direction.

"She saw your note on the tree," he said. "I can't take any credit there, and Denise and Denver wouldn't have missed this. I'm just here for the lemon cake."

I laughed at the not-so-subtle reminder of his favorite dish. "Oh, I have your lemon cake," I said, a furious blush rushing across my cheeks. "It's upstairs. I only made one, and I didn't want it to be accidentally shipped off with a delivery."

Grady smiled. "Well, I'd love to come up and get it when we're done here. Maybe we can share the first slice."

"I'd like that," I said, pushing a swath of hair behind my ear.

"You got bangs," he said, scanning the change.

I waited while he made his evaluation, knowing I shouldn't care, and caring so much I almost asked what he thought.

"I like them," he said finally, brushing the strands carefully aside.

I cleared my throat and fought against the heat wave rolling over me. "Has there been any more news on Janie?" I asked. The holidays had slowed things at the courthouse, but I knew she'd been transferred to the mainland this morning. Charm simply wasn't equipped to hold anyone for an extended length of time, and Janie would likely be behind bars for quite a while.

"We've got an airtight case," Grady said, pride curving his lips. "I thought I had the killer when I left you at the hospital that day. We matched the SUV leaving the fire to one that had been at the post office the day your first threat letter was mailed."

"Lanita's SUV," I said, knowing how that story went.

"Janie was smart not to use her own car," Grady said. "Smart not to use an established local transportation service too, but she sealed her fate when she called Lanita for those Pick-Me-Ups. That kid keeps better records than half the businesses in town, and she's only here for winter break. She'd already pointed me in Janie's direction when Wyatt called." His smile faded. "I hate getting those calls."

"Sorry," I said.

He reached for me with one arm and pulled me a few more steps in his direction. "I'm glad you're okay."

"Thanks to you," I said. "And Wyatt."

Grady's smile slipped again. "I owe that guy."

"Me too."

He tracked Aunt Fran across the room with his gaze. I watched with him as she stopped to talk to

Senator Denver, then the women laughed. "Is she still running for mayor next year?" he asked.

"I think so," I said. "What about your mother-in-law?"

He pulled me a few more steps toward the café's threshold. "I think she might give that a rest."

"If you help find her husband?" I guessed.

He nodded.

Lanita opened the front door and stomped snow off her boots. "I'm back for another round of meals," she called out. "Are there more ready to go?"

An older couple manifested beside Grady and I, hurrying packed bags to her hands.

"Be careful out there," I told her.

She saluted before vanishing back into the night.

"I'm going to miss her," I said, turning back to Grady, who'd moved closer while I wasn't looking. The scent of his cologne and warmth of his body lightened my head until the busyness around us faded.

When he spoke, there was heat in his usually brooding eyes. "Every family on the island is going to have a feast tonight because of you," he said.

"Not just me," I said. "Look around. This is possible because of our neighbors, their families, our friends. You."

He shook his head and latched his hands to the small of my back, towing me in until the toes of our shoes bumped. "This is all you, Swan. These people love you, and they followed your lead tonight. You did good."

My cheeks heated at the compliment. The rest of me heated at his touch. I tipped my head back and rolled my eyes up to the mistletoe hanging above us. "What about you?" I asked. "I followed your lead all the way to the mistletoe. Now what are you going to do about it?"

Something warm and bright flashed in his eyes, but Grady didn't look up. He'd known exactly where he'd been taking me. "Merry Christmas, Everly," he said softly as he lowered his mouth to mine.

SIMPLE SWAN FAMILY RECIPES FIT FOR A HOLIDAY GATHERING!

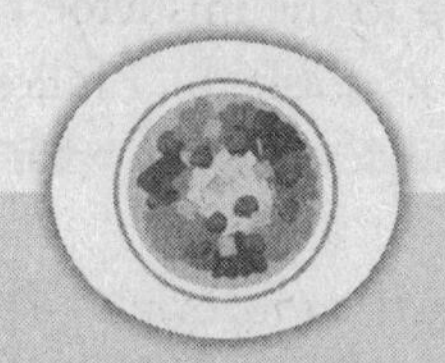

Simple Caesar Salad

Ingredients:

2 hearts romaine lettuce

1 English (seedless) cucumber, chopped

1 cup grape tomato halves

1 cup creamy Caesar dressing

1 cups Italian-seasoned croutons, crushed

Directions:

Wash romaine and separate into leaves.

Arrange cucumber and tomato evenly on leaves.

Drizzle with dressing.

Sprinkle with croutons.

Serve!

Gingerbread Bars

Ingredients:

1 pouch of your favorite sugar cookie mix
¼ cup all-purpose flour
½ cup butter, softened
2 large eggs
3 tablespoons light molasses
1 teaspoon ground cinnamon
1 teaspoon ground ginger
¾ teaspoon ground allspice
½ teaspoon ground cloves
Your favorite cream cheese frosting

Directions:

Prepare a 9-by-13 pan with cooking spray.

Preheat oven to 350°F.

Place all ingredients in medium bowl and mix well.

Spread resulting (thick) batter in pan and bake approximately 25 minutes, or until a toothpick inserted in center comes out clean. Cool completely before frosting.

Ice cooled bars with cream cheese frosting and sprinkle with additional cinnamon.

Refrigerate before serving.

Cranberry Christmas Iced Tea

Ingredients:

6 cups cranberry juice cocktail
4 tea bags black tea
6–12 mint leaves
6 tablespoons sugar

Directions:

Heat cranberry juice cocktail to boiling.
Remove from heat. Add tea bags and mint.
Steep 10 minutes.
Strain.
Stir in sugar.
Chill and serve over ice.

READ ON FOR A LOOK AT

BOOK #1 IN THE SEASIDE CAFÉ MYSTERIES SERIES

CHAPTER ONE

"Welcome to Sun, Sand, and Tea." I perked up at the precious sound of seashell wind chimes bouncing and tinkling against the front door of my new café. "I'll be right with you."

A pair of ladies in windbreakers and capri pants smoothed their windblown hair and examined the seating options. Sounds of the sea had followed them inside, amplified briefly by the opening door.

I bopped my head to a Temptations song and tapped the large sweet tea jug behind the counter. Until three months ago, owning and operating an iced tea shop on the shore of my hometown had been nothing more than a childish dream. I'd thought being a grown-up meant working a job I hated while wearing uncomfortable clothes, so I'd toed the line for a while, but my looming thirtieth birthday and a broken heart had changed all that.

Now I did what I wanted—in comfy clothes for significantly less money, but at least I could wear flip-flops.

I set a lidless canning jar of Old-Fashioned Sun Tea in front of the man sitting at my counter and beamed. "Let me know if I can fix you anything else, Sam."

He frowned at his phone, too engrossed or distracted to answer. Sam Smart was a local real estate agent. He'd arrived in Charm during the years I'd been away from home, and from what I could tell, he was a type-A, all-stress all-day kind of guy—a little sweet tea was probably just what he needed. I nudged the jar closer until his hand swept out to meet it. "Thanks."

"Everything okay?" I asked.

He flicked his gaze to mine, then back to his phone. "It's Paine." He shook his head and groaned.

"Ah." I grabbed a thin stack of napkins and patted Sam's shoulder on my way to welcome the newcomers. "Good luck with that."

Benedict Paine had been a thorn in my side since the day I'd approached our town council about adding a café to the first floor of my new seaside home. Owning a sweet-tea shop was my dream come true, and honestly, I couldn't afford the house's mortgage payments without the business income. Despite the home's fixer-upper condition, the price tag had been astronomical, making the café a must, and Mr. Paine had fought me the entire way, complaining that adding a business to a residential property would drag down the neighborhood. I could only imagine the kind of headache a man like Paine could cause a real estate agent.

The space that was now my café stretched through

the entire south side of the first floor. Walls had been strategically knocked out, opening the kitchen and formal dining area up to a large space for entertaining. The result was a stunning seaside setup, perfect for my shop.

From the kitchen, a private hallway led to the rest of the first floor and another thousand or so square feet of potential expansion space. A staircase off that hall provided passage to my second-floor living quarters, which were just as big and full of potential. The stairs themselves were amazing, stained a faded red, with delicate carvings along the edges. They were mine alone to enjoy, shut off from the café by a locking door. I could probably thank the home's history as a boarding house for my substantial second-floor kitchen. The cabinets and fixtures were all older than me, but I couldn't complain—the café kitchen was what mattered, and it was fantastic.

Seating at Sun, Sand, and Tea was a hodgepodge of repainted garage sale and thrift shop finds. Twenty seats in total, five at the counter and fifteen scattered across the wide-planked, whitewashed floor, ranging from padded wicker numbers with low tables to tall bistro sets along the perimeter.

The ladies had selected a high table near a wall of windows overlooking my deck.

I refreshed my smile and set a napkin in front of each of them. "Hello. Welcome to Sun, Sand, and Tea."

They dragged their attention slowly away from the rolling waves and driftwood-speckled beach beyond the glass, reluctant to part with the amazing view for even a second.

"Can I get something started for you?"

The taller woman settled tortoiseshell glasses onto the ridge of her sunburned nose and fixed her attention to the café menu, scripted on an enormous blackboard covering the far wall. "Do you really make twenty flavors of iced tea?"

"Yes, ma'am. Plus a daily array of desserts and finger foods." The selection changed without notice, sometimes with the tide, depending on if I ran out of any necessary ingredients.

"Fascinating. I came in for some good old-fashioned sweet tea, but now you've got me wondering about the Country Cranberry Hibiscus. What's in that?" She leaned her elbows on the tabletop and twined her fingers.

"Well, there—there's black tea, hibiscus, and, uh, rose hips, and cranberries." I stammered over the answer to her question the same way I had to similar inquiries on a near-daily basis since opening my café doors. It seemed a fine line between serving my family's secret recipes and sharing them ingredient by ingredient.

The woman glanced out the window again and pressed a palm to her collarbone as a massive gull flapped to a stop on the handrail outside the window. "Dear!"

"Oh, there's Lou," I said.

"Lou?"

"I think he came with the house."

She lowered her hand, but kept one eye on Lou. "I'll try the Cranberry Hibiscus," she said. "What about you, Margo?"

Her friend pursed her lips. "Make mine Summer Citrus Mint, and I'd like to try your crisp cucumber sandwich."

I formed an "okay" sign with my fingers and winked. "Give me just a quick minute, and I'll get that over here for you."

I strode back to the counter, practically vibrating with excitement. After only a month in business, each customer's order was still a thrill for me.

The seashell wind chimes kicked into gear again and I responded on instinct. "Welcome to Sun, Sand, and Tea." I turned on my toes for a look at the newest guest and my stomach dropped. "Oh, hello, Mr. Paine." I shot a warning look at Sam, whose head drooped lower over his tea.

"Miss Swan." Mr. Paine straddled a stool three seats down from Sam and set his straw porkpie hat on the counter. Tufts of white hair stretched east and west from the spaces below his bald spot and above each ear. "Lovely day."

I nodded in acknowledgment. "Can I get you anything?"

"Please," he drawled, giving Sam a thorough once-over. It wasn't clear if he already knew Sam was mad at him, or if he was figuring that out from the silent treatment.

I waited, knowing what the next words out of Mr. Paine's mouth were going to be.

Reluctantly, he pulled his attention back to me. "How about a list of all your ingredients?"

Sam rolled his small brown eyes, but otherwise continued to ignore Mr. Paine's presence.

I grabbed a knife and a loaf of fresh-baked bread and set them on the counter. "You know I can't give that to you, Mr. Paine. Something else, perhaps?" I'd been through this a dozen times with him since Sun, Sand, and Tea's soft opening. Swan women had guarded our tea recipes for a hundred years, and I wasn't about to hand them over just because he said so. "How about a glass of tea instead?"

I cut two thin slices from the loaf, then whacked the crusts off with unnecessary oomph.

Sam took a long pull on his drink, stopping only when there was nothing left but ice, and returned the jar to the counter with a thump. "It's very good," he said, turning to stare at Mr. Paine. "You should try it. I mean, if you'd had it your way, this place wouldn't even be open, right? Seems like the least you can do is find out what you were protesting."

I didn't bother to mention that Mr. Paine had already tried basically every item on the menu as I plied him with free samples to try to get in his good graces.

Mr. Paine frowned, first at Sam, then at me. Wrinkles raced across his pale, sun-spotted face. "It's a health and safety issue," he groused. "People need to know what they're drinking."

"Yes." I arranged cucumber slices on one piece of bread. "I believe you've mentioned that." It had, in fact, been his number one argument since I'd gotten the green light to open. "I'm happy to provide a general list of ingredients for each recipe, but there are certain herbs and spices, as well as brewing methods, that are trade secrets."

"He doesn't care about any of that," Sam said. "He just wants to get his way."

Mr. Paine twisted on his stool to glare at Sam. "Whatever your problem is, Sam Smart, it's not with me, so stow it."

Sam shoved off his stool. "And your problem isn't with her." He grabbed the gray suit jacket from the stool beside him and threaded his arms into the sleeves. "Thanks for the tea, Everly." He tossed a handful of dollar bills onto the counter and a remorseful look in my direction.

I worked to close my slack jaw as the front door slapped shut behind him. Whatever grudge match Sam and Mr. Paine had going, I didn't want a ticket for it. I put the unused cucumber slices away and removed a white ceramic bowl from the fridge.

Mr. Paine watched carefully, teeth clenched.

"Maybe you'd like to try the Peach Tea today," I suggested. "Whatever you want. On the house."

Preferably *to go*.

"How much sugar is in the Peach?" he asked, apparently determined to criticize. "You know I don't like a lot of sugar."

I pointed to a brightly colored section on my menu that highlighted sugar-free options. "How about a tea made with alternative sweeteners, like honey or fruit puree? Maybe the Iced Peach with Ginger?" I turned to the refrigerator and pulled out a large metal bowl, then scooped the cream cheese, mayo, and seasoning mixture onto the second bread slice, turning it face down over the cucumbers. "There's no sugar in that at all."

"Fine." He lifted his fingers in defeat, as usual, pretending to give up but knowing full well he'd be back tomorrow with the same game.

I had quit hoping he'd start paying for his orders two weeks ago. That was never going to happen, and I had decided to chalk the minimal expense up to community relations and let it go. Though if he kept walking off with my shop's canning jars with , he'd soon have a full set—and those weren't cheap.

"Great." I released a long breath and poured a jar of naturally sweetened peach tea for him. He was lucky I didn't serve it in a disposable cup.

"What's in it?" he asked.

"Peaches. Tea." I rocked my knife through the sandwich, making four small crustless triangles.

"And?" Mr. Paine lifted the tea to his mouth, closed his eyes, and gulped before returning the half-empty jar to his napkin. He smacked his lips. "Tastes like sugar."

"No," I assured him. "There's no sugar in that." I plated the crisp cucumber sandwiches, then poured the ladies' mint and cranberry teas, grateful that they were too busy ogling Lou out the window to notice the delay. "Fresh peaches, honey, ginger, lemon, and spices. That's it."

I knew what my tea really tasted like to him: *defeat.* He'd tried to stop me from opening Sun, Sand, and Tea because businesses on the beach were "cliché and overdone." According to Mr. Paine, if I opened a café in my home, Charm, North Carolina, would become a tourist trap and ruin everything he lived for.

Fortunately, the property was old enough to have been zoned commercial before Paine's time on the town council. Built at the turn of the nineteenth century, my home had been a private residence at first, then a number of other businesses ranging from a boarding house to a prep school, and if the rumors were true, possibly a brothel. Though, I couldn't imagine anything so salacious ever having existed in Charm. The town was simply too…charming. And according to my great aunts, who'd been fixtures here since the Great Depression, it had always been that way.

The place was empty when I bought it. The previous owner lived out of town, but he'd sent a number of work crews to make renovations over the years. I could only imagine the money that had been slowly swallowed by the efforts. Eventually it went back on the market.

Mr. Paine eyeballed his drink and rocked the jar from side to side. "I don't see why you won't provide the complete list of your ingredients. What's the big secret?"

"I'm not keeping a secret. The recipes are private. I don't want them out in the world." I wet my lips and tried another explanation, one he might better understand. "These recipes are part of my family's lineage. Our history and legacy." I let my native drawl carry the words. Paine of all people should appreciate an effort to keep things as they were, to respect the past.

He harrumphed. "I'm bringing the ingredient list up at our next council meeting. I'm sure Mayor Dunfree and the other members will agree with me that it's irresponsible not to have it posted."

"Great." He never seemed to tire of reminding me how tight he was with the mayor. He'd used their relationship to the fullest while trying to keep my shop from opening, but even the mayor couldn't prevent a legitimate business from being run in a commercially zoned space. I refilled Mr. Paine's jar, which had been emptied rather quickly. "Let me know if there's anything else you'd like to try."

Mr. Paine climbed off his stool and stuffed his goofy hat back on his mostly bald head. "Just the tea," he said with unnecessary flourish.

"See ya." I piled the ladies' teas and sandwich on a tray and waved Paine off. "Try not to choke on an ice cube," I muttered.

~

The afternoon ebbed and flowed in spurts of busyness and lulls of silence. I supposed that was typical of a new business in a small town, not to mention that Sun, Sand, and Tea hadn't had its official launch yet. I was due for a big grand opening, but fear and cowardice kept me from planning it. What if no one came and the whole thing was a flop?

I flipped over the CLOSED sign promptly at five and went upstairs to trade my sundress for exercise gear and hunt for my track shoes. I'd gotten out of shape while I was away, loitering behind a table at culinary school, in a city where I never felt completely safe, eating take-out and every meal on the run because I didn't have time to cook for myself while studying the art of haute cuisine.

Now none of my clothes fit and I wasn't happy about it. Luckily, Charm was a great place to get out and get moving, whether hiking the dunes, playing volleyball on the beach, or swimming in the warm, blue ocean. I hit the boardwalk with a brisk stride.

Waning sunlight glistened on the water, reflecting shadows of soaring birds and the occasional single-engine plane, and the heady scent of home hung in the air. It was the salty, beachy fragrance that clung to my skin and hair long after I'd gone inside, the humidity and seagrass, wet sand and a hint of sun-block. I could never quite put it into words, and my attempts had been wholly lost on the friends I'd made living inland. Maybe rather than just a smell, it was a sensation you had to experience to understand. Kind of like that perfect glass of iced tea. Or maybe it was just me. Some days I wasn't sure if it was sweet tea or saltwater flowing in my veins. Probably a little of both.

I turned away from the beach and headed through the marsh, following the wooden planks beneath my feet. Tenacious green stems poked through stringy bundles of dead seagrass. Spring in Charm was lovely, but soon everything would be in bloom, lush and wild, the way I loved it.

Too soon, the bushy marsh shrank away, revealing a glimpse of Ocean Drive, the main road in town, in the distance. I slowed at the sight of an extra-large moving truck parked across multiple spaces outside the Gas-N-Go.

Was I no longer the newest full-time citizen of Charm? A curious thrill buzzed over my skin. Was the person with the truck new-new, or newly returned, like me? Did I know them from my previous life here? Or was I about to meet a new friend?

Booted feet moved beneath the truck's long metal belly, nearing the back corner at a clip. I nearly held my breath in anticipation.

The boots arrived in full view a moment later, attached to a pair of nicely fitting jeans and six feet of serious.

I gave a low whistle, and the man's head turned sharply in my direction. Keen gray eyes fixed me in place.

"Oh." He'd heard that? My heart raced and my cheeks burned with humiliation. I'd been caught whistling at a strange man. What was next? Catcalls from my porch?

ACKNOWLEDGMENTS

Thank you, dear reader, for joining Everly on another adventure in Charm. You make my dream possible, and I can't thank you enough for that. Also, thank you, Anna Michels and Sourcebooks. I'm humbled and honored to be a part of your amazing team. Thank you, Jill Marsal, my blessed literary agent and personal cheer squad. I don't know how you do it, but you keep me busy and I love it! Thank you to friends who help me plot murder: Jane Ann Turzillo, Kathy Long, Cari Dubiel, Shellie Arnold, and Wendy Campbell. Also my critique partners, Jennifer Anderson and Danielle Haas: you make my stories better. And finally, thank you to my family: Noah, Andrew, Lily, and Bryan. I realize that I'm usually daydreaming, alone at my desk and in my pajamas, but you are my world, and I wouldn't replace you with a million fictional ones. Not even if those worlds had free books and chocolate.

ABOUT THE AUTHOR

Bree Baker is a Midwestern writer obsessed with small-town hijinks, sweet tea, and the sea. She's been telling stories to her family, friends, and strangers for as long as she can remember, and more often than not, those stories feature a warm ocean breeze and a recipe she's sure to ruin. Now she's working on those fancy cooking skills and dreaming up adventures for the Seaside Café Mysteries. Bree is a member of Sisters in Crime, International Thriller Writers, and the Romance Writers of America.